DEATH IS A GREAT DISGUISER

A SANTA CRUZ MURDER MYSTERY

LINDA S. GUNTHER

Charleston, SC

www.PalmettoPublishing.com

Death Is A Great Disguiser

First Edition

ISBN: 978-1-63837-042-0

DEATH IS A GREAT DISGUISER

A SANTA CRUZ MURDER MYSTERY

LINDA S. GUNTHER

A Note to the Reader:

THIS SUSPENSE NOVEL IS A WORK OF FICTION. THE CHARACTERS IN THIS story are not intended to resemble or reflect real-life people. Character names and their backgrounds are also fictional, made up solely for story-line purposes. The novel is mainly set in September, 2020, during the COVID-19 pandemic crisis in Northern California, and in 2019, in Merida, Mexico.

Dedication

MY INSPIRATION FOR WRITING THIS MYSTERY NOVEL CAME FROM MY dear friend, Bill Mowatt.

He shared an idea for a debut novel and asked me to critique some of his draft chapters. The plot centered on a college English literature teacher, Brian McCallam, and his dog, MacGregor (aka Mac). It was an intriguing concept for such an unlikely duo to become entangled in a brutal murder case.

Sadly, Bill passed away at the age of eighty-three, in January, 2020, and was unfortunately unable to move forward with more work on his novel. Like me, he was a resident of Santa Cruz County, loved this area as much as I do, and was intent on having our Central California coast as the setting for this story. With his love for English literature, Bill chose the book title, *Death Is A Great Disguiser,* a quote from William Shakespeare's *Measure for Measure.*

Bill was an amazing friend with a big heart and a zesty sense of humor. I met him at Cabrillo College, where I was teaching a one-day workshop on the subject of indie book publishing. It was a full house that day in my classroom, but Bill stood out like a sparkling diamond. We became good friends, often meeting for breakfast at The Dolphin Café on the Santa Cruz Wharf. He came to all of my book signings at various venues around town and even to those held in more distant counties. He was one of my most enthusiastic and supportive fans.

His dear wife, Gail Mowatt, gifted Bill's incomplete skeleton manuscript to me. From there, I decided to write a new story line with an alternative persona and background for the protagonist, brand-new secondary characters, and subplots, and deepen the book's intensity with complex family relationships. Gail asked if I would keep Mac, the dog, and the name, Brian McCallam, for the lead character, and if I'd retain Merida, Mexico, an enchanting town in the Yucatan, as a second setting in the story. Merida was a place Bill and Gail visited many years ago and this location held precious romantic memories for them as a couple. The only other thing Gail requested was that I retain Bill's book's title, *Death Is A Great Disguiser*. I gratefully agreed to these few things, both of us knowing that I would craft a fresh story line from my own imagination.

Because I wrote this novel during the COVID-19 pandemic era, I made the decision to honor what we were going through during this exasperating period in California. Readers will see several references to characters being frustrated and troubled with the virus that truly took over our lives.

I often think of Bill when I walk along the beach, feel a breeze on my face, or look at a stunning sunset. I miss that sparkle in Bill's eyes, his unrelenting positivity, his distinctively warm voice, his constant curiosity, and most of all, his delightful laugh.

Acknowledgements

IN THE MIDST OF A GLOBAL PANDEMIC, WITH ALL THE STRESSES AND DISruptions to our normal lives, several people generously gave me their hearts, minds, and time in reading the draft of *Death Is A Great Disguiser,* chapter by chapter.

Because this was the first time I'd attempted a novel where my lead character was male, I am especially thankful for the two male perspectives for providing their invaluable critique.

Thank you to all of these extraordinary beta readers:

Melodie Nelson: Your encouragement and contributions to plot points and the character's decisions, challenges, and vulnerabilities helped me make leaps in my writing as I grew this story.

Rick Riccardi: Like you did on my last novel, *DREAM BEACH,* you came through on this one with immediate feedback, spotlighting specific and important details that needed clarification. You held my feet to the fire on any holes in the plot!

Kathy Buchanan: Your highlights on characters you liked and those who were not so likeable helped me commit to the contrasting personalities and the underlying motives of my protagonist and secondary characters.

Brandon Harwood: Your knowledge and expertise on firearms and your experience having read numerous suspense novels over the years greatly helped me to heighten the action, suspense, and tension in this tale.

I'd like to also express my appreciation to my dear writing coaches, Roxan McDonald and Jane Edberg, as well as to all of my Thursday Writer Group colleagues. Digging into dialogue, settings, and transitions helped bring my characters alive, and as our two gurus described so well in our craft talk sessions, the importance of weaving in a clear through line as the heart of the story.

To my amazing cover artist, Julie Tipton, my heart is also full of thanks. Your cover-art creations for all six of my novels have inspired me in so many ways as I worked to complete each project. You took the cover concept vision I had in my head and turned it into beautiful art, amazing me each and every time.

Laurel Ornitz, my editor of all things grammatical, thank you for your recommendations and suggestions.

Finally, I'd like to express my thanks again to dear Bill Mowatt, who has passed on from this world, but left the wonderful seeds for building a rockin' murder mystery. And to Gail Mowatt, my sincere appreciation for gifting me the opportunity to take those seeds, plant them, and grow them into what I hope is a riveting page-turning work of fiction.

CHAPTER 1:
"The Empty Vessel Makes the Greatest Sound."*

–WILLIAM SHAKESPEARE

B RIAN McCALLAM'S WEATHERED LEATHER JACKET FELT SNUG AROUND his gut. He was likely carrying an extra eight to ten pounds, which he had packed on over the late spring and summer of 2020. With the full-blown COVID-19 pandemic in play, he had sunk into a lazy routine over the past few months, eating too much junk food and entirely laid up for the last two weeks with an ear infection. The pain had thankfully subsided, but had left him with a half-stuffed ear, which would not relent, despite the medication the doctor had prescribed. He self-administered three drops of the liquid religiously three times a day for eight days, leaning his head over on his bed pillow and feeling the dribble of the cold drops stream into his ear and ooze into the canal or wherever the hell they went inside his head.

As he walked on the bluffs over Santa Cruz, his ear still felt packed, but his brain seemed to be operating a lot better than it had ten days ago. Dr. Bering had refused to give him a COVID test, as he had no sign of fever,

---

*   "The empty vessel makes the greatest sound." Henry V, William Shakespeare, Act 4, Scene 4

nor any problems breathing and no apparent cough, the key symptoms of the virus. *Damn doctor, I bet I had the freaking disease*, he thought.

He was feeling better, but it was cold for late September, the wind sending a chill down his golf shirt. He had forgotten to wrap a scarf around his neck. It had poured down with rain the last couple of days, an unusual event so early in the fall season. The grass felt slippery under his feet and his socks were moist at his ankles. He had worn his warm jacket, but failed to put on the right shoes for a walk in the mud.

"Come on, Mac, nothing to smell there," he called out, pulling on the leash. "If you want to go, let it rip." Mac ignored him, yanking toward some white plastic thing that the dog had spotted in the taller grass near the edge of the bluff.

"Damn it." The hefty Airedale, a sixty-five-pound, brown, curly-haired dog named after Brian's great grandfather, MacGregor, tugged again so hard that Brian's wrist burned, as the taut fabric of the leash dug into his skin. "Mac, no!"

Mac put his nose to the ground, and with his teeth, snatched up the wet plastic white thing. "Oh God!" Brian recognized it to be a latex glove, part of a pair like many people had been wearing when out and about shopping. You could find one or two discarded gloves or even a face mask at a glance on a patch of ground or sidewalk and they were often left behind in grocery carts. Brian shook his head in disgust. We controlled the use of plastics, didn't we? he cynically thought.

"Drop it, Mac."

The dog surprisingly obeyed, as he seemed to eye something more interesting just a few feet away, closer to the cliff's edge, but stopped short to take a dump. "Good dog." Brian reached for the poop bag in his pocket. He was wearing an old jacket that he had nabbed from an Army Surplus store twenty years ago when he was a young thirty-something.

He bent to pick up the poop. He could probably get away without retrieving it, but he didn't want to see others leaving dog poop behind on such a stunning stretch of earth that sprawled out over the Pacific Ocean. He knotted the bag and walked a little further, the Airedale at his side. The dog looked up at him and seemed to question why they were out in the rain as if he sensed that the worst of it was yet to come. Brian shook his head. He had a damn smart dog.

He reached down to give Mac an apologetic pat, realizing the dog was sopping wet, his woolly red-brown coat pasted down from the rain. Mac's curly brown eyebrows stood out in stringy strands resembling some poorly glued-on false eyelashes. Brian couldn't help but laugh out loud at the sight.

"You're a soggy mess." Brian said and patted his pet again.

Standing at the edge of the bluff, he glanced down at the turbid ocean crashing against the jagged rocks and imagined how many small boats and even large vessels lost in the fog had been crushed to splinters over the many years before the lighthouse was erected. He read in a local paper that the structure had been built in the late-1860s, but not before many lives had been lost to the unforgiving, sometimes invisible Northern California coastline. Maybe he'd write about it. *Yeah, maybe a sea rescue suspense novel,* he thought.

He missed his girlfriend, Ivy.

"Come on, Mac, time to head home." He could feel the ping of rain-drops hit the crown of his head. He tipped his neck and brushed his hair. A few drops drizzled down to the tip of his nose. He regretted not having snagged the 49er cap from the hook by his front door. Foolish at the tail end of a nasty ear infection, he thought. He tugged the leash and started down the hill back to the Jeep Cherokee.

He hadn't seen Ivy for over three months. She took care of her two granddaughters ever since the pandemic had taken over the world and expressed that she didn't want to chance Brian visiting her, put any of them at risk, including Brian himself. Ivy's daughter, Becky, was an ER nurse at Dominican Hospital and regularly exposed to the deadly virus. The little girls had been living with Ivy 24/7. She was the youngest-looking grandmother he knew, and the prettiest.

The rain started to pelt down. About to reach the road where the Jeep Cherokee was parked, the Airedale suddenly turned, jerked on the leash, signaling a desire to go back up the hill.

"Jesus, Mac! We're getting soaked." Brian pulled on the leash. Mac wrig-gled his body back and forth, and managed to maneuver his neck out of the collar, a trick the dog had discovered some months ago.

Brian recalled Mac's prankster behavior surfacing on a hot day at the park back in July, when Mac was determined to separate some kid from his skateboard. The Airedale detested the sound of the moving board rumbling on the pavement and had barked in response, appearing vicious to people who walked close by. There were at least a dozen skateboarders around that afternoon, screeching and zigzagging across the blacktop, taking full advantage to jump every speed bump in the expansive parking lot. Twisting out of the collar had become Mac's new habit, often pulling this Houdini-like stunt when Brian least expected it.

"Mac!" Brian called out, as his dog ran up to the top of the bluff. The cold rain slid down the back of Brian's jacket, the wet cotton shirt pressed against his skin.

The dog darted back to something in the dirt, to an object that had caught his attention earlier when he went for the plastic glove. Although wet and cold, Brian was amused. "What now, Mac?" He had to admit that he was kind of envious of Mac's ability to surprise humans, change his canine mind on a dime, be spontaneous. Brian trudged up the slippery hill after his determined pet. Mac pawed an object that stuck out above the surface of the puddled ground. The thing moved in the slate-colored mud. A rivulet of murky water swooped around it. It looked like a human hand.

"Holy crap." He felt sick, nauseous, the same queasiness he experienced whenever a grim discovery had been made while he was on the detective beat. The ten years since the last time he eyed such a sight seemed to melt away.

The light-skinned hand seemed to come alive with the water rushing around it. The nails looked professionally manicured with a candy-red polish. The fingers were long, slender, the wrist small, and protruded from what looked like a red jacket sleeve that almost matched the nail lacquer color.

"Leave it, Mac. Come on." He bent down and made an attempt to get the collar back on the anxious dog, clamoring back to the hand. Brian's knees were weak. His stomach somersaulted. Mac won the battle. Using claws and teeth, the dog yanked eagerly at the red fabric, swinging his muzzle back and forth, then abruptly changed focus from the wriggling human hand back to Brian. The dog sat up on his back haunches in the mud and waited obediently for Brian to refasten the dog collar. This ritual seemed to be the dog's favorite part of the "escape the collar" game, surprise the master by allowing him to regain control of the situation.

Once he refastened Mac's collar, Brian's eyes shot back to the bobbling hand. The dog pulled again, desperate to get over to the hand, which moved about like a broken marionette.

"Oh God," Brian yelled out and plucked the cell phone from his jacket pocket. He needed to phone Tim Carrick immediately. He pulled Mac away from the grisly discovery. Clicking on his ex-partner's name, he listened for the ring tone.

"Come on, be there," Brian muttered to himself.

"Carrick. Santa Cruz PD."

"Tim, it's Brian McCallam."

"McCallam, what the hell. Good to hear your voice, man. Ready for a drinking session now that this pandemic crap is—"

"Tim, that's not why I phoned," Brian interrupted, "though I wish it were."

"What's up?" Tim said.

"I'm on a walk out here with Mac, on the bluff, by the beach and...shit, we discovered something bad... something grim!"

"Nothing could be worse than this fricking COVID shutdown. What is it?"

"Well, it's a—"

"Spit it out, McCallam. You're the smartest guy I know, but never good at handling the unsavory stuff."

"I know that." Brian raised his voice above the noise of the pounding rain. "We found a human hand. My dog, Mac, found it."

"Damn, that *is* grim. A hand sitting there on its own?" Tim chuckled into the phone. They had spent ten years together on the beat in Santa Cruz and another five years partnered as detectives. "You were always the sensitive type," Tim teased.

"What's the hand look like?" Tim asked.

Brian felt the bile rise in his throat. "What's it look like? Looks like a body is buried here in the mud, a female hand sticking out above ground. It's grotesque." The rain pelted down. More rain had slithered down his back to the waistband of his jeans, and he was still holding a bag of dog poop.

"I see," Tim said. "So, the hand is attached to a body?"

"Very funny. It wouldn't be moving around if it weren't attached to a body. No rings on the fingers of the one hand. I can't see the other." He looked over at it and felt a shiver crawl up his spine.

"Man," Tim said, "you still got the observant eye. Well, that's something."

"It was Mac who spotted it, not me."

"Shit," Tim said. "Mac's a fucking canine metal detector."

"Yeah, he's full of curiosity." Brian looked down at Mac. The dog yanked on the leash, anxious to get his chops back to the hand. "Mac, leave it." He tightened up on the leash. "Tim, you'll send someone out here?"

"Thirty minutes. I'll need to pick up the forensic guys. Where exactly are you?"

"Up on the bluff, just across from the Davis mansion."

"Be there in thirty. Haven't seen you for almost a year. Hope I recognize you."

"I'm the one who looks like a drowned rat attached to the leash of a sixty-five-pound sopping wet Airedale. You can't miss us."

"Still got that sense of humor—just hang in McCa—"

His phone went dead. He pulled on the leash again and headed down the hill back to his Jeep. "Want treats, Mac?" The dog's ears perked up. "Treats. Let's go get them."

Brian stepped down the muddy hill, Mac following without resistance. The feel of the cold wind and rain battered his face. He reached to pull his jacket's zipper up as high as it would go, but it jammed three or four inches from the top. "Crap. Figures."

At the bottom of the hill, he tossed the poop bag into a trash bin. He yanked open the passenger door. Mac eagerly jumped in. It was as if a bucket of water had been doused onto the leather seat and worsened after Mac wriggled his body, sluffing off his wet fur. "Mac!"

Brian shut the door and rushed to the driver side, sliding in behind the steering wheel. He reached his hand to the backseat. "Towel back here?" Mac vigorously shook, his dog collar tags ringing out like a baby rattle, sprays of water flying everywhere. "Hey, come on, Mac!"

No damn towel. He spotted a crumpled cotton jacket, the black one with the DeLaveaga Golf Course insignia, which he kept in the vehicle.

He grabbed it and wiped the water from his face, then swabbed it across the steering wheel.

Mac voraciously licked his front paws. "Let me help you out, buddy." Brian twisted the jacket into a thick wad, rubbed it across the dog's back, his underbelly, and legs, and attempted to soak up water from the seat. "This thing is useless." The smell of wet dog wasn't helping. "You stink, mate." Brian shook his head and glanced at himself in the mirror. "We're a right pair. Man and his dog."

He threw the soaked jacket to the back and reached down behind the passenger seat for Mac's bag of treats. "The cat will mew, and the dog will have his day," he orated like an English professor, his coveted career for the last four years. Mac tilted his head to one side.

"That line was from *Hamlet,* in case you're interested." Brian pulled out two brown milk bones from the bag and placed them by Mac's paw. The dog immediately snatched one up and started to crunch on it.

"Geesh, that was a dismal find, wasn't it?" He realized the dog was paying no attention to him.

He massaged the ache at the base of his neck and bent his head left and right a few times until he heard the cracking sound. He couldn't shake the image of the animated hand out of his mind. He noticed that the fog had rolled in. His was the only vehicle in sight. Reaching in his pocket, he pulled out his cell phone and plugged it into the charger. He was stressed if his phone wasn't charged.

He was always prepared, prepared for responding quickly to his daughter who often had anxiety about law school, prepared with detailed lesson plans for teaching his English lit classes, prepared for birthdays and holidays with gifts and cards. Always on time for appointments, he didn't like it when others were late, and generally wasn't keen on surprises.

That's why police work hadn't been his life's ambition, that, and the fact that every day the police department had been fraught with one harrowing scenario after another. It was a murder suicide, blood everywhere, at the crime scene, that finished him off for homicide detective work. The nightmares followed. Three months later, he switched over to Police

Department Community Outreach, and finally, left his police career altogether, to teach English lit, after he finished his master's degree.

The weather seemed to have changed for the worse, the sky now a steel-gray with black patches of clouds, a steady drizzle dotting the Jeep's windshield.

He ran his hand across Mac's back. "Almost dry, buddy."

It would be another ten to fifteen minutes before Tim would arrive with the forensics team.

He texted Ivy:

Can't wait to see you Saturday. It's been too long.

Ivy would be handing off her two grandkids back to her daughter, Becky, who planned to take some weeks off from her nursing job after months of crazy work hours responding to dozens of Coronavirus patients. And likely, as Ivy had described, she was dealing with plenty of emotional angst not seeing her daughters over an extended period. Now that some local restrictions had been lifted, Becky was taking the girls away to Sebastopol to visit Grandpa, Ivy's ex. That meant Ivy would be completely free to spend time with Brian.

A text came back from Ivy:

Me too! Come early. How about around five? Your ear better?

A photo came across. It was a picture of Ivy and the two little girls sitting at the kitchen table engaged in a crafting project. Colored paper, glitter, crayons, scissors, stickers, were scattered in front of them, across a daisy flowered plastic cloth. It looked like Ivy's arm was held out taking the selfie. Bridget and Tia sported zany expressions. Ivy beamed with a sweet, dimpled smile and wore a pretty scoop-necked royal-blue blouse. At the age of fifty, she was still sexy. Brian grinned, admiring her shoulder-length brown page-boy cut and her chestnut eyes, the centerpiece of her olive-skinned face. She had the knack of always looking happy, healthy, and fresh.

Another text:

The girls miss you. They'll be gone by early Saturday, so you won't see them. But they wanted me to say hi.

Brian tapped:

You're the best grandma on the planet.

Three emoji hearts followed. *So, your ear is better? I've been worried about you.*

Yes, my ear is good. Just that something ugly came up today.

She texted back:

You okay?

Oh God. He didn't intend to alert her. He quickly typed back:

I'm fine. Tell you about it when I see you. No worry.

He glanced over at Mac. Both dog biscuits were gone. He was curled up on the wet seat. Brian grinned and lowered the phone in front of Mac's sad-looking eyes. "You are handsome. Look at you."

He took the photo and forwarded it with another text:

Mac can't wait to see you. But for different reasons than his master.

A text came back:

Hope he's willing to watch us slobber over each other. I mean it's been more than three months!

I'll be counting the minutes, he tapped back.

He put the phone down and looked up to see heavy streams of water running down his windshield.

Glancing into the side mirror, he spotted a green-and-white police van come up alongside and slide into the parking spot in front of him.

"Okay, Mac, time to go back up that hill." Brian got out of the Jeep, leaving the dog inside.

Tim stepped out of the back of the police van and stood under his sprung-open oversized black umbrella. "Where's that mutt of yours?" he shouted over to Brian. "I've got a reward for him."

Two men jumped out of the front seats of the van, one medium height and husky, the other tall and lanky. All three of the men wore black rain slickers with Santa Cruz Police printed in bold yellow across the front.

Tim rushed over, stood next to Brian, and knocked twice on the passenger window, where he could see the Airedale staring at him. "Hey Mac, how ya been, ya big dude?" Reaching into a brown paper bag, Tim pulled out what looked like a huge hunk of meat on a bone. The dog watched him from inside the Jeep, his paw clawing on the window.

Brian grinned. "That a spare rib? Where the hell did you get that?"

Tim dropped the rib back into the paper bag.

"I snagged it off the desk of one of my reports. I'm the boss now, so the guy didn't even flinch—a lot of meat on that bone." Tim handed the crumpled bag to Brian.

Brian shook his head. "Stealing from your own squad? I'll keep it for later as his reward. Mac is probably the only one of us who can locate that hand again with all this rain. I should have marked the area, but I didn't." He half-unzipped his jacket and stuffed the paper bag inside. He didn't want the dog to smell it just yet.

"Okay, let's go." Tim called out to the young officers who were lifting things out of the back of the van. "Hey, bring my black binder. It's in the backseat." The tall one gave a thumbs- up.

Brian opened the car door and Mac jumped down, splattering mud in all directions.

"Whoa," Tim said and jumped back. "Someone's excited!" He looked over at the two men who had come up close to them. Their rain jacket hoods were up over their heads. Tim did introductions. "Brian, this here's Eric and Samuel, our best forensic guys."

Brian nodded, without reaching out to shake hands, the right protocol in the Coronavirus era.

The shorter one tapped his finger to his head in a half-salute and hand-ed Tim the black portfolio. Eric, the tall one, had a dark-green oversized gym bag slung over his left shoulder.

Tim looked over at Brian. "Since I don't have you as my partner any-more, I'm the one taking all the notes." He tapped Brian's sleeve. "You were good at that, man. Detailed documentation—I miss it."

Brian laughed. It was nice for Tim to give him the compliment.

Mac yanked on the leash, eager to head up the hill.

"And this," Tim said to the men, "is my old beat partner, Brian McCallam, and his private-eye mutt, Mac."

The dog jumped up on Tim's waterproof pants.

"Okay, guys, enough of this meet-and-greet crap. Grrrr," Tim growled at Mac, whose tail gave a hearty wag. "Let's follow the anxious mutt, shall we?"

As they turned uphill, Mac tugged on the ten-foot leash.

With the mud beneath his feet and the rain coming down, it wasn't easy for Brian to keep his balance going up the slope. I'm so out of shape, he thought. He noticed that Tim had the same problem. Eric and Samuel seemed to leap through the sludge and were far ahead of them. "Nice to be fucking young," Tim shouted out. He looked over at Brian. "Remember those days?"

"Carrick," a voice yelled from behind them.

"Gavin, glad you made it," Tim called out. The heavy-set man wearing the same uniformed black slicker, his hood up, unsteadily started up the muddy hill toward them. "That's Gavin McAfee, our new County Coroner," Tim whispered.

"Right," Brian nodded. "The Coroner needs to be here with you."

"Yeah, the guy's way more out of shape than we are." Tim laughed. "Came here from L.A., too full of himself, pain in the ass, as far as I'm concerned."

Tim waved over at McAfee, who lost his footing halfway up the hill, falling onto one knee. The Coroner struggled, but was able to right himself and continue up the hill.

At the top of the bluff, the wind was wild. Small tree fragments and debris wheeled in the air. Brian looked down at the angry white caps in the ocean below. He had never learned to swim, although his parents had encouraged him over the years. As a young boy, he preferred indoor board games and reading. Outdoors, he did some mountain biking, but that was about it. As he gazed over the cliff, past the jagged rocks and out to the ocean, a moment of fear gripped him.

Mac veered off to the right, pulled hard on the leash, vociferously sniffing. Within seconds, the dog found the hand, lowered his snout, and with his teeth, started to yank on the red sleeve of the jacket.

"Brian, can you pull Mac away? We need to examine the area without the damn dog messing with the corpse. As you know," Tim emphasized.

His words came out like a command. Was he showing off to the new Coroner?

"Come on Mac," Brian said. "I've got something for you." He moved about ten feet away from the men and reached inside his jacket for the paper bag. He waved the spare rib in the air. "Here boy!" He threw the meat on the ground. The dog bolted after it.

From a distance, Brian watched the men gather around the grim site. Through the shapes of their bent bodies, he could see the hand seem to wave in the harsh wind.

McAfee, the Coroner, was knelt down by the corpse. The wind had picked up even more, but the rain seemed to have retreated. McAfee struggled again to get up from the ground. Once he regained his balance, he directed the two young men to begin the work. The tall one, Eric, plunked down in the mud near the hand, his body sprawled out, his chin almost level to the dirt, his elbows planted. With a telephoto lens on a small pocket camera, he took photos of the landscape around the moving hand, then, of the hand itself, the exposed fabric of the red sleeve, and various spots around the area. Samuel kneeled close by, a clear plastic bag in one of his blue-gloved hands, and scooped up samples of mud. He made notes on a white slip of paper, slid it inside, and sealed the bag. He pulled out a second bag, then a third, picking up small things in the mud that might be of evidential value. Tim stood over the two men, his shoulders hunched, the black umbrella close over his head. He hurriedly wrote notes in the binder.

The rain started pounding. Mac settled in the muck and gnawed at the bone as if at a picnic on a sunny day. Brian felt a nervous tick start in his left lower eyelid.

Tim walked back to Brian and placed the umbrella over his friend's head. "You're getting soaked, pal. You run out of hats? Don't make much money in that college teacher job, do you? You should have stayed with the police department."

Brian shrugged. "Forgot my hat. Didn't expect we'd be caught in a downpour."

"Here, take my umbrella. You need it," Tim said. He handed it to Brian. "And can you hold this damn thing? I'll do more notes later." Brian took the binder. Tim raised the hood of his slicker and walked over to the men working. Brian watched from a distance as Samuel dug with a shovel, moving quickly, first edging a narrow ditch around the perimeter of the body and then going around a second time, digging out larger chunks of mud. Eric continued to take photos, as the body was pulled out into full view, the female face-down in the dirt.

"Turn it over," the Coroner instructed. Tim stood close to McAfee.

Brian turned away. He didn't want to see any more.

A few minutes passed. "We're done," Samuel yelled out. "I'll get the body bag, right sir?"

McAfee nodded.

Tim walked back to Brian and stood with him under the umbrella.

McAfee tossed his van keys over to Samuel, but they didn't make it over, and dropped into the mud. Samuel reached for the keys. Tim rolled his eyes. "He does things like that on purpose."

Samuel started down the hill. "The bag's in the back hatch." McAfee shouted. "And don't fuck with anything else in there."

Tim rolled his eyes again. The rain pelted down. Mac sat undisturbed in the mud, his teeth still on the rib. "Could have picked a better day to be a sleuth," Tim said. "The reluctant sleuth—didn't you say you were writing a murder mystery? That's a good title, *The Reluctant Sleuth*. Ya think?"

"Yeah, you could be my muse. You're pretty enough." Brian joked, thankful for some light conversation. Samuel ran back up the hill with the body bag. Tim and Brian watched the action from a distance; McAfee hovered over the men. Brian could see the body of the petite woman wearing a red jacket and blue jeans. The men slid the body into the black vinyl sack. Samuel zipped it up.

"The shoe," Tim yelled out, and pointed to the ground. "You left one of the shoes. Get it in there. Come on guys."

Brian stared at the abandoned red leather ankle boot; a black tassel attached to its side. The sight of it in the mud made him queasy. His neck ached. The boot was more proof of a real person, a woman who was walking, talking, breathing, had gone shopping one day, and out of all the shoes in the store, had chosen the red leather ankle boots with the black tassels.

The men put the body bag down on the ground while Eric retrieved the boot from the mud and partially unzipped the body bag to toss the boot inside. Samuel took some wooden stakes from the duffel and a roll of yellow barricade tape.

The Coroner called out, "Make sure those stakes are dug in there as deep as you can get 'em. Eric gave him a thumbs-up. The Coroner spit on the ground.

"He spits," Tim said, "disgusting. I heard he smokes in his office, too."

Brian shook his head.

Samuel finished setting up the rectangular barricade using the stakes and the tape. Printed across the tape were the words: "POLICE LINE, DO NOT CROSS."

The Coroner called out, "Looks good."

Tim elbowed Brian. "That's a joke. That tape will never hold. The guy's a dope, does things for show."

Brian nodded. "I see what you mean."

The two cops lifted the body bag and moved down the hill back to the Coroner's vehicle. McAfee followed behind, barely keeping himself upright in the mud.

Up on the hill, they watched. "The guy walks like a penguin," Tim said, nudging Brian.

"I guess I'll head out now," Brian said. He bent down to nudge Mac, who appeared to have finished devouring the rib.

"Yeah, I'm outta here, too," Tim said. "You, my friend, are drenched, and look at that mutt."

Brian half-saluted his friend and yanked on the dog leash. Mac sprang up out of the mud, a small chunk of bone between his teeth.

They started down the hill both under the black umbrella. Rivulets of water made the descent tricky. They stepped sideways to keep their balance. Mac trailed behind, not anxious to get anywhere. Once near the Jeep, Tim glanced over at Brian, grinned, and said, "Thanks for all this. It was a great date."

Brian bent over, feeling queasy.

"Hey buddy, you feeling okay?" Tim asked. "You look hella green."

"I'm okay." The Coroner's van left the scene. Brian handed Tim his dripping leather binder.

"Listen, how about lunch at Rosie McDougal's tomorrow? It's Friday. I'm working half day. Rosie's is full-fledged back open. You free at twelve-thirty?"

"It'll be my first outing since the pandemic started." The sight of the moving hand still lingered in his head. "Okay, see you at Rosie's," Brian managed.

CHAPTER 2:
"Love All, Trust a Few, Do Wrong to None."*
—WILLIAM SHAKESPEARE

AFTER HOSING OFF MAC IN HIS SIDE YARD, IT WAS CLEARLY NOT ENOUGH to get the grit out of the fur. The dog smelled like he had spent a week in a swamp. Brian sniffed inside his leather jacket—the same musty odor. When he took off the damp jacket to hang it on the coat hook, the empty brown paper bag that had held the rib fell out onto the wood floor. The grease from the rib had stained his blue golf shirt. "Damn it."

He coaxed Mac into the downstairs bathroom, closed the door, stripped off his clothes, and threw all of it into the wicker hamper. He led Mac into the shower and stepped in beside him. *The benefits of living alone*, he thought, and grinned down at Mac. The mutt looked up at Brian's naked body, his head tilted to one side, his brown eyes big, his fur matted down to the point where he no longer resembled the Airedale breed. Brian recalled only ever having Mac in the shower with him maybe two other times, but not since the puppy days.

Mac let out a yelp and barked. Brian removed the dog collar. Cracking the shower door, he tossed it onto the granite countertop. Mac, calmed,

---

*   "Love all, trust a few, do wrong to none." All's Well That Ends Well, William Shakespeare, Act I, Scene I

sat down on the tiled flooring and lowered his head on his front paws. Brian realized that he'd have to use his own bar of soap for Mac since he had forgotten to grab the doggie shampoo from the cabinet. "All in the family. Right?"

It took about twenty minutes to towel-dry Mac—a bonding ritual, Mac on the bathmat, Brian, cross-legged on the tile floor in his terrycloth robe. "You're the best dog." With an extra- soft towel, he rubbed back and forth over Mac's back, his legs, and underbelly. The image of the dead girl's body laid out in the mud flashed in his mind.

He lit a fire in the living room. The crackling of the log soothed him. He could hear the rain pelt down on the glass of the oak-framed skylight.

"Alexa, play J.J. Cale," he called out.

Flashes of the flopping hand shot back into his head.

The song was "Closer to You," the title track on an album from the mid-nineties. The image of the hand and the woman's lifeless body started to gradually melt away.

By the fireplace, he scarfed down a frozen lasagna, sharing bits of beef with Mac. Once the food was gone, the dog sprawled out on the burgundy throw rug and fell asleep.

As Brian sat in his La-Z-Boy chair, the back of his neck ached. He moved his head to the right and left until he heard the two desired cracks.

The easy lyrics of the song shifted his thoughts to Ivy. He poured himself a shot of whiskey and sat back in the overstuffed chair. After he downed the shot, he leaned against the headrest, his thoughts still on Ivy—the photo she texted him in the car, the smile on her face sitting at the table with her granddaughters.

Shit, I forgot to turn off the headlights. The "auto-off" setting had been failing for a month, but he'd put off scheduling the repair, with the virus outbreak going on for months and the earache in play for the past two weeks.

He grabbed the car keys and plodded down the stairs to the front door. Mac woke up and started to bark. When Brian stepped outside, cold splashes of rain fell from the top deck, hitting the top of his head. *Damn it, another repair I haven't had done.*

He slid behind the steering wheel to turn the headlight switch off and noticed that there was something on the dashboard window set under the windshield wiper, a slip of white paper.

He got out, snatched the slip of paper from the windshield, and rushed upstairs to the front door and inside the house. His robe and slippers were soaked. Annoyed, he opened the folded damp paper. The note was hand-written, printed with a thick black felt-tipped pen.

It said, **LOOK AT YOUR EMAIL NOW.**

"What the hell?"

Upstairs, he took off the wet robe and grabbed the frayed gray robe, shook off his wet slippers, and rubbed his head dry with a hand towel.

Glancing at himself in the mirror, he looked worn-out. He ran a comb through his salt- and-pepper mop of hair and realized that he hadn't shaved for two days. Even when he shaved, the dark outline of his whiskers was visible. His daughter thought it made him look rugged, like a lumberjack, that, and his broad shoulders and six-foot-one height. A compliment, but these days as a college instructor, he was going for more of a distinguished look. His hazel eyes, probably his best feature, were blood-shot. He grabbed the Visine out of his shaving kit, sprinkled two drops in each eye, and downed two melatonin capsules. He wanted to sleep, but he had the jitters, and the whiskey hadn't yet done the job.

In the living room, Mac was out cold again on the rug by the fireplace. J.J. Cale was halfway into the third or fourth song, but Brian's mellow mood was spoiled, bothered by the Shakespeare quote on the note and for being directed to look at email. The laptop was downstairs in the office. It was the last thing he cared to do before bed.

He poured another whiskey, sat down in his easy chair, and debated whether to head down to the office or turn in. He closed his eyes and thought of Ivy, how good it would be to see her again. His cell phone jingled, the tune to *It's A Hard Knock Life*. Although his daughter was in her mid-twenties and in law school, it was still her favorite song from the musical, *Annie*. She had insisted that he use it as her identifier.

"Astrid?"

"Hi Dad." Her tone was flat. Most times when he picked up, she'd sound joyful, instantly start to talk nonstop about one of her arrogant professors or the great time she had with her fiancée on a weekend getaway.

"I wanted to hear your voice," she said. A long pause followed.

"Astrid? You still there?"

"I'm here. Um...how's your earache? I've been worried about you."

"Better. I think I'm recovered."

"I'm glad." There was no energy in her voice.

"Astrid, is something going on? Bad grade? You sound..."

"Dad," she interrupted. "Nothing to do with school. It's Dennis, he broke up with me."

Brian wasn't skilled at giving advice on issues of the heart, especially when such matters centered on his own daughter. But he was a good listener. That's the attribute he'd default to whenever mushy things came up with her. She'd often go to him instead of his ex-wife, Barbara. It baffled him every time.

"Tell me what happened," he said. *Good*, he thought. *Dennis wasn't the right guy for her, too selfish.*

"Well, you know that Dennis and I have been glued together for the past three months," she said, "in this tiny apartment 'sheltered in place.' I guess it highlighted the gaps."

"The gaps?" he said. "So, you had arguments?"

"A lot of them; I had my law classes online, and had to study all day into the night...and finals were delayed because of the pandemic. She raised her voice. "It was intense, Dad." Brian took a gulp of his whiskey.

"My study period dragged out for weeks, and Dennis didn't like that. He played video games and got really bored...and wanted me to focus on him." Her voice cracked.

Brian picked up the handwritten note from the car and looked at the words again,

LOOK AT YOUR EMAIL NOW. The ache in his neck sharpened. "Damn note," he blurted out.

"Dad? Are you listening to me? Should I call you back later?"

"No. I mean yes, I'm listening. Go on honey."

"Dennis wasn't working at all. And I think he was sort of fired."

"So, Dennis was basically unemployed and your school was 24/7."

"Yes," she said. "We'd argue like crazy. I'd get stressed out, tell him to just leave me alone, and be quiet, for God's sake. I guess I got my wish. He's gone." He could hear her sniffling.

Bravo, Brian thought, and raised his whiskey glass in the air. *Hope that jerk's out of her life for good.*

"I'm so sorry, Asti."

"That was four days ago," she said. "I haven't heard from him since."

"Maybe he's just upset and he'll come back," Brian said, hoping to sound supportive.

"No Dad, he took all his stuff. Said he was moving in with his mom in Tahoe and planned on doing real estate business up there."

Good, far enough away, he thought, and took another sip of whiskey.

"Honey, what can I do to help?"

"I-I don't know, Dad. We dated for two years, lived together for the last year. Wham, three years of my life down the tubes."

He could almost see the tears trickle out of her blue eyes and down her cheeks. When she was worried, as a little girl, she'd bite her lip and anxiously twirl a long blonde curl around her index finger. He wondered if she were doing the same thing at that moment and wished he could hug her.

"Can you meet me for breakfast on Monday?" she asked. "Does eleven work? I have a legal contracts class at one o'clock. First day of new semester and on campus since 'shelter in place' has been lifted."

Thankful she had changed topics, he replied, "So, Santa Clara U. is back on track. Sure. Let's do breakfast on Monday."

"Thanks Dad."

"Wait," he said, "you sure you don't want me to come over this weekend?" I have some plans with Ivy, but I can rearrange it."

"No, it's okay. I'm going to Napa for the weekend with a girlfriend. A chance to unwind, get away."

"Good for you. What about Paisley?"

"No worry. The Bed and Breakfast takes small dogs."

"So then eleven on Monday at Albie's," he said. "Outside dining okay? I'd like to bring Mac."

"Mac! Oh, I miss that big boy. Yes, see you there. I'll bring Paisley, too," she said. "Love you Dad."

"Astrid?"

"Yes."

"Honey, if you need me before Monday, will you call me?"

She cleared her throat. "I will. Thanks Dad."

He put the phone down and took the last slug of his whiskey. He was a good problem-solver, a competent associate English lit professor, but without skills when it came to counseling on affairs of the heart. He was a loner, with a few good friends, a loving daughter, and an easy-going girlfriend.

Oh God, better look at that email. Whatever was waiting, nothing could be worse than a broken-hearted daughter.

He picked up the note, which he had half-crumpled up. **LOOK AT YOUR EMAIL NOW.**

He started to feel a buzz from the whiskey. As he rose from the easy chair, his legs felt wobbly. His neck ached like hell. Mac nudged Brian's knee to signal that he needed to do his business outside. He grabbed the damp note from the table and headed downstairs, opened the inside door to the garage, and let Mac out.

His office smelled good. There were floor-to-ceiling walnut bookcases full of books. The tri-level shelving on the right wall was devoted to Shakespeare, his works, and several biographies of the bard's life. The rest of the bookcase held a variety of European authors. He especially enjoyed English historical novels and had a decent collection. The bookcase to the left was loaded with novels that he cherished by the greats, like Steinbeck and Hemingway, and contemporaries, like Grisham, Brown, and Crichton. Two mahogany cane-backed chairs with end tables topped with small brass lamps afforded Brian a quiet place to read. He'd often sip his Oban whiskey and sink into a good book after dinner. Inspired, he had started to write a murder mystery over the summer, but with the pandemic, and his laziness, he hadn't gotten very far.

He sat down in the leather office chair and drew up his email, looking for any hint of reference to the handwritten note. There were about twenty-five to thirty new emails he had yet to review. Mostly garbage here, Brian thought, as he scanned the addresses: ads for Rite-Aid, Safeway, vacation deals, food delivery services. His email was bombarded with junk mail. Even when he had clicked "Unsubscribe" to many of them, they found their way back into his inbox within a couple of days. He wanted to go to bed. The note on the Jeep was likely some sort of joke. Odd that someone would bother to go out of their way for some stupid prank on a stormy night.

He heard Mac come up the steps from the garage. He heard the paws thump into the room and turned to see the muddy tracks across the wood floor. "Geesh, Mac!" The dog lay down at his feet.

He shrugged and looked back at the screen. Tomorrow, he'd delete all this crap from his email. He saw nothing in the list of emails that might relate to the hand-printed note. He went to shut off the laptop, but was stopped when Mac jumped up and placed his wet snout on his knee.

"Hey boy, time for bed!" He nudged the dog, but Mac wouldn't move. He looked up at the screen again without disturbing his dog to eye the list of emails one more time. The last unread email address he didn't recognize, Viking@gmail.com.

An advertisement? He opened it. Subject line: **VIKING.** The body of the email: **DEATH IS A GREAT DISGUISER.***

It was a direct quote from *Measure for Measure,* his least-favorite Shakespeare play. Was this the email that the paper note was referring to? He looked down at Mac and realized it was his dog who had alerted him to take another look at his email before signing off.

He saved it on his laptop in a folder, which he titled, STRANGE SHAKESPEARE NOTE. He felt exhausted.

Once he slipped between the sheets, Mac jumped onto the bed, and snuggled up to his feet. Brian stared up through the skylight at what

---

* "Death is a great disguiser." *Measure for Measure,* William Shakespeare, Act 4, Scene 2

looked like maybe a full moon, a fuzzy cotton blob with its frayed fingertips of white reaching out behind the obstruction of a dark cloud, reminding him of the fingers on the dead woman. The image of the hand on the bluff sharpened.

The streams of water on the glass above seemed to break the visible portion of the moon into shards. He had downed another shot of whiskey before bed, which had softened the jagged edges of his day. He reached over to turn on the sound machine. He liked the soothing sound of the ocean before sleep.

CHAPTER 3:
"Suspicion Always Haunts the Guilty Mind."*

-WILLIAM SHAKESPEARE

THE CLIMB TO THE TOP OF THE STAIRS AT ROSIE MCDOUGAL'S PUB IN downtown Santa Cruz was not as easy as it used to be. Brian felt out of shape, and by the sixth or seventh step, promised himself to get back to running, something he used to do three or four times a week. But during the past three months he had failed to exercise, although it was encouraged during the COVID-19 outbreak.

He put on his face mask, and before he reached the top step, a tall, slender woman he recognized stood behind a glass partition fixed to the podium. It was Rebecca who for a brief time had dated Tim. What looked like a heat lamp hung from the ceiling next to the hostess station.

"You passed the scanner test," she said through her face mask. "Your temperature is exactly 98.6°. Welcome back to Rosie McDougal's. You're meeting Tim, yes?"

"You just took my temperature?"

She nodded.

"Wow. High tech."

---

* "Suspicion always haunts the guilty mind." King Henry VI, Part III, William Shakespeare, Act 5, Scene 6

"You're Brian, do I have that right?" she said, and smiled. She had a blonde pixie haircut and dark-brown eyes.

I wonder why Tim stopped dating this one, he thought.

"Brian, that's me," he said.

"Tim's already seated and waiting for you." She pointed to a booth by the window.

He nodded and moved toward the booth with a view adjacent to the sprawling oak bar. A huge rectangular mirror hung on the wall behind the bar. Its giant black letters read, GUINNESS, a gold harp embossed to the right of the lettering. It was the most popular beer on tap in the Irish pub.

"Good to see you in the flesh, man," Tim greeted him, wearing a gray wool sport jacket and a black turtleneck sweater beneath it. He looked lean and fit, a contrast to how Brian felt.

"You got the best table," Brian said, sliding into the seat. He took off his face mask and stuffed it in his pocket. "The benefits you get as a local police officer, right? And the fact that Rebecca is still the hostess."

Tim's raised his eyebrows, seeming puzzled by the comment. He looked over at Rebecca and then back at Brian. "Oh. Yes, we did date for a month or so, but that was years ago." He shrugged his shoulders. "Honestly, I almost forgot about it."

The waiter approached, wearing a black cloth face mask, a green T-shirt imprinted with the Rosie McDougal's logo, black jeans, and one gold hoop through his right ear. "Ready to order?" he asked.

Tim glanced at Brian. "Burgers? Two Blue Moon's on tap? Will that work?"

Brian nodded. "Perfect, you had me at burger." He looked up at the waiter. "No cheese on mine."

"I'll take his cheese," Tim said.

"Got it." The waiter nodded and left.

Tim leaned back and clasped his hands together on the tabletop. "We found out the dead girl's identity." He opened up his black leather binder. Brian noticed a page full of scribbled notes inside. Tim turned to the first blank page.

"And is she local?" Brian asked. "How old was she? She looked young."

"Yeah, young, twenty-six. Her name's Consuela Rae Malecon."

"Consuela Rae Malecon?" Brian's thoughts swirled.

Tim turned back in his notes and eyed the words on the page. "Yeah, looks like she was shot in the back and then strangled. There was a business card with her name on it in her pocket, and she was wearing a gold bangle bracelet centered with a heart and a small diamond. There was an inscription on the inside of the bracelet."

"An inscription," Brian repeated.

Tim flipped to another page in his binder. "Here it is, the inscription: "Consuela, this heart is ever at your service." Tim closed the binder. "I'm thinking maybe a jealous lover did the dirty deed."

Brian felt the shiver go up his spine and settle at the base of his neck, which furiously ached.

The waiter arrived at the table with two Blue Moon beers, the traditional slice of orange hinged on the edge of each glass. "Here you go," he said.

Tim raised his glass for a toast, but Brian couldn't get himself to pick up his beer. The waiter left.

"Consuela Rae Malecon died about a year ago in a plane crash in Mexico," Brian said. "That dead girl on the bluff must have been someone else."

"You knew her?"

"Consuela was my daughter, Astrid's, school roommate and best friend. Yes, I knew her."

"Well, this young woman, the one you found with Mac, died just forty-eight to seventy-two hours ago, some coincidence, about your daughter's roommate. Same exact name." Tim took a gulp, downing more than half the beer.

Brian wished he had a whiskey.

"How old was your daughter's friend when you say she died?" Tim asked, and flipped open his binder to make a quick note.

"Twenty-three or twenty-four," Brian said. "Consuela went off to live in Mexico. Actually, she quit grad school before she finished her coursework and left for some job in the Yucatan."

Tim scratched his head, and made more notes. He slugged down the rest of the beer, signaled the waiter who stood near the bar, and pointed down at his glass for a refill. Rebecca passed by and seated a couple in the booth behind them. Tim watched the hostess as she moved and smiled at her.

Brian's mind shot back to the last time he saw Consuela. It was at a surprise dinner that Astrid had arranged for her friend. Surrounded by six or seven grad-school friends, Brian had been honored to be invited. Astrid would often bring Consuela over to the beach. Sometimes the two girls would stay the weekend at his house. He enjoyed having his daughter visit and thought Consuela was a beautiful, interesting girl. When Astrid had told Brian of Consuela's death in the horrid plane crash, it had troubled him for weeks. He realized that he secretly had strong feelings for the young woman.

"Here you go," the waiter said. He placed the two plates down on the table. Both burgers came with a heap of steak fries. Tim picked up the bottle of ketchup, shoved the fries to the side with his fingers, and squeezed a big red blob onto his plate.

"Consuela Rae Malecon, that's a unique name," Tim said, and took the first sip of his second beer.

"I agree," Brian responded. His stomach felt queasy.

They sat in silence while Tim ate most of the burger and half of the fries. Brian managed a bite of his burger and took a few sips of beer. The sight of the hand on the bluff, the painted polish on the fingernails snapped back into his head. He flashed to the celebration dinner for Consuela before she left for Mexico, recalling that she always wore shiny red polish on her fingernails. Her hair was long and dark, and usually curled in soft ringlets at the ends, which rested loosely on her shoulders. He remembered that she wore classy clothes, even when in a casual setting, and she was bright, almost brainy, when she spoke.

Tim squeezed more ketchup onto his plate, dipped two fries, and pushed them into his mouth. Tim was good-looking, tall, with a thick salt-and-pepper head of hair, and although in his mid-fifties, was highly sought-after by the local single women. But he was a messy eater. Often Brian would wonder if women were turned off by it, especially if they had dinner with him too often.

"I think the dead woman you found has to be the same woman you used to know," Tim said, his brow furrowed.

Brian reached up to rub the back of his neck. The pain seemed to be getting worse.

"That's impossible," Brian replied, as he fidgeted with the paper napkin. "She died over a year ago in that plane crash. Everyone on that plane perished. Consuela was coming back to California for a visit because her grandmother was dying from cancer." Brian had torn the napkin in little pieces as he spoke.

Tim glanced at the shreds of napkin on the table. "Well, something's not kosher," he said, taking another gulp of beer.

"You think I'm not leveling with you? Not telling the truth?" Brian asked.

Tim shrugged, slipped the pen into the binder, and closed it. "No, not necessarily, but I doubt if there are two Consuela Rae Malecon's."

"The one yesterday had to be a different Consuela," Brian insisted. "I'll prove it to you."

"You will? How?"

"I'm going to my dentist tomorrow over in Los Gatos. Consuela used to go to the same dentist, Dr. Snyder."

"Good to know." Tim's eyebrows rose. He opened the notebook again, picked up the pen, and jotted another note. "I'll need to subpoena her dental and medical records. That'll take a while, maybe a week, at least."

"Well, what if I can snag the dental records quickly and get them to you?"

"I doubt you can," Tim snapped. "And remember, you're not associated with the police department anymore."

He peered at Brian and pressed his lips together. "Did you ever have a relationship with the girl?" he asked, stuffing two more fries into his mouth.

"No, of course not."

"I believe you." Tim nodded. "You're a stand-up guy. I can't see you with a twenty- something year old anyway."

The words had come out of Tim's mouth, but Brian wasn't sure he quite trusted that this career policeman, even though a good friend, didn't suspect him of maybe being involved somehow.

"I'm going to get Consuela's dental records and bring them to you on Monday. You'll see that they don't belong to the girl we found yesterday."

"Good luck with that. If I don't hear from you by Monday afternoon, I'll be pursuing the subpoena process. What's the full name of that dentist?"

"Dr. Bernard Snyder. I've been a patient for over fifteen years."

"Okay, good." Tim wrote one last note on the pad and smacked the portfolio shut. "And if you have any success, remember that the envelope needs to be properly sealed. Hey, you don't have any vacation plans with Ivy, that girlfriend of yours, do you?"

"Nothing scheduled. I've got the new semester coming up. Lots of work to do."

"Yeah, English lit stuff. Sounds like a lot of work," Tim said sarcastically, then transitioned the subject to football. He complained about the games planned without real fans in the stands because of the damn pandemic. He finished the last gulp of beer and insisted on picking up the check, which was unusual for him.

"Next time, it'll be on you, my friend," Tim said, as he plugged his credit card into the machine on the table, "and we'll have a fancy meal at Shadowbrook." Brian nodded, and put on his face mask. He wanted to get outside and away from the conversation with Tim.

As they approached the stairs back down to the street, Tim stopped at the hostess station where Rebecca stood. "Going to visit here for a few," he said. "I'll be in touch, McCallam."

Brian gave him a quick wave before he descended the steps. He had planned to say something to Tim about the email he received with the Shakespeare quote, but had decided against it. His stomach churned, his thoughts jumbled, and his mind swept from the memory of Consuela to the dead girl he found yesterday. He headed down Pacific Garden Mall to his Jeep Cherokee. *How could the dead woman on the bluff be wearing the same bracelet I gave Consuela?*

He remembered when he handed her the bracelet, the light that shined in her eyes when she opened the box. It was the night of her going-away dinner. He handed it to her across the table at the going-away dinner event and said it was from her two biggest fans. He and his daughter grinned at each other, excited to give Consuela such a special going-away gift. But the inscription had been a personal message from him alone, a

Shakespeare reference: My heart is always at your service.* Astrid had asked him to pick up the gift because the clasp needed fixing. He hadn't told Astrid about the last-minute inscription he had the jeweler etch on the back of the bracelet.

On the drive home from the Rosie McDougal's, he thought about his friendship with Tim, who had been his only male confidante over the years, someone who Brian could say just about anything to, at any time. He had shared his self-doubts with Tim, as he tackled the process of quitting the police force and shifting to a more low-key career. Through his studies and the grueling thesis process, Tim bolstered Brian with support, humor, and encouragement to finish his master's degree in English literature. Brian felt depressed thinking their friendship was strained and maybe even spoiled.

When he arrived home from the pub, he found Mac in the backyard sprawled out on the deck. The rain from yesterday had vanished, the morning fog had cleared, and the afternoon sun felt warm. Brian looked out at the flowers in the garden. The tiny pink tea roses were in full bloom. The lemon tree was full of fruit. He'd need to pick some of the darker ones before they got too ripe.

He sat down on the wooden patio bench and reached down to pet Mac. The lunch conversation with Tim had worn him out. He felt sad to think that his friend didn't trust him.

The girl can't be dead twice. The thought raced through his head.

He recalled the day, a year ago, when he got the phone call from Astrid. Between the tears and sniffles, his daughter told him of Consuela's death, about the plane that had plunged down in the Yucatan just after takeoff.

Astrid learned of the tragedy from a grad-school friend on Facebook. "Dad, look at the news article. I just sent it to you on email. I can't believe that she's gone," she cried. His daughter had sobbed while he silently read the article on his computer screen.

---

* "My heart is always at your service." Twelfth Night, William Shakespeare, Act I, Scene 2

He recalled how he had sunk back in his office chair, shaken. He didn't know what to say to her. All he could muster was, "I'm so sorry, Asti. She was a beautiful girl."

Sitting on his back deck, Brian still felt the sting of Tim's veiled accusation suggesting that he had a romantic connection with the girl.

Brian's thoughts went to the unforgettable afternoon he had spent alone with Consuela. His daughter and her friend were having a beach getaway weekend at Brian's house. It was a Friday afternoon, about four months before Consuela left home to start her new life in Mexico. It was a Friday afternoon. The girls had just arrived at his house in Santa Cruz.

While they all sipped iced tea, and started to enjoy the weekend, Astrid sprang up from her chair and announced that she had to go back to San Jose to retrieve her laptop, which she had forgotten at home. She had a school paper due that Monday and had planned to finish it while spending the weekend at the beach. It was at least a two-hour drive back and forth between Santa Cruz and San Jose.

She insisted that Consuela stay put in Santa Cruz. "Why bother to get in the car and get stuck in beach traffic with me? Ridiculous. You stay here with my dad," Astrid had said.

He recalled their first few minutes alone together after Astrid left. Consuela had thumbed through one of the Shakespeare textbooks on his coffee table.

"I love Shakespeare," she said. Her eyes lit up as she shared her passion for her favorite play of all time, *The Taming of the Shrew*. She liked the way Katherine, the gutsy heroine, had defied her husband, but realized that she loved him in the end, without having to give up her freedom or her true voice. Consuela had even memorized Katherine's final speech.

"Would you like to hear me recite it for you?" Consuela asked Brian.

He laughed. "I'm an English lit teacher with a specialty in Shakespeare. Yes, please."

She stood up, stepped to the center of his living-room rug, placed her hands, palm-over- palm, on her heart, cleared her throat, and shook her shoulders a few times, her long dark curls splayed over the navy-blue Peter Pan collar of her pale-yellow cotton sundress.

"Fie, fie, unknit that threatening unkind brow and dart not scornful glances from thine eyes to wound thy lord thy king, thy governor. It blots thy beauty as frost do bite the meads..."* She moved across the rug animated like the young queen in *The Taming of the Shrew.*

Brian was in awe of her talent, how she finessed the challenging monologue, how she drew him in. Her dark eyes danced from spot to spot around the room as if all of the king's court in the last scene of the play was there to hear her speech. Her ability to capture the lilting rhythm of the iambic pentameter impressed him.

Brian's cell phone rang out, jolting him out of his reverie of that one afternoon alone with Consuela.

"Hello," he said into the phone.

Silence on the other end, a click and a dial tone.

He tapped to phone the number back, but it was blocked.

"Damn robocalls." Mac pushed his snout under Brian's hand, insisting to be pet. Brian stroked his dog's head. "Let's go inside, Mac, get a cold drink."

Mac headed straight for the water bowl. Brian poured himself some lemonade.

He wanted to pick up the textbook he needed to review for his course, but thought he'd first check his email. When he sat down behind his desk and pulled up the string of usual junk mail, his eyes immediately went to VIKING@gmail.com, the second one from the mystery sender in the last two days.

Yesterday, the first email read, **Death Is a great disguiser,**** a quote from Shakespeare's *Measure for Measure.* Today's one-liner, **The better part of valor is discretion.*****

---

*   "Fie, fie, unknit that threatening unkind brow..." The Taming of the Shrew, William Shakespeare, Act 5, Scene 2

**   "Death is a great disguiser." *Measure for Measure*, William Shakespeare, Act 4, Scene 2

***   "The better part of valor is discretion." *Henry IV, Part 1*, William Shakespeare, Act 5, Scene 4

Was it a joke from a past student? Were the emails meant to scare him, warn him? Somehow connected to the body on the bluff?

He got up from his desk and reached up to the top shelf on the bookcase for his copy of *The Taming of the Shrew*. A year ago, he had printed the article Astrid had emailed to him, had placed it between the first two pages of the Shakespeare play. It was still there. He unfolded the paper.

Plane Crash Kills Eight: September 24, 2019

The Cessna Citation Longitude, a chartered Contour Airlines plane, plunged into the Yucatan jungle in a fiery crash. The airplane was headed to San Francisco, California. Listed as fatalities were Consuela Rae Malecon, an American passenger working for Venture Horizons Real Estate Development in Merida, Mexico, Ernesto Diente, a second passenger from a government agency, the pilot, Fernando Chavez, the flight attendant, Talia Alvarez, and four other employees from a local agricultural company, not to be publicly released before close relatives are contacted. All eight souls on board perished.

CHAPTER 4:
"The Eyes Are the Window to the Soul."*
-WILLIAM SHAKESPEARE

MAY, 2018: A NEW DOG PARK IN DOWNTOWN SAN JOSE HAD JUST opened. Although she felt somewhat apprehensive about taking the small white Scottie into a crowded dog park, she wanted her puppy to be able to play with other dogs in the neighborhood. She stood at the entrance to the park. There were three long runs, with more than a dozen dogs of all sizes playing, retrieving balls being thrown, a frenzied bed of activity, and with no separation or barrier of any kind between small and large dogs.

"Let's not do this, Paisley." Consuela shook her head, left the park, and headed back to the car.

Within moments, an untethered husky brown dog came running up and aggressively nudged the small terrier.

Consuela tried to shoo the big dog away with her hands, then realized that the owner was close by. She yelled out to the man who stood about ten feet away, swinging a red leash in one hand.

"Can you get your dog?" she called out.

---

* "The eyes are the window to the soul." King Richard II, William Shakespeare, Act 5, Scene 5

He wore ear buds and didn't seem to hear her.

She yelled louder, "Can you get your dog?" She moved closer to the tall slender man and waved her hands in front of his face, gesturing for him to rein in his pet. She tried to pick up Paisley, but the large dog continued to chase the small Scottie around Consuela's legs.

Finally, the man started to move in to leash the brown dog but didn't appear to be in much of a hurry. He smiled and flipped his ear buds out from his ears. She noticed the gold nugget dangle from a long narrow gold chain around his neck, highlighting his golden tan. His dog darted in all directions, signaling the man to chase him.

"Smudge! Come on, we are not there yet." He spoke with what sounded like an Eastern European accent. He looked over at Consuela. His eyes were a light shade of green she'd never seen before. *He must wear contact lenses for that color*—the thought skipped through her mind. He was attractive in a rugged sort of way. His dark-gray T-shirt fitted nicely on his muscled frame. His brushed blue jeans fell loose and casual. He looked healthy, like a surfer.

"My dog, he just playing," the man said, raising his shoulders. "No worry."

"No worry? You're not in the dog park yet. Your dog could have injured mine."

"Smudge? You can see he is playing. *Da*?"

"The only thing I see is a large dog loose on a public street attacking my tiny dog."

"Your dark eyes are so fiery when you get angry. Forgive Smudge. He loves the girls. How about we go together to park? What do you say?"

"N-no, I don't think so."

"But you were headed there. I saw you hesitate at entrance. I can see you want to go back." He flashed a dimpled grin. His green eyes reminded her of amethyst.

"We have to go. My dog is thirsty."

"Thirsty, *da,* aren't we all?" he muttered.

"Excuse me?"

"Aren't we all?"

Consuela scrunched up her nose and bit her thumbnail. "Did you actually just say that to me?"

"No, guess not. I am too straightforward," he said, and started to walk backward toward the park. He seemed to move like a skilled ballet dancer, one foot to the left and one foot to the right, a smirk on his face.

"Nice to meet you, too," he shouted. His dog seemed to counter the young man's movements in an orchestrated, even rehearsed, way. Consuela almost grinned, but stopped herself. She continued back to her car with Paisley when a small stick came flying past her.

She didn't turn around, but stopped and pulled out her cell phone to text Astrid, her closest friend and roommate.

Just met an incorrigible man, she typed.

A text came back: *Does that mean you're in love again? I pray YES.*

Flashes of Victor, her ex-boyfriend, swooped through Consuela's mind. Astrid had never liked Victor, and after the messy break-up, had predicted that Consuela would soon meet the true love of her life.

"Hey, you drop this." She heard his voice come from behind her.

She turned to face him.

"Lucky my dog picked it up."

"What? You almost hit me with that stick."

She had dropped the embroidered cloth pouch she had purchased in the Mexico City airport. Damn, she thought, I had a chunk of money in that pouch. Even when roaming in the neighborhood, she always had cash with her, a practice her mother had drummed into her when she was a little girl.

"I-I must have dropped it when I took out my phone," she said. "Thanks."

He looked to be about twenty-six or twenty-seven years old. Her plan was to avoid getting too close to the rude man with the special green eyes and streaked blond hair.

He glanced at her outstretched hand and gave her a wry smile. "Thanks? Is that all Smudge gets?" He pointed to the dog. "It was hundred dollars in purse."

"Oh, well, then should I marry your dog?" she replied sarcastically.

"Will you settle for not-so-good-looking one?" He straightened, puffed his chest out, and pointed to himself. His streaked blond hair flopped forward as he moved with an unusual gracefulness.

Consuela stuffed the cloth pouch back into her shoulder bag. "And to set the record straight, there was exactly $81 in that purse, not even close to a hundred."

"$80, now."

"Huh?"

"Smudge insisted on taking tip. But...less than ten percent. He's gentleman. Usually, he take twenty or thirty percent."

Paisley pulled toward Smudge.

"Oh, someone's in mood," the man said, raising his eyebrows. His accent now seemed thicker. "But I'm not saying who."

"Keep the dollar." She turned away, and pulled on Paisley's leash. The terrier stood there, fixed, refusing to move.

Consuela bent down and picked up the seven-pound dog.

The man held something out in the palm of his hand. "A gift from Smudge Petrovsky," he announced. "When we give treats, they promise to be delicious." He quickly looked away.

"What?"

"Yummies for your dog."

"No, thank you." She grinned and realized that she was softening.

He moved closer. She looked at him with his striking green eyes. No sign of contact lenses, she thought. There was a faint smell of coconut as he leaned in.

"Here," he said, "some treats for road." She noticed his carefully trimmed nails, maybe manicured and with a coat of clear shiny polish.

She put Paisley down on the ground and opened her hand to accept the treats. She started to reach for the car keys in her purse but found it difficult to take her eyes from his.

He looked at his dog. "Come on," he said. "Look at these two, falling in love. Or maybe it's only *toska*."

"*Toska?*"

He peered into her eyes. "*Da, toska*. Russian word; it means 'a longing.'" He tapped his hand to his heart and held his palm out to Consuela as if to take hand for a dance. She felt flushed. "No matter," he said, tossing his hair back, and shrugged. "They want to play together."

"Well, I guess since my dog has been *seduced* into it," she said, and smiled. "All right, we'll come with you."

She saw the triumphant look in his eyes, as he brushed his hair back. She spotted the tattoo around his left wrist, a narrow dark-green-and-black braid resembling a bracelet of tightly woven leaves of grass. Consuela didn't like tattoos, but admitted to herself that this one was tasteful. The man had a mix of sophistication and recklessness about him. A walk in a dog park with this curious man would do her no harm and it would be a refreshing break from the type of men she usually met.

That was how Consuela met Leonid Petrovsky, the man who would entangle her in provocative situations that would frighten, thrill, and challenge her all at the same time. He'd turn her emotionally inside out. She would grow to admire his confidence and love his passion. She would open herself to learning everything from him about making big money, leverage her deep knowledge in accounting and her fluency in Spanish. She would effectively manage the finance side of his thriving Mexico real-estate business, Venture Horizons Development. They would leave California and move to Merida, Mexico, the colonial-architected gateway to the Yucatan, often called the "white city."

CHAPTER 5:
"In My Heart of Hearts"*
-WILLIAM SHAKESPEARE

B RIAN ARRIVED THIRTY MINUTES EARLY FOR HIS DENTAL CHECK-UP. Outside the entry door stood a tall face-masked female at the side of a table. She held up an electronic thermometer with one hand and waved at him with the other. Brian stopped in his tracks, turned, and rushed back to his car to retrieve his face mask. *Damn it, when will I ever get used to wearing this thing?*

When he got back to the table, a voice came from behind the face mask. He thought he recognized her from last year but wasn't sure. With the accent and what looked like a heavy-duty mask, her words were muffled.

"Say again?" he requested.

She spoke louder. "Mr. McCallam, welcome back," she said in a Dutch accent. "We missed you over the past several months. You're way overdue."

It was Lila, his dental receptionist. She had frizzy dark hair and green eyes, and stood at least six feet, her eyes level with his. He hadn't realized before that she was that tall, as he'd only seen her seated behind a desk.

"Please stand back a little and I will reach to your forehead."

He obeyed. "Perfect," she said, "you may go in. Please be seated in the waiting area. We're doing one entry at a time. Good news, the hygienist

---

*   "In my heart of hearts." Hamlet, William Shakespeare, Act 3, Scene 2 and Dr. Snyder are both ahead of schedule. So, you'll be called in less than ten minutes."

"Lila, I'd like to talk to Dr. Snyder alone before my appointment."

"You tell Katarina inside when she does your cleaning. Okay?"

He nodded.

Katarina greeted him as he entered. She was Dutch like Lila, petite, and with a hint of an accent. Her face mask was a lilac color.

"Ah, you're lucky, Mr. McCallam. No X-rays today," she said. "The machine is on the fritz. Dr. Snyder will refer to your pictures from last year."

Good, he thought. He hated X-rays, having to clench those cardboard things in his mouth was so uncomfortable.

"Please," she said, "I take you back for your cleaning now."

Katarina chattered away the whole time while she did his cleaning, at first about the hassle of having to teach her two children at home during the COVID-19 shutdown, and later while removing the tartar, she complained about her husband being furloughed because of the pandemic. The headlight from the contraption on her head shined down, blinding him. Brian shut his eyes and thought about what he was going say to Dr. Snyder to get him to hand over Consuela's dental records. Katarina scraped harder, poked his gums, and continued to gripe about her frustration with her husband's disintegrating career.

"All good now," she said. "You can sit up and rinse."

Brian opened his eyes and sat up. She handed him a small white paper cup filled with water.

"I'd like to spend a few private minutes with Dr. Snyder before the exam," he said, as she placed the tools in the cleaning bowl.

She looked over at him, her eyes narrowed. The crease at the top of her nose deepened.

She thinks I want to complain about her.

He took a sip of water, swished it around in his mouth, and spit into the sink. "Katarina, that cleaning was very good, very thorough. Thank you. I actually want to talk to Dr. Snyder about something personal, maybe privately in his office?"

"Ah, okay. Let me ask him," she said, and left.

Two minutes later, she returned. "Yes, Dr. Snyder will see you in his office."

He followed her lead around the corner and into a cubby hole of an office.

The gray-haired, half-balding Dr. Snyder sat behind his desk, wearing a blue face mask and a crisp white lab coat. His chubby hands worked briskly across the computer keyboard. Katarina moved close to the dentist, lowered her face mask, and bent down to whisper something in his ear. She straightened and adjusted her mask. Snyder brushed his shoulder lightly against her hip, making slight contact, glanced up at her, and winked before she turned and walked out the door. The brief encounter could have gone unnoticed, but Brian remembered what he heard about the dentist's personal life from his daughter. Astrid had caught Dr. Snyder fondling Katarina about a year ago when she had accidentally opened the door to his office before the start of her dental cleaning thinking it was the door to the restroom. Brian filed the salacious morsel of information away in a far corner of his brain.

"I just need to enter this," Dr. Snyder said, as he tapped the keys. He glanced up at Brian who stood patiently by the door. "You're looking trim, Brian. Not like most of my other patients after this long 'shelter in place' period.

"Think so?" Brian said. "I'm sure I gained eight or nine pounds."

Snyder laughed. "You're wearing it well," he said, and motioned to Brian. "Sit, please. What can I do for you?"

Brian's neck ached. Was it discomfort from the dental chair or was he tense because of what he was about to ask? "You remember Consuela Malecon, your patient? She died in a plane crash about a year ago."

"Consuela? Yes. Tragic. Marianna Alvarez, her aunt, lives right here at the corner of Kennedy Drive. She's also a patient of mine. The poor woman still grieves."

"I can only imagine. It was a shock for everyone. My daughter and I miss her very much." Brian cleared his throat. "Doctor, I'm working with a Santa Cruz police detective on a case that may involve Consuela's death. We need her dental records. I'd like to take them with me today—sealed, of course."

The dentist glared at Brian. "You know I can't do that." He rolled his eyes, turned back to his computer, pressed down on a key to shut it down, and stood up. "You used to work for the police department, didn't you? You know they need a subpoena. Takes a week or two. Why would they need those records now, anyway? Hasn't it been over a year since her death?"

"Doctor, I know this is a big deal, and outside the normal process, but it's important that I get the records today. Otherwise, I'd never ask this."

The dentist shook his head. "Not possible."

"Um," Brian hesitated, "I don't mean to pry, but I have a hunch that Mrs. Snyder wouldn't want to hear about you and Katarina." Brian tilted his head and raised his eyebrows, almost disbelieving the words that had just dribbled out of his own mouth.

The dentist dropped back down in his chair. "You're bribing me? Come on."

Brian folded his hands on the desk like a guilty schoolboy. "I admit this style is not usually in my lane, but I promise you, the urgency is warranted."

"Who's the detective in the police department who will receive the records?" the dentist barked. He tossed a pad of paper across the desk. "Write down the full name and job title. I'll have the photos sealed with my signature. You've got some nerve, Mr. McCallam." He threw a ballpoint pen, which ricocheted off Brian's index finger and landed near the white pad.

"Thank you," Brian said. "I really—"

"Enough. I'll need to rush your exam today. We have a tight schedule," he grumbled.

Brian jotted down Tim Carrick's information, got up, opened the office door, and headed back to the dental chair. Katarina was busy spraying Lysol across the countertop and wiping it down.

To Brian's surprise, the dentist worked with the same care as usual until the very end of the exam when Brian felt the sharp prick of the metal tool dig too deeply into his gum. It was a fleeting yet painful probe. He knew it was intentional.

Dr. Snyder whispered something to Katarina, but Brian couldn't make out his words. The dental hygienist responded, "Yes, I'll go get them right now." Snyder worked for another minute in his mouth, using a contraption to spray air in every crevice of his mouth. Katarina returned and placed an oversized manila envelope on the chair in the corner where Brian had left his jacket.

"Done," Snyder bellowed. He pulled off the blue paper bib covering Brian's chest and pushed a button to raise the back of the dental chair. "Time to sit up, Mr. McCallam." The dentist was gone from the area by the time he put his legs on the floor. Katarina gathered the tools and sprayed more disinfectant.

"More water?" she said.

"No, I'm fine." Brian stood, reached for his jacket, and plucked the manila envelope from the chair. "Thanks Katarina. You do a really good job." The corners of her eyes indicated a smile behind the face mask.

His heart pounded as he rushed back to his Jeep. He laid the envelope on the floor mat under the passenger seat, discerning the embossed seal and Snyder's signature over it. He was light-headed and needed some lunch, but first he wanted to walk down Kennedy Drive. Curious about Consuela's Aunt Marianna, he hoped that maybe he could talk with her about the plane crash, reconfirm the details of her death.

Kennedy Drive was known as one of the most beautiful streets in the Los Gatos area. Brian had heard his daughter talk about it after Consuela had taken Astrid to visit her Aunt Marianna. As he walked down the street, he remembered that he had met Marianna Alvarez at Consuela's memorial service. That was a little over a year ago. After the service, Astrid had introduced the handsome woman as Consuela's aunt, the older sister of Consuela's mom, who had passed away from breast cancer some years before. He recalled Marianna cupping his hand in hers, her warm smile, her eyes, tired and tearful. A tiny elderly woman in a wheelchair was by her side and seemed very frail. Astrid introduced the old woman as Consuela's grandmother.

He remembered that both women wore delicate gold crosses on chains around their necks. He vividly remembered that. What caught his eye about Marianna was that at likely sixty or sixty-five years of age, she had an unusually thick head of wavy black hair that finished a few inches below her shoulders. A pure white streak of a long curl fell in a tight spiral on one side of her head. There was an elegant air about her, her neck long, her clothes sophisticated. Maybe she'd remember him from the memorial service. He hoped so.

Halfway down the block, he recalled that Dr. Snyder said Marianna lived in the house on the corner. He stopped, turned around, and looked back up the tree-lined street. It could have been the first house where he had made the initial turn onto Kennedy. He hadn't paid attention. Could be either end of the street. He kept walking. As he approached the next corner, to his right, he spotted a stunning lilac jacaranda tree in full bloom set on a spacious green lawn of a grand white house. A winding brick path up a slightly graded hill led to the front door.

The house was a sprawling colonial-style one-story. Two white columns flanked the lacquered front door, which was painted a dark-blue and featured a brass knocker in the shape of a bell; under the knocker hung a large brass cross. He recalled that Marianna was religious, much like the rest of Consuela's family. This could be her house, he thought. It looked peaceful.

He opened the wrought-iron gate and started up the walkway.

Pink and white impatiens bordered the brick path. He heard footsteps behind him, heels clicking. He turned and saw a petite young woman headed toward him. She wore faded blue jeans, thigh-high black leather boots, and a white chiffon scarf wrapped around her neck, which partially fell over the top of her black leather jacket. Her hair was burgundy red, a short pixie cut; spiked bangs brushed to one side. A red long-strapped purse crossed her body. Something black was tucked under her arm.

"You here to see Marianna Alvarez?" she asked. "Is she at home?"

"Uh, I'm hoping she's at home," he said. The young woman rushed up close to him. They stood side by side facing the front door.

"Me too," she said. "So, you're a friend of Mrs. Alvarez?" The woman, about five-foot-two, had clear light-green eyes and long eyelashes.

"Well, I-I met her once," he said.

The woman smiled. She looked to be in her late-twenties. He noticed the tiny diamond stud sparkle on one side of her small upturned nose. He tapped the brass door knocker on the front door a few times.

The young woman pulled a blue face mask out from inside her red purse. "Oh God, I keep forgetting to put this thing on," she said.

"Right," he said, and scrambled to take the black face mask out of his jacket pocket and place it over his mouth and nose, stretching the elastic bands behind each ear.

She fidgeted, opened up a black binder, took out a pen, and looked down at something printed on the first page.

"So, do you know Marianna?" he asked. He reached out to ring the round mother-of-pearl doorbell.

"Maybe you don't want to ring that bell," she said, putting her hand up.

He raised his eyebrows. "Why is that?" he said. "I already banged the door knocker."

She closed her binder and held it up. The embossed white lettering on the front cover read, "Santa Clara County—Official Business."

"You're here on business, then?" he asked.

"I'm a COVID-19 Contact Tracer. I need to talk to Mrs. Alvarez about someone she may have been exposed to who tested positive for the virus. Oh shit." She stepped back, pressing her palm against her face mask. "I shouldn't have told you all that."

Brian grinned under his mask. "Well, if we're making confessions, I'm here to see her about a possible murder. Oh, I shouldn't have said that."

The woman's green eyes opened wide. She stifled a giggle. "Well, it looks like Mrs. Alvarez isn't at home," she said. "I'll come back tomorrow. Maybe you should phone her instead of seeing her. That's what I'd recommend. I should probably do the same."

She turned away and started down the brick path. The front door opened.

Behind him, he heard the young woman's heels clatter back up the path. She came up next to him and they both stood facing the woman who opened the door.

Marianna Alvarez looked much like he remembered her from a year ago the day of Consuela's funeral. He recognized the same beautiful head of wavy black hair, the narrow white streak of a long corkscrew curl on one side. A navy-blue wool shawl was wrapped around her shoulders set over a black sweater and gray skirt. She wore the same gold cross on a delicate chain around her neck. But she seemed older. Maybe seventy or so, he thought.

Marianna squinted. She reached behind the door and put on a pair of black eyeglasses. Crystals adorned each side of the filigreed metal frames. In a weak voice, she said, "I think I know you, don't I?"

He nodded. "Yes, we met once before. I'm Brian McCallam, Astrid's dad. She was Consuela's friend and roommate."

Marianna's dark eyes watered. She looked up as if to the heavens for a moment, lowered her gaze, and let out a deep sigh. Her small freckled hands seemed to tremble. At first, he thought the shaking was because of her sadness, but realized that it was likely a medical condition, maybe Parkinson's.

"Ahh, Astrid," Marianna said, her voice raspy. "Such a charming girl, Consuela's best friend; how is she?"

"She's doing well, second year of law school at Santa Clara U. Look, I'm sorry to show up without warning," he said. "I was around the corner, seeing my dentist, Dr. Snyder. Thought I'd stop by and visit but—"

"Yes, Dr. Snyder. He's my dentist, too. I'm glad you came by." She looked over at the young woman and tilted her head to one side. "You're not Astrid, are you?"

"No, no," the young woman said. "I'm here for a totally different reason. We just happened to arrive at the same time. My name is Savannah Romeo, from the County Health Department. I need to talk with you privately about the COVID-19 virus...about an exposure you may have had."

Marianna crinkled her brow, grabbed a flowered fabric face mask from inside the door, and struggled to put it on, her hands shaking. Once she positioned the mask, she touched her forehead with a trembling hand. "Oh my. Please forgive me. I-I need to rest for a while. Just came from the doctor, and, well, he gave me an injection. Can you both come back in an hour or so?"

Brian and Savannah glanced at each other.

"Sure," Savannah said. She looked down at her wristwatch. "It's eleven-thirty now. How about if we come back at one-thirty? Actually, would you rather I come tomorrow morning? Or, I could phone you if you give me your contact information?"

Marianna's quivering hand reached up to her temple. "Today at one-thirty is fine. I look forward to it." Her eyes creased at the corners with gratitude. "See both of you then. Goodbye for now." She shut the door.

They stood for a moment in silence. Brian glanced over at Savannah. "Do you want to see her first before me? Then I'll come in after you—you at one-thirty, me at two o'clock?"

"You hungry?" she asked, closing her binder, and placing the pen in her jacket pocket.

"Always hungry," he said. "My weakness is definitely food."

"How about lunch? she asked. "Panera Bread? We'll go Dutch, of course. It's just around the corner on the boulevard."

"Sure. I'm in."

They turned from the front door and started the walk down the path passing the Jacaranda.

"I love that tree. I love anything purplish," Savannah said. She handed him her cell phone. "Take my photo, will you?" He noticed the gracefulness of her petite frame, as she moved, the way she took small leaps back to the lavender-colored tree, her black boots coming high off the grass. Once under the tree's canopy, she placed her black binder down on the grass, took off her face mask, and pressed her body against the gray-brown bark, a rosy-cheeked smile on her red-haired-framed face. He took several shots with her iPhone. She rushed back to his side, clicked through the photos he'd taken, giggling as she peered at each shot. "Perfect! Thanks," she said, and tucked the phone in her purse.

They continued down the path to the iron entry gate and out onto the sidewalk. Savannah bolted away, toward a black motorcycle parked on the street. A red helmet hung from the handlebar of the bike.

"I don't need this binder at lunch." She opened up a side compartment and placed it inside. "I'll take a chance and leave the helmet here, too. Nice neighborhood, right?"

She came up next to him and they headed down the street together.

"Cool motorcycle you've got there," he said.

"Thanks. I *live* to ride my Ducati. And I work my ass off to afford the payments."

"So, you're a Contact Tracer? Must be interesting work," he said.

"Contact Tracing Investigator, that's my actual job title. Part-time, twenty hours a week. I track down people who were exposed to the virus, ask who they've been in contact with, and make recommendations for testing. Oh, and I also help them mentally prepare to quarantine. It's kind of like being a private-eye and a therapist all in the same job."

"Sounds intense," he said.

"It is, but I'm helping people. I also do taxes. And, I'm a website designer." She laughed. "I've got three jobs. Multitasking, that's my premiere talent."

"Not mine," he said. "I usually take one career at a time."

When they entered the café, Savannah waved for him to go ahead of her.

"Next," the woman called out.

Brian moved to the counter. "I'll have a tuna sandwich on sourdough, a bag of chips, and a lemonade."

"Got it," the cashier said. He paid and moved off to the side, waiting for Savannah to step up and place her order.

"Same as that guy," she said, pointing to Brian.

He spotted an open booth. Savannah followed, but stopped at the drink station. Brian's cell phone rang out just as he sat down. He could see Tim's name spring up on the display.

"Hey, Tim," Brian answered.

Savannah sat down across from him.

"Good, I wanted to catch you." Tim said. "About those dental records, I don't think it's—"

"They're already in my hands," Brian interrupted. "Well, I mean, they're in my Jeep. I'm having lunch in Los Gatos right now."

Savannah picked up his drink cup from the table and walked away.

"You managed to wrangle the records from the dentist? How the hell you'd do that?" Tim asked.

"I used my cracker-jack influencing skills," Brian joked. He followed in a more serious tone. "Don't worry; they're in a sealed envelope. Dr. Snyder's signature is over the seal and your name is on it as the receiver."

Tim's tone sharpened. "I was calling to tell you that it wasn't kosher for you to handle those records. I thought more about it this morning."

"Oh," Brian said.

"Too late now," Tim said coldly. "Can you drop them off to me early on Monday? I'll be in my office at 7:30."

Savannah approached. She placed his lemonade and a straw on the table.

"Sure, I can come by your office," Brian said, rolling his eyes.

"I'm trusting you won't tamper with the envelope," Tim said sternly. "Hey," he softened, "I don't know why I just said that. See you Monday, pal. And um, give my love to Ivy, will you?" He disconnected. Brian slapped the phone down on the table.

"Ouch," Savannah said. "That sounded bad." She took off her face mask and placed it on the paper napkin on the table.

"Yeah, that was my good friend Tim. He's not too happy with me." Brian removed his face mask and pushed it into his jacket pocket.

"Wow, you have a nice mouth," she said. "I mean...a nice face...I mean... Oh God." She cupped her hand to her chin, her head tilted to one side, and a smile on her face.

He was flattered.

The server arrived with two plates full of food.

Savannah tore open her bag of chips and took off the top slices of bread on both halves of her tuna sandwich. She placed two potato chips inside each half and reassembled the sandwich.

"So, you like potato chips on your tuna. I mean, right *on* your tuna," he said.

"I like sound effects when I bite into my sandwich. Want to know why?" She took her first bite. He grinned when he heard the crunching sound.

"Yes," he said, "I am curious."

"Back in high school, my boyfriend and I would sneak over to his apartment after class when his parents were at work. We'd fool around for hours while listening to heavy metal music." She brushed her red bangs out of her face. "You know, so the neighbors wouldn't hear us. Afterward, he'd make tuna sandwiches and we'd always put potato chips between the bread. It was our thing." She shrugged her shoulders.

"Sounds fun," Brian said.

"And the best part was that we ate them stark-naked in bed between more heavy necking."

49

Brian almost spit out the first bite of his sandwich.

"Sorry," she said. "Too much information... What about you? What was your favorite pastime in high school?"

"Well, high school was a long time ago for me." He took another bite and thought about it. "As I recall," he said, "I played softball, did a lot of mountain biking. Oh, I also did a lot of reading. Shakespeare was my favorite. Now, I teach English lit to college students."

"Oh," she said, and stretched out her arms. "Romeo, Romeo wherefore art thou Romeo."* She giggled. Not very good, am I? My name is Savannah *Romeo*, and that's the only quote I know from Shakespeare." People kid me all the time about my name.

Brian laughed. "Right. Savannah Romeo. You have an intriguing name."

"My friends call me Savvy. I think you and I are going to be friends." She crunched down into the other half of her sandwich.

She's a free spirit, he thought.

"Are you in college now? I mean outside of your three jobs?" he asked.

"Me? I'm done with school, finished with an AA in Broadcast Communications at community college. That was a few years ago. I got into San Jose State's bachelor's program, but I decided not to go. I needed to earn a living. I'm thirty-eight years old. More school is not in the cards for me."

"You're thirty-eight? You look twenty-four."

"You're delusional, Mr. McCallam. But I like that about you." She crunched down the last bite of her sandwich

They walked from the café back to Marianna's house, an easy silence between them. The sun had lowered in the sky. Brian noticed that the shadow of the oak trees that lined Kennedy Drive created the illusion that the two of them were stepping across the tops of the trees instead of on the gray pavement. Once they got to Marianna's gate, Savannah veered off to her motorcycle parked on the street. "My helmet's still here," she shouted out. "Good neighborhood." She plucked her binder out of the

---

*   "Romeo, Romeo, wherefore art thou Romeo?" Romeo and Juliet, William Shakespeare, Act 2, Scene 2.

side compartment of the bike. Brian opened the iron gate and they started up the path to Marianna's front door.

The color of the Jacaranda tree on the hill seemed to have changed from a lilac to a deep shade of violet. The wind had picked up. Clusters of the small trumpet flowers were sprinkled on the grass in a wide berth around the tree. More flowers cascaded down like a gentle rain as they gazed at it.

Savannah stopped halfway up the path. "This afternoon light, it's magical," she said. "Stand by the tree. I want to take your picture."

He shook his head. "No, I don't do photos. I'll take yours."

"Get under the tree." She raised the black binder above her head, pretending to swat him. "Come on, get going," she teased.

He shrugged his shoulders and moved toward the tree, his hands in the pockets of his khakis.

"Look happy," she coaxed, and placed the binder down on the grass. "Forget about that phone call."

Just before she tapped the key to take the shot, Brian embraced the tree, flashing his best smile.

"Awesome. Keep it up," she yelled out. She tapped the phone, then stepped to the right to catch a different angle. She moved close to him, kneeled down on the grass, and tapped again. She lay down, rolled over on her back, and took a shot upside down, over her head. "Great one," she said. She got up and backed further away to capture one final shot.

"Oh shit," she shouted, waving for him to come quickly.

He went to her. "What's wrong? Did I break your phone?" he asked.

Savannah fumbled to put on her face mask, picked up the black binder from the grass, and pulled him close. "Mrs. Alvarez, she saw me acting goofy," she whispered. "She's watching us from the window." Savannah tilted her head in the direction of the front door. "Oh God, I looked totally unprofessional," she said.

She hesitated a moment, played with the zipper on her leather jacket, looked up at him, and burst out laughing.

"It was worth it. Right?" she said. "You were a delicious subject."

He said nothing, not knowing how to respond.

Savannah pushed her phone back inside her pocket, opened up her binder to the first page, and took out her pen. "Let's shape up, shall we?" She cleared her throat like a grade- school teacher. You got me carried away," she said, and smiled.

"Yeah, it was all my fault." He pulled the face mask from his pocket.

Marianna opened the front door. "I heard your voices," she called out. "My window is open. Glad you both came back."

"Thank you," Brian said. "I think Ms. Romeo will see you first, if that's okay. I'll come in when she's ready to leave." He glanced over at Savannah.

Marianna smiled and opened the door wider. "I have some iced tea for you, dear," she said, as she gestured for Savannah to enter.

As the door closed, Brian turned to gaze over at the Jacaranda tree. He laughed aloud, recalling the look on her face when Savannah realized she was busted by Marianna at the window. He walked down the path through the iron gate and headed to her motorcycle parked on the street.

The Ducati insignia was painted with white script lettering under the left pedal and again lettered in a chrome relief across the top of the bike. Sleek, contemporary, he thought. The frame was a jet-black, except for a zigzag of red pipes in the middle of the frame. *It's a beauty*, he thought. What struck him as a unique feature was the streamlined design of the seat, held out like the wing of a beautiful, yet powerful bird. It welcomed the rider to the Ducati experience. He came around the front and noticed a small square of metal about six-inches by six- inches set between the handlebars engraved with the words, **Fly Savvy Fly**. He reached out to run his fingers across the relief of the lettering.

"Hey, you better think again about stealing that bike." He turned to see Savvy open the iron gate and step out on the sidewalk. She pulled off her face mask, stuffed it in the pocket of her leather jacket, and headed toward him. "You like my wheels? Italian design, you can't beat it."

"It's a stunner," he said. "I've been admiring it. So, you're done? That was some fast COVID-19 counseling."

Savvy opened the side compartment on the bike, placed her binder inside, and took out a pair of black leather gloves. She tossed them into the helmet that hung from the left handlebar.

"Terrific news," she said. "Mrs. Alvarez was not exposed to the virus. She didn't even attend the community event. She was at home not feeling well but had already RSVP'd. My source who is now in hospital with the virus used the RSVP list to identify attendees. Zero exposure for Mrs. Alvarez."

She clapped her hands together. "Ain't life grand?"

"Agreed, ninety-nine percent of the time." He grinned and held his thumb up.

"So, you can go up and see her now. And as a bonus," Savannah said, reaching out to touch his shoulder, "Mrs. Alvarez has homemade cookies."

"Just what I need after that lunch," he said. He stepped out of the street, back onto the sidewalk, giving her the space to get her bike ready.

She lifted the helmet from the handlebar of the motorcycle and held it dangling by the strap on one wrist. She came up close to him, took his hand, turned his palm face-up, and took out a ballpoint pen from her pocket. "Don't be a stranger." She jotted something on his palm. "Now, never wash this hand."

He looked down to see a phone number.

"What's yours?" she asked. "Here, write it on my palm." She handed him the pen.

He took the cue and wrote down his number.

"Like getting tattoos," she said. "Romantic." She laughed, took her gloves from inside her helmet, and put them on. After brushing her red spiked bangs out of her eyes, she placed the helmet on her head, fastened the strap, and tightened it under her chin. "Happy Saturday," she said.

With her signature bounce, Savannah Romeo sprinted back to her motorcycle. She jumped on it like a performer, her left leg hiked over the chassis, revved the engine, tapped her helmet to bid him goodbye, and accelerated straight ahead about twenty feet. Tilting her body to the left, she leaned in as close as possible to the handlebars and performed a trick like a U-turn. She tapped her helmet again with a brief salute. His hand went to his eyes to avoid the glare of the sun as he watched her head down Kennedy Drive to Los Gatos Boulevard.

He missed her energy as soon as she was gone.

CHAPTER 6:

"O, Full of Scorpions Is
My Mind..."*

−WILLIAM SHAKESPEARE

B RIAN OPENED THE GATE. HALFWAY UP THE PATH TO MARIANNA'S FRONT door, he stopped and stared again at the Jacaranda. The wind had picked up. More blossoms had fallen to the ground, creating a lavender carpet of trumpet flowers. The moment felt empty without Savannah Romeo standing there to behold its beauty. Her lively spirit intrigued him. The buzzing iPhone interrupted his thoughts. It was Ivy texting him.

Just ninety-two long minutes till I see you. Can't wait.

Another buzz on his phone from a number he didn't recognize, or did he? He looked at what Savvy had jotted on the palm of his hand. The text was from her.

She had sent him a photo of him hugging the Jacaranda, a broad smile on his face. He laughed. Never could anyone else get him to be so uninhibited. How could that happen for the first time at almost fifty-one years old? he mused. Tempted to forward the photo to Ivy, he realized it would take some explanation, and he wasn't prepared to do that.

He took a fresh photo of the Jacaranda and texted it to Ivy, with a caption,

---

* "O, full of scorpions is my mind." Macbeth, William Shakespeare, Act 3, Scene 2

Finished with the dentist—one more stop and I'll be on my way over the hill. A beautiful tree I came across today. At your place a bit later than 5.

Ivy responded, *Gorgeous tree. No prob. Dinner will be at 6 then. Miss you.*

He texted her back, *Perfect. I'll swing by my house and pick up Mac, and my clothes for the weekend.*

He felt guilty. Marianna opened the door. "Good, I was hoping you'd still be here. Come in. I'd hug you a proper hello, but this virus." She shrugged her shoulders. "A different world now."

"Sure is," he said. He smelled the roses as soon as he stepped through the doorway and spotted them arranged artistically in a tall ceramic vase on the table in her foyer.

Marianna led him into the elegantly decorated living room. "Please, have a seat on the sofa. I'll get us some iced tea."

He noticed her hands tremble when she took off her face mask. She placed it on the arm of the dark-blue velvet easy chair that sat adjacent to the upholstered floral-patterned sofa. "Thank you," he said. "You certainly have a beautiful house."

"You're kind to say that. I'll be right back. Get comfortable," she said, leaving the room.

Brian sat down on the sofa, which was set back against the picture windows at the front of the house. All three windows were adorned with vertically striped blue-and-white scalloped fabric treatments at the top and pulled-back white-lace curtains, a tasteful contrast to the royal-blue carpeting.

Antiques were everywhere in the living room. In one corner was what appeared to be an authentic oak Singer sewing machine table, with its original pedal and iron Singer embellishment. The piece, likely from the early 1900s, had been converted into a beautiful end table. A hexagonal stained-glass leaded Tiffany lamp sat on top of it. To the right of the end table was a majestic walnut etagere that held a large flat-screen television. An electric fireplace was built into the bottom of the etagere. Red, blue, and yellow flames glimmered, giving the large room a warm feel.

Adjacent to the etagere was a three-tiered walnut breakfront. On the upper shelf sat several small-framed photographs, some in a sepia tone. On the middle shelf was a set of tiny crystal cordial glasses arranged in a circle on a silver-rimmed mirrored tray. In its center sat a long-necked glass decanter half-filled with what looked like brandy. The bottom shelf was waist-high, marble-topped, and featured one eight-by-ten wood-framed photograph of a young woman. A row of small red glass votive candles sat in front of the photograph, creating a somber, yet serene tableau. A black iron cross mounted on a distressed white block of wood was positioned on a metal stand to the right.

Brian took off his face mask and stuffed it in his pocket. He removed his jacket, laid it down on the sofa, and walked over to the breakfront to take a closer look at the framed photograph. It was Consuela's high-school graduation picture, likely taken when she was seventeen or eighteen years old. The flickering of the votives reflected on the glass and highlighted her features: large dark eyes, the chocolate dot of a beauty mark just above one cheekbone, the perfectly oval face, the raw innocence in her hopeful expression.

In the high-school photo, she wore a single strand of white pearls and an off-the-shoulder scoop-necked black dress. Her loose dark curls brushed the tops of her bare shoulders. The pretty smile on her face reminded him of the afternoon he had spent alone with her in Santa Cruz. He felt a lump form in his throat. His eyes moistened.

"I see you found my angel," Marianna said from behind him. He wiped his eyes quickly and turned to see her place a small silver tray on the coffee table in front of the sofa. She smiled at him, but her eyes seemed distant.

"Looking at her lovely face, it's easy to forget she's gone," he said. "My daughter continues to grieve."

In a soft voice, Marianna said, "Consuela spoke highly of you and dear Astrid. She told me that she enjoyed talking with you about Shakespeare."

She carefully held onto the arms of the easy chair before setting herself down. He noticed that her hands never stopped quivering. "Come, sit," she said. "I've made some chocolate-chip cookies."

He came around the back of her chair and sat down on the sofa.

"They were Consuela's favorite." Marianna smiled. "With pecans." She loved pecans. "First time I've baked in a long time."

"I'd love one," he said. He picked up a cookie from the flowered plate. It was sweet, chewy, rich with chunks of dark chocolate and bits of pecan.

"Are you feeling better?" He asked. "I won't stay too long if—"

"No, no. I'm fine. And good news, Ms. Romeo was mistaken. I wasn't exposed to COVID- 19 because I never went to that event. Now, tell me about your Astrid, in law school? Such an achievement."

"Yes, I'm very proud of her," he said. "I must confess that I came here to visit with you but also to ask you some questions about Consuela, about the plane crash."

"Plane crash?" She held a trembling hand to her temple. She closed her eyes for a moment.

"Yes," he said. "Something strange has occurred. I don't want to upset you. But I know that you're Consuela's closest-living relative, so I think it's important to tell you this."

"Of course, what is it?"

He took a sip of iced tea. His neck felt tight and started to ache. "This is difficult to talk about." He paused. "The body of a young woman was found a couple of days ago near a beach in Santa Cruz. The police identified the woman to be Consuela."

Marianna leaned forward in the easy chair. Strands of her thick black hair fell around her face. She lowered her chin to her chest and stared down at the blue carpet. She struggled to stand up, hesitated, and moved slowly to Consuela's framed photograph. The light of the votive candles shimmered under Marianna's chin as she gazed at the image. Reaching out, she brushed her hand over the glass and stroked the girl's face.

"My niece died over a year ago at the age of twenty-five." Enunciating each word, she continued, "She couldn't have died all over again." Marianna, feet faltering, began to lose her balance. Brian sprang up from the sofa, rushed to her, and took her arm, giving her support to move back to the chair and sit down.

"I-I shouldn't have said all that," he said.

"No. You had to tell me. But you know she died in that plane crash. How could they say it was Consuela's body found by the beach?"

"Exactly what I thought." He nodded. "But the police found personal identification on the body and some jewelry, a bracelet with an inscription."

She shook her head. "It doesn't make sense. How do they know the bracelet was Consuela's?"

"Because I gave her that bracelet; I mean Astrid and I gave her the bracelet before she went off to take the job in Mexico."

"Oh, you did?"

"Yes, we did. Can you tell me everything you might recall about her death?"

Through tears, Marianna went over the details. They were the same facts he had gathered from the newspaper article he had saved. She went on to explain that there was a plane crash observed by several eye witnesses in the Yucatan just outside the Merida Airport. The results later referred to undetected mechanical problems. The authorities notified Consuela's grandmother, who was in the San Jose hospital, battling cancer. Hospital staff reached out to Marianna since she was Consuela's aunt and only other known close relative. Unfortunately, Consuela's grandmother, Marianna's mother, passed away from heart failure less than a week after Marianna was notified of her niece's death.

"Was there anything unusual about the communication you received about the crash?" he asked. "I don't know what that might be, but—"

"Nothing that I recall," she replied. "Consuela's body came to us within a few days. I arranged the transfer from the airport with the funeral home. I didn't view her body because...because..." Marianna burst into tears. She reached up to cover her eyes. Her shoulders shook. "I just couldn't bear it."

Damn it, Brian thought, *I'm just causing her more grief*. He kneeled down on the carpet in front of her chair.

"Oh God. I upset you. That was not my intention."

Her hands came down on her lap. Her eyes were wet and reddened. He reached over to the coffee table and handed her a napkin from the silver tray. Her trembling hand dabbed the moist, crinkled skin under each eye.

"You had to tell me," she cried. "I'm glad you told me."

He picked up his jacket from the sofa.

"You need to rest. I can see that."

Marianna struggled to stand up. "Yes," she said. "I'm still feeling under the weather, the injection and all." She shook her head.

He walked ahead of her to the front door and opened it.

"Brian, please come back and visit me again. Won't you?"

He nodded.

She whispered, "You did the right thing." It was the second time that day he felt heavy with guilt. The first was when he received a text from Ivy after getting butterflies talking to Savvy. He said goodbye and started down the brick path to the front gate.

Before passing the jacaranda, he heard her call out, "Brian, wait!" She gestured for him to return to her.

He rushed back. "There's one thing I do recall that bothered me," she said.

"What is it?"

"Yes, it's probably nothing, but at Consuela's memorial service, which was delayed a few weeks, I noticed this odd little man standing at the back of the church. He didn't look familiar to me, and I hadn't greeted him before we all sat down for the service. He had a dark mustache, wore a black trench coat, and had a hat on, some sort of fedora. Frankly, I was annoyed that he was wearing his hat inside the church."

"And?"

"Well, I wanted to introduce myself and see who he was. When I got up, right after the prayers ended, he was gone. I looked to see if maybe he had sat down in a pew, but I didn't see him anywhere. I walked outside to try to catch him before he went to his car. No luck."

"So, you didn't know this person at all."

"No, and honestly, I thought maybe it was a woman dressed in men's clothes. Sounds crazy, I know, but it was something about the walk. I asked people later at the reception whether they knew the mustached man in the black trench coat and fedora. Nobody did."

"Thank you for telling me. Time for you to get some rest." He touched her shoulder tenderly. "I'll be in touch. I promise," he said, and left.

CHAPTER 7:
"Thy Life's a Miracle."*
–WILLIAM SHAKESPEARE

H E STARTED THE DRIVE OVER THE MOUNTAIN TO THE BEACH WITH the radio turned up. Stravinsky's *Firebird* would help his troubled thoughts. Brian knew each and every treacherous curve of Highway 17 like the back of his hand. This enabled him to operate on autopilot most of the drive. *I screwed with peoples' lives today*, he thought. He had caused Marianna's reawakened grief. He blackmailed the dentist he'd had for almost fifteen years. And he flirted with a woman whom he thought was twenty-four but turned out to be thirty-eight. Savvy's energy had ignited something inside him he hadn't felt since first dating his ex-wife, Barbara.

He thought back to the marriage to Barbara, which ended seven years ago. They were together for eighteen years. Brian wasn't happy for at least the last five of those years. He recalled the night they had the awkward conversation. Astrid was in her last year of high school and would be going away to UCLA for university. It was a Friday night and she was at a friend's sleepover party. Just after dinner, Barbara and Brian were on their second glass of wine. He broached the subject by asking her if she was happy being married.

---

*   "Thy life's a miracle." King Lear, William Shakespeare, Act 4, Scene 6

"What a question," she said, her forehead wrinkled. "Are you asking me because you're unhappy?" She rolled her eyes. "Marriage has its ups and downs." She shrugged and took a sip of her wine.

Her response fueled him to proceed forward, thinking they were likely on the same page. The timing seemed right. He suggested that perhaps they should think about a separation, maybe even consider a divorce. "We barely talk to one another," he said, "unless Astrid is around us. You feel it too, I know. Even when we do talk it's usually about what's for dinner or should we have family Christmas at our house this year?"

She dropped her head in her hands, hiding her eyes, her shoulders slumped.

He leaned across the table. "Barb," he said, his voice turned to a whisper, "when we're alone together, you ignore me. It feels like you don't want me around. We've grown apart for a long time."

She nodded slowly. "I know," she said. "I know how it seems to you."

She straightened, sat back in the chair, and drank the rest of her wine in silence. She stood and started to gather the dinner plates. The clanging of the knives and forks as she threw them onto the soiled plates stirred feelings of guilt inside him. She headed to the kitchen, but stopped and turned to him before leaving the room. Some of the silverware dropped from the plates to the wood floor. She kneeled to pick them up. When she stood up, her expression was cold, her lips tightly pressed together. She stared above his head out the lace-curtained window to their back garden. "A divorce is fine with me," she said. She went to the kitchen without returning for the salad bowl or wine glasses. He sat there for several minutes, bewildered and regretful.

I'm a heartless husband, he remembered thinking. He had hopelessly misjudged Barbara's readiness for divorce, failed to test the waters over time, instead of dumping the bombshell on her without warning.

He recalled that an hour later that evening he came out of the bedroom and was outside the bathroom door upstairs, and from down below, he could hear her talking to her sister on the phone. Her voice was light, a playful lilt in her tone. "Oh Lisa, I'm so relieved that he wants out, too. A divorce will set me free. Thank God he realized it."

Why didn't she just tell me she wanted out? Why did she fake it? Hearing her on the phone call had angered him. Or was she only pretending to be happy with her sister?

He had been distant with his wife throughout the marriage—a curse he had carried since childhood, "Don't share your real feelings or emotions," his mom had drummed into his head for years, before she passed away with cancer, two days after he turned thirteen. "You need to toughen up," she told him the night she died, her voice a raspy whisper, strained from the throat cancer, which had spread to her lungs. "You be strong for your dad. No tears, you hear me? No big dramatics when I'm gone."

"But Mom..." he had said, unable to hold back the tears trickling down his face. On the edge of her hospital bed, he looked down at the pale, chalked pallor of the face, which was once his beautiful mother.

"Stop it," she said. With a boney index finger, she gestured for him to come closer. She whispered, but with the same command he knew well, the soundtrack he had listened to day after day over his childhood years. "Promise me," she said, "you'll keep your private feelings tucked away. Don't let anyone ever see you cry. Don't be emotional. It weakens you. "

"I promise, Mom." He drew in a breath and wiped away the tears.

She gave him a weak smile. "And second, do some good in this world." She pressed her fingers into his arm. "Become a cop like your dad and your granddad." She paused, her eyes closing for a moment. "Tell me you will." Her hand fell away from his. The machine that kept her breathing sounded a loud buzzing alert. Doctors rushed in. She was gone in the next few minutes.

Brian kept his promises, worked hard to suppress his emotions, kept his fears and worries well hidden, graduated college, and joined the police force. It didn't mean that he didn't have friends, but he just held back. He never cried in front of his family members, didn't laugh too loud, didn't boast, and rarely showed extreme happiness or sadness. He could see how disappointed Barbara had been with a marital relationship devoid of true intimacy. She had tolerated him spending hours in the cave of his home office, where he'd read on most evenings. Once they were in bed late at night, she'd complain to him. "You're like a stone," she'd say. "Why don't you ever tell me what you're really thinking or feeling? A wife needs that from her husband."

"It's just my way," he'd respond. "Just the way I'm wired. That's all."

After a while, Barbara stopped pressing him. She chose to ignore him and be quiet about his issues.

In contrast, his daughter seemed to accept him the way he was. Since she was small, Astrid would frequently show up in his office, the room stacked high with books. She'd drag in her oversized pink "Dora the Explorer" pillow and ask him to read to her.

"Okay, fetch me one of your picture books and I'll read to you."

"No, Daddy. I want you to read me what *you* like to read. One of those books up there. I'll just listen and we'll share my Almond Joy." He'd nod and pick out something from one of the crowded bookshelves, get down on the carpet, and sit close to her. "Share my pillow with me, Daddy," she'd insist. She'd hand him a piece of her candy bar each time he'd pause to turn the page.

She likely didn't understand the Shakespeare or Dickens or the Chaucer, but she didn't seem to mind hearing it. She'd encourage him to keep reading, even when he suspected that her mind had strayed somewhere else. "Daddy, I love your voice," she'd say. "Gentle. Smooth. Calm like the water in Lake Tahoe. Please don't stop reading."

He'd tickle her until she'd wriggle and giggle. "You're my own sweet Almond Joy, aren't you?" he'd tease her. He'd continue reading and she'd fall off to sleep on her pillow next to him. It touched his heart every time.

She had been a blessing to him. In high school, she'd often slip into his office and spill the events of her day, her first crush, a recent heartbreak, details of a new friend she made at the "Y," anecdotes about teachers, her anxiety before taking the SATs. She even gave him a heads-up before she had her first experience with marijuana. "I can't tell Mom this stuff," Astrid would say. "Only you, Dad." He knew that her candor with him was an outcome of his tendency to not show an extreme reaction to anything he heard.

When Barbara and Brian told their daughter of their plans to divorce, Astrid collapsed on the sofa in tears. They both assured her that they would still be a family, split their time with her, whenever she returned from college for holidays or summers, and would stay in the house together through the rest of Astrid's senior year in high school.

A blinking sign ahead brought Brian back to Highway 17, back to his drive over the Santa Cruz mountains. About to approach the summit, he saw that off to the right shoulder was a neon sign: CAUTION—ONE LANE AHEAD. *Damn!* He detested being late for anything. Disappointing Ivy was the last thing he wanted to do that day. He turned the radio station from classical to 80's rock. Sting's voice sang out from his police days: "Every breath you take, every move you make..." Brian's thoughts morphed to the image of Savvy Romeo riding down Kennedy Drive on her black bird of a motorcycle.

The dashboard in his car buzzed. I was Ivy. He lowered the music and pushed the phone icon button on the steering wheel.

"I'm sorry. Traffic's a bitch," he said.

"Where are you now?" she asked.

"At the summit, but evidently there's only one lane open for who knows how long over this mountain."

"No worry. I'll cook more slowly." She laughed.

"Thanks for understanding. Listen, I'm a little worried about Mac," he said. "Since the pandemic started, I've been with him all day every single day. Today I've been gone over ten hours. Hope he's not freaked."

"You want me to drive over to your place? I can bring him here."

"No, it's okay; he's got access to the backyard. I'll be there soon enough. *Toute suite.* Well, *toute* slow."

"I have a silver lining for you," she said. "I'm making your favorite meal, homemade lasagna from scratch and Caesar salad. Sound okay?"

"Lavish me with lasagna!" he said. "That should have been a Shakespeare quote, right?"

She giggled. "I was calling to see if you could pick up a bottle of vino on the way over. I haven't been drinking at all since the grandkids were here full-time."

"Coppola Cabernet coming your way. I'm afraid my ETA is now six-thirty."

"Oops, gotta go. Nothing worse than burnt lasagna." She disconnected.

He had dated Ivy for the last four years. Never was there any pressure from her to live together or see each other more frequently than on weekends and occasionally one other night during the week. He had kept space between them and she respected it. He and Mac would arrive on Friday night at her small cottage, a short block away from Seabright Beach. They'd take long walks at sunset, play fetch with Mac on the beach, have Sunday breakfast at Linda's Café, read their individual books for hours together in her back garden, where the hummingbirds would visit the glass feeder, the gentle sound of her rock fountain in the background. Sometimes they'd take in a movie in downtown Santa Cruz. On Sundays, he'd leave her house in the late afternoon, stop at the dog park for Mac to socialize, and then head home to get ready for his classes, which kicked off early on Monday mornings. That was his routine life before COVID-19. He couldn't wait for things to get back to normal and this weekend with Ivy would be the start to all that.

He noticed that two cars in front of him a man wearing an orange vest reached down from the flatbed of a truck and was picking up orange construction cones from the right-hand lane of the highway, hoisting them, one by one, into the truck bed. The winding road turned back into two lanes. The rest of the journey to his house on the west side of Santa Cruz was thankfully hassle-free. As he pulled into his driveway, he heard Mac barking from behind the side gate that led to the backyard. His dashboard clock read 6:07. If he grabbed some weekend clothes and Mac's food, he could make it to Ivy's house by six-thirty. He noticed the side gate was slightly ajar. *Damn, did I forget to latch it?* He opened the gate and bent down to pet Mac, who returned the greeting with a voracious series of tongue licks on Brian's face. "Hey boy, stop that." Brian laughed.

The dog waddled over to the glass-topped wicker table up on the redwood patio. His snout was down on the deck and pulled on something with his teeth. Brian came up the three wooden stairs. He spotted a slip of white paper set under the foot of the table. "What's that, Mac?" The dog wagged his tail. Brian reached down to tug the paper out from under the table.

It was a handwritten note in bold black felt-tip pen. *Damn, somebody's been here.* Brian stood up and read the note, **BETTER ONCE THAN NEVER, <u>BUT NEVER TOO LATE</u>.***

Another Shakespeare quote, but from what play? He couldn't place it. And the last part of the sentence underlined.

He looked at his phone. *Crap, 6:15. The hell with the note.* "Let's go, Mac." Mac followed him inside the house. He grabbed his overnight bag and stuffed it with jeans, his sweats, a couple of golf shirts, underwear, and toiletry bag. In a plastic Trader Joe's sack, he put a bag of dog food, two bowls, the dog leash, and some rawhide treats. He whistled for Mac to follow him out to the Jeep. *Lock the gate,* he reminded himself. Mac jumped up into the passenger seat. Brian rushed back into the house, out to the backyard, and latched the side gate shut from the inside. *Nobody comes into my space without being invited,* he said to himself. *Nobody.*

---

*   "Better once than never, but never too late." *The Taming of the Shrew,* William Shakespeare, Act 5, Scene I

CHAPTER 8:
"Love Sought Is Good,
but Given Unsought Is Better."*
—WILLIAM SHAKESPEARE

IVY OPENED THE FRONT DOOR. THE AROMA OF THE LASAGNA AND THE warmth of her embrace were an instant elixir for any stress Brian felt from the day. He missed having her close to him, the way she easily fit in his arms, the way her head rested against his chest. She kissed him sweetly on his lips, brushed his cheek with the palm of her hand, and kissed him again, a tender lingering kiss. She stood back and glanced down at Mac. His tail wagged as he circled around them.

"Mac, I have something for you." Ivy picked up a stuffed toy hedgehog from the velvet cushioned chair. "Catch," she called out, and tossed it to the Airedale.

They watched Mac start to gnaw away at the toy, already intent on extracting the hidden squeaker, something he did within the first few minutes of being introduced to a new plaything. "Oh, you need a grooming session, my canine friend," she said.

Brian watched as Ivy sat down cross-legged on the braided rug close to Mac. "Gimme that toy," she said, and patted her thigh a few times. The

---

*   "Love is sought is good, but given unsought is better." Twelfth Night, William Shakespeare, Act 3, Scene I

dog dropped the hedgehog in front of her. In her tan pedal pushers and flowered peasant blouse, her large chestnut eyes shining, Ivy looked both comfortable and pretty. She wore dangly fleur-de-lys-shaped silver earrings. Her dark-brown hair page-boy cut seemed shorter than he recalled it from three months ago, the last time he saw her. She rarely used makeup and wasn't into nail polish or anything artificially manufactured that would touch her body.

She glanced over at Brian. "When was the last time Mac had a beauty treatment?" she asked.

"Well, I hosed him down a couple of days ago. Does that count? Oh, and he had a quick shower with me."

"Say no more," she laughed. "Mind if I treat him to an old-fashioned bath in the morning? Mac looked up, seeming to recognize the word *bath*.

Ivy smiled and stroked Mac's head. "Bubbles? Lavender-scented doggie shampoo? Blow-dry? The works." Mac dropped the stuffed hedgehog in her lap.

"Sure," Brian replied. "And if you'd like a partner in crime—"

"Absolutely," she said, and threw the hedgehog near the front door. "You scrub and I'll dry."

He laughed and sat on the tapestry-covered sofa. Ivy liked to collect comfy used furniture, her prize possession, a king-sized brass bed, which barely fit in her small bedroom.

Whatever she put in her cottage had to be accommodated by the thirteen hundred square feet of living space. With her English garden sanctuary of wildflowers, roses, and home-grown vegetables in the backyard, and the generous front porch, the property was just shy of a half-acre. She had purchased it "for a song" when the market crashed in 2008, a fortunate find less than a block from Seabright Beach.

Her steady income as a school counselor had enabled her to save enough and cash in her 401K to afford to buy the place on her own. Ivy's daughter was a love child from a boyfriend she had in the late 80's. She never married Carl, the father of her child, whom she touched base with now and then. Ivy was a frugal woman who spoiled her grandkids, instead of herself, savored her romance novels, and pruned her roses daily, and took care of the front and back gardens, which looked like they came out of a country photography book. She had opted for early retirement when she turned fifty, just a few months before the Coronavirus outbreak had taken its brutal hold on America.

"I'll be in the kitchen," she said. "Dinner in a few minutes. You relax." Mac followed Ivy to the kitchen, the dog toy in his mouth.

"Can I help?" Brian asked.

"No, just show up at the table in five minutes," she shouted from the kitchen.

He sat back on the sofa and thought about what parts of the mess he was embroiled in he would share with Ivy. Reluctant to disturb this peaceful oasis, he felt like leaving everything else behind. But the tone of the interactions with Tim and the mysterious notes and emails churned inside his head. He looked down and noticed that the phone number Savvy wrote on his palm with the black pen was still there. *Shit.* He went into Ivy's bathroom, took his phone out of his pocket, and tapped Savvy's phone number into his iPhone Notes, then washed his palm with soap and scrubbed it with the nail brush he found near the sink.

He looked in the mirror and thought the guilt he felt inside must show in his face. He headed to Ivy in the kitchen. The oak dining-room table was set with crystal candlesticks, the two candles already lit. The teal-colored wine glasses were filled with wine and the food set out on plates ready to eat.

"Sit," Ivy said. "I'm just warming the focaccia."

The two lead-framed windows were cranked open to the back garden, which made the cramped kitchen space feel roomy and fresh. The wind chimes, the salt air, and the smell of the roses in the garden took him to a deeper level of serenity. Mac sat outside on the patio at the back door chewing on a rawhide treat.

The dinner conversation was filled with an animated Ivy talking about her two granddaughters, sharing funny anecdotes about them, how Bridget and Tia would wake up early and set the table for breakfast or craft a "Good Morning" card and put it on the coffee table, surrounded by chocolate kisses, as a surprise for her, how she helped the girls learn to sew colorful cloth face masks to wear when they accompanied her to the grocery store. He could listen to her heartwarming grandma stories for hours.

Ivy served up her homemade coconut ice cream for dessert, a favorite Brian had missed over the past three months. When she got up from the table to pour him a cup of decaf, he peered out at the garden and thought of Savvy bringing him lemonade from the drink station at Panera Café and the pixie-like expression on her face when she stood under the Jacaranda tree, the way she jumped onto her motorcycle like a stunt driver earlier that day in Los Gatos.

"You daydreaming?" Ivy asked.

"No. I'm...I'm enjoying being here with you. I've missed you." He took a sip of coffee. "Mmm, you'd never know this was decaf. Really good."

Ivy sat down across from him, and scooped up the last spoonful of her ice cream. "You seem preoccupied," she said. "Got a lot on your mind?"

He reached across the table and squeezed her hand. "To say the least, I've had quite the eventful last forty-eight hours."

"Want to share some of it with your Santa Cruz girlfriend?" she said, and bit her lip.

Santa Cruz girlfriend? Did she suspect him of being with another woman?

"Tell me what happened," Ivy said. "Maybe you need to get it off your chest."

He appreciated her matter-of-fact style. Like him, she listened without overreacting or inserting a hasty solution.

His phone buzzed. It was a text from his daughter, a photo of Astrid and her friend, Laura, having a champagne toast, a sprawling orchard on rolling hills behind them. The caption read, *GETTING OVER MY HEARTBREAK. IT'S A NEW DAY!*

"Astrid," Brian said, looking over at Ivy. He put the phone in his pocket. "Her fiancée moved out, broke her heart. She's off on a weekend in Napa with a girlfriend. That's just a small window into my last forty-eight hours."

"I'd like to hear the rest of it over another glass of wine." She picked up the bottle and poured more in each glass.

"Let's just say Mac and I made a grim discovery on our walk by the beach yesterday during that rainstorm that seemed to come out of nowhere. Look, how about we not talk about it tonight? I'd rather chill, enjoy our reunion." He raised his glass in a toast.

"Something grim? What happened?" she asked. The crease at the top of her nose deepened. "I worry about you, especially when you say something like that." She looked at him harshly.

"It's morbid, gruesome. Can we do this discussion tomorrow? Really, I'm fine and I'd rather focus on us tonight."

She sighed. "Okay. Your wish is granted. Since we're focusing on us, may I share something personal? It's a little delicate."

"Of course, you know you can," he said, and took another sip of wine. The words on the mysterious note he found on his back patio earlier that evening flashed before his eyes. **BETTER ONCE THAN NEVER, BUT NEVER TOO LATE.***

"Well, I've been thinking," Ivy said.

"That's very like you, always thinking, and doing." He reached over to give her a slow tender kiss. He sat back in his chair. "Maybe I should just shut up and listen."

Ivy laughed. She pulled her chair closer to him and touched his sleeve.

"I've missed you way too much over these past few months." She grinned, her eyes warm and caring. "This pandemic made me think about the short journey we have left on this earth, and the brief time you and I have to spend together. We need to make the most of it."

"I feel the same," he said. "God, I hope we don't have another surge of this virus, and another lockdown. It would be unbearable not to see you."

She pressed her lips together and nodded. "Do you think that maybe we should move in together?" she asked.

His neck ached. It was the first time he ever heard Ivy ask for more than their weekends together and the occasional weeknight taking in a movie. He bent forward, his head in his hands, looking at his feet. He stayed there for a minute without responding. He reached for her hands and pressed his lips to her palms.

---

*   "Better once than never, but never too late." The Taming of the Shrew, William Shakespeare, Act 5, Scene 3

He sat up, his back pressed against the slatted wood of the straight-backed chair. "Yes," he said, "it's something for us to think about. I-I love being with you. There's no question." Mac swaggered over to the table and placed his head on Brian's knee.

Ivy looked away, then stood and went to the kitchen pantry. "Mac, time for another treat." She pulled out a stick of rawhide from a plastic bag."

Brian went to her, took the treat out of her hand, and threw it by the open patio door. "There you go, boy. Have at it." He pulled Ivy to him and whispered in her ear, "You are the best thing in my life." He hugged her tighter and stared out the back window at the roses. "It's just that I've lived alone for quite a while. It's hard for me—"

She took his arms from her waist and stepped back. "Brian, the last thing I want to do is spoil what we have; it's so good." He could see the tears brimming over her eyelids. "Let's put this topic on the back burner," she said, "and enjoy the weekend, like you suggested. We don't need clutter." She brushed her arms down in the air as if to shoo away the difficult subject.

"Okay," he said, "but I do want to come back to it." He had only told Ivy he loved her once when they were in the heat of making love. He didn't want to disappoint yet another woman with his need to be alone for hours each day, his need to remain aloof, to be separate, his need to be free.

His cell phone rang out. The number looked familiar, but no name came up on the display.

"Take the call," Ivy said. "Sit in the garden."

"Thanks," he said. "Probably another robocall."

"I bet you're missing me," the woman's voice on the phone teased.

His chest felt tight. "Savvy?" he asked in a hushed voice.

"I was thinking about you, Brian McCallam. I have a proposition."

"You do?" He sat down on the white iron bench set on the edge of Ivy's back garden.

"I remember you saying that in high school you did a lot of mountain biking. Do you still have a bike?"

"Yes, in my garage. Probably haven't ridden it for five years. Savvy, it's hard for me to talk now," he whispered.

"This won't take long," she replied. "How'd you like to mountain-bike with me, tomorrow, at Wilder Ranch? They finally opened the trails again after the fire." She has a radio voice, he thought, smooth and clear.

"Tomorrow?"

"Why not?" she said. "Good exercise. It's a Sunday, but I don't think it will be too popular because most people don't even know it's opened up."

He got up from the bench and went to the furthest spot away from the back door to the kitchen. "Savvy, I guess I didn't tell you that I have a girl-friend. I'm sorry. My fault."

"I'm not inviting you to have sex. A bike ride, that's all." She giggled. "As friends."

"I-I can't. I'm busy all weekend. But," he hesitated, "maybe another time." He wanted to get off the phone, but not say goodbye forever.

"Okay, but if your plans change for tomorrow, you have my number. I hope you didn't wash it off," she teased. "Anyway, it's now in your phone. Have a good one, Mr. McCallam." She disconnected.

His head felt light, his mind full of guilt. His heart fluttered.

Brian stepped over Mac, who sat on the floor at the kitchen door, fin-ishing up his second rawhide stick. Ivy was busy at the sink scrubbing the casserole dish.

"Important call?" she asked, without looking up. "Astrid?"

"It was the university. A student had a question about my distance learning protocol."

"The university? Calling you on a Saturday after 6:00 p.m.? Wow, that's dedication."

"Uh, yeah, Registrar's Office, must be working overtime during the pan-demic," he said, rushing his words. "I agree, it is odd, but classes start soon, week, so... Hey, how about another cup of that decaf?"

"Sure. You get comfortable on the sofa." She turned to him, her hands full of suds. "Maybe find a movie on Netflix, if you like. Or we could just snuggle." She grinned and bit her lip, then pivoted back to scrubbing the dish. He came up behind her and gently squeezed her shoulders. "Whatever we do is fine with me." He kissed her tenderly on the base of her neck.

They spent the evening watching an old film, *The English Patient*, which neither of them had seen before. On the sofa, his head on her lap, and Mac at their feet, curled up on the braided rug, Brian unraveled from the day. He had wanted to make love to her, but instead fell asleep, as she ran her fingers through his hair. She knew he needed rest, to turn off whatever noises were in his head. When Ivy saw that he was asleep, she kissed his forehead, turned off the television, and reached for the white lamb's wool throw to cover him. She regretted having brought up the awkward topic of living together when it was clear he was struggling with something serious.

Her cell phone jingled. It was the tune, "Let It Go," from the movie *Frozen*, her daughter, Becky's, signature ring. She eased Brian's head off her lap, slid out from beneath him, got up to grab her shoulder bag from the wall hook, and took out her phone.

"Becky? Anything wrong? The girls okay?"

Brian stirred. He opened his eyes and looked over at Ivy. She was listening into the phone for what seemed like a long time, every now and then responding with "Uh huh" or "Oh no." Her shoulders were hunched over. When she turned back to him, he saw the grimace on her face.

"No, no, it's not a problem," she said into the phone. "I'll be there in the morning, around ten-thirty or so. Will that work?"

She listened again. "Don't worry, baby, we'll figure it out. See you tomorrow." She put the phone down on the coffee table.

"What's wrong?" Brian asked. "Bad news? Becky all right?"

"Becky and the girls are fine. It's her dad, Carl, my ex." Ivy sat down in the velvet easy chair. Her face looked pale. "He's been diagnosed with brain cancer. He just told Becky tonight, and she says that he's refusing to do chemo or have the recommended surgery. Refuses! The girls are wondering what's wrong with grandpa. He's groggy, on pain pills. Becky doesn't know what to tell them, or how to influence her dad."

Brian had never met Carl. From Ivy, he knew that Carl was a fisherman working off the California coast and that he was a macho guy. She had described him before as "tough as nails."

"He's just being stubborn." Ivy sighed. "Becky wants me to come to Sebastopol. Talk some sense into him." She rose from the chair and paced the room. She talked at a fast clip. "He won't get on the phone with me, despises talking to anyone on the phone. He's got no other relatives in California. Oh God, he's got to re-think this. Not just for him." She threw up her hands, exasperated.

"And you want to help him," Brian said, not knowing how to comfort her. He would listen. That's all he knew how to do. He didn't remember ever seeing Ivy so upset in their four years together.

"Yes, I want to help," she said. "Who else will do that? For some reason, I still have influence with him, even though it's been well over twenty years since we broke up." She sat on the sofa next to Brian. Mac got up from the rug and wagged his tail. Ivy stroked the dog's back, biting her lip, her brow furrowed. "Becky sounds frantic and she's got the two girls there. I'll need to leave for Sebastopol early in the morning. Carl is as stubborn as a mule." Ivy slapped her hands down on her thighs. She turned to Brian, and softened. "I'm sorry, love. This totally spoils our weekend together."

He put his arm around her and pulled her close. Her head slipped comfortably in the space between his chin and shoulder like she belonged there. "We'll have plenty of weekends together," he said.

"You'll spend the night, right?" she asked. "I'll get up at five o'clock, but you can sleep in. Just close up the house when you go."

"You sure you want me to stay?" he asked.

"Yes, I'll pack my bag tonight and be set to leave first thing."

She took his hand, pulled him up from the sofa, and led him into her bedroom. The brass bed was decorated with an antique-looking blue-and-white flowered quilt and matching pillows. A square of ivory lace was set over a dimly lit Tiffany lamp set on a side table, the patterned shadow of the lace outlined on the wall behind it. The scene invited comfort and intimacy.

"Oh, I almost forgot." He rolled his eyes. "I need to take Mac out for a walk."

"That works. Go," Ivy said. "Gives me a bit of time to pack. I'll be waiting under the covers." She tilted her head playfully, back and forth, her silver fleur-de-lys earrings dangling.

"Deal," he grinned. "Hey, Mac, ready for a walk?" Brian grabbed the dog leash and a poop bag out of the plastic sack he had left in the living room by the front door. Mac sat obediently waiting to be leashed. Outside, the air was fresh. No fog. He walked a short block down to Seabright Beach. It had turned chilly. He was fatigued, but it didn't stop him from thinking about Savvy, wondering if he should take her up on the Sunday-afternoon mountain bike ride. He needed the exercise and he couldn't deny that he wanted to see her again. And Ivy would be off to Sebastopol early in the morning.

His phone vibrated in his pocket. A text—he stood at the end of Seabright Avenue on the path just above the beach. The full moon lit up the white froth of the waves. Mac stopped at a patch of grass to do his business. There was little wind and the stars twinkled like crystals. He took the phone from his pocket and read the text.

*DEATH IS A GREAT DISGUISER.**

It was the same cryptic Shakespeare quote as the first email he received two days ago.

Who is this? he typed, and tapped the phone to send a return text.

Blocked, the display on his phone said.

Death Is a great disguiser? What the hell did it mean? He pulled hard on Mac's leash. "Sorry, Mac," he apologized. He stuffed the phone back in his pocket, bent down, and threw the soiled bag into a nearby trash bin.

He started back down Seabright Avenue, wishing that he could explain everything to Ivy, the dead body on the bluff, the accusations from Tim, the blackmail he committed with his own dentist, the discussion with Consuela's aunt, and these damn mysterious notes with one-liner Shakespeare quotes. But with Ivy's stressful family predicament, it would not be a good time to dump all of his troubles on her, and learning that Ivy wanted to live together only added to him feeling overwhelmed and full of guilt. He had never before felt the need to pretend anything with her.

He and Ivy met at a university gathering. It was four years ago at a fall garden party hosted by the chairman of UCSC's English Department. It was Brian's first semester teaching. After several years working for the

---

*   Death is a great disguiser." Measure for Measure, William Shakespeare, Act 4, Scene 2

Santa Cruz Police Department, studying for a master's degree at night and on weekends, he was finally doing what he had dreamed of, teaching Shakespeare at the university level as an adjunct faculty member. He remembered how intimidated he felt by the other faculty at that party, most of them Ph.D.'s and several holding full tenure. Afraid of fumbling his words or somehow making a fool of himself, he stood against a wall, below the radar, with a neat glass of whiskey in hand.

A slender woman, medium height, probably five-foot-five, approached him and stood by his side, her back against the wall like his, joining him in gazing out at the crowd of partygoers. He glanced over at her, curious to take a good look. She had shiny brown straight hair that fell almost to her shoulders and wore long dangly gold earrings shaped like autumn leaves. Her sleeveless, scooped-neck, royal-blue velvet dress stopped just above her knees. He remembered how healthy she looked. He glanced down and noticed how her calves were well-shaped and muscular, the black suede pumps giving her a few inches of lift. Although dressed simply, she looked elegant.

"See that woman over there?" she said and tilted her wine glass toward a tall blonde-haired woman who was talking to Dr. Mathews, the Department Chair. Several men, mingling around them, were listening closely to the Chair, but staring at the blonde. The woman at Brian's side nudged him. "She's the one with the 1940's-style black pillbox hat and veil, red lipstick, low-cut black dress. You see her?"

"Yes," Brian replied. "She certainly gets attention from the men. Maybe she's a little too full of herself though." He took the last sip of whiskey in his glass.

"She's my sister," she said nonchalantly. "Always gets more attention than me." He had put his foot in his mouth, without even trying, and almost gagged on his drink.

She giggled and turned to face him. Her bare freckled shoulder pressed against the wall. "I'm Ivy Davis," she said, "and that woman, the Chairman's wife, my sister, Laura, set me up tonight on a dreadful blind date." She tilted her head to the left. "You see that skinny tall man with the bushy mustache, wearing a burgundy crew neck sweater and a plaid bow tie?"Brian nodded hesitantly, grateful that he had chosen a dark-brown corduroy blazer and muted checkered shirt for his wardrobe that evening. Ivy continued, "He's my blind date and that's why I'm standing here with you."

It was Brian's turn to laugh. Ivy sighed and said, "He teaches English grammar and punctuation. I don't mean to make fun of him, but I'm just not into him." Brian and Ivy stood there together, like two partnered wall-flowers, happily people-watching for the rest of the evening. At times, they didn't speak for several minutes, but it felt comfortable. At the end of the party, he asked her out to dinner for the next Friday night.

They immediately clicked, and from there, slipped into a steady rhythm of weekend romance and the occasional mid-week movie date. She was his first and only long-term relationship since his divorce. Unlike his ex-wife, Ivy gave him no pressure, no drama, and had no complaints about his unwillingness to dig into deep feelings or express strong emotions. The ease between them, Ivy's simple elegance, and most of all, her positivity, kept him faithful and content over the past four years. But there was something about Savannah Romeo, the feisty red-haired pixie, he met that morning in Los Gatos, that he found fascinating, seductive. And he wanted to see her again.

CHAPTER 9:
"The Course of True Love Never Did Run Smooth."*
—WILLIAM SHAKESPEARE

H E STRIPPED OFF HIS CLOTHES AND GOT INTO BED WITH IVY. THE moonlight crept in from the skylight, throwing a streak of white onto the wall. He noticed her packed suitcase, which stood by the oak dresser, a jacket draped over it. Ivy peeked out from beneath the sheets, a welcoming smile on her face. Mac curled up on the blanket Ivy had laid out on the wood floor for him, the one she kept solely for their sleepovers.

"I see you're ready for a quick escape," Brian whispered.

She wrapped her leg around his thigh. "Yes, all packed," she said.

He brushed the strands of hair from her face. "I want to come back to the subject of us living together," he said. "Don't think I just pushed the idea away."

She placed two fingers on his lips. "Shh," she said. She skated her fingertips across his bare chest. He pulled her to him and gently stroked high on the inside of her thigh. He looked into her eyes and saw tears stream down her cheeks. "What's the matter?" he asked.

---

*   "The course of true love never did run smooth." A Midsummer Night's Dream, William Shakespeare, Act I, Scene I

Ivy turned away and sat up. "I'm just worried about Carl."

She pulled the sheet around her, dropped her chin down on her raised knees, and stared at the wall opposite the bed. "Becky is very close to her dad. She's been so stressed, nonstop nursing during this pandemic, and..." Ivy laid her head down on the pillow and faced him, "this whole thing has unnerved me. Carl's always been as strong as an ox, a dedicated father and grandpa. Now this." She sighed.

Brian slipped his arm under her back, bringing her close, her head tucked in the crook of space between his chin and shoulder. They both gazed up at the skylight above the bed, the moon bright in the dark, a tiny lone star just below it. He felt lost on how to comfort her. The strong feelings she had for Carl made him wonder if she still loved the man. Maybe she was realizing it.

"Let's get some sleep," he said. "You need to be wide awake for that long drive."

"I'm sorry," she whispered. He stroked her hair until she fell asleep, held her all night long. He had forgotten what it was like to sleep next to Ivy. It had been three months, but like before, it felt like a safe haven, a tranquil place. He recognized the familiar scent of lavender in her room. It relaxed him.

Over their four years of dating, it had been Ivy who had provided the emotional support in their relationship, encouraging him whenever he showed hints of self-doubt about teaching at the university level, coaching him when his daughter faced some new trauma and he struggled over how to respond. This was the first time he could remember where he needed to step up and play that same role for her. But he didn't feel adequately equipped for the task.

Ivy left at six o'clock the next morning. He half-opened his eyes and saw her wheel her suitcase out of the room. Mac woke him about an hour later, the Airedale's wet nose nudging Brian's foot. The morning dove cooed from the back garden.

He got out of bed, pulled on his sweats, grabbed his cell phone, the dog leash, and took Mac out for a short morning walk. As they started down Seabright Avenue, Brian's phone beeped. A text from Ivy:

I miss you already. Blueberry muffins for you in the bread bin. xoxo.

There was another text, one that he had missed. Was it another Shakespeare quote to taunt him?

At Panera Café, thinking of you, Wilder Ranch parking lot, noon today? Hoping you changed your mind. Your FRIEND, Savvy.

He wouldn't have had the guts to connect back with her. But here she was, checking in. I'm a shit, he thought.

He tapped a text back:

I think I can make it. See you there.

He sent it. His neck ached.

A text came back:

My dream came true. I'll be in a red pickup.

His stomach did a somersault. It was eight-fifteen. He'd need to get home, pump the tires on the mountain bike, hose it down, and make sure it was operational for the ride. Mac would stay at home, have the run of the backyard.

Before he left Ivy's place, he tidied the bed, grabbed a muffin from the bread bin in the kitchen, collected his overnight things, and locked up the cottage, leaving the key in the magnetic holder under the front porch.

On the way home, he stopped at the dog park so Mac could run free for twenty minutes, the least he could do for his dog. He threw out a tennis ball. The only other dog in the park, a greyhound, got in on the action, vying for the ball. Brian threw it down the run several times.

The two dogs seemed to be having a good time. Twice, Brian took his phone out to text Savvy to cancel the date, but each time he stopped himself and put the phone back in his pocket. He had to see her again.

He leashed up Mac, ready to head home, and threw the tennis ball to the owner of the greyhound, who wore a blue face mask. He felt guilty that he'd left his face mask in the car. Fifty percent of people still wore a mask in public, and the rest refused to do it. "Keep the ball," Brian shouted to the white-haired man. The man caught the ball and waved.

As he approached the exit to the park, about to go through the iron gate, Brian noticed someone staring in his direction from a light-blue late-model Honda. It was parked across the street.

A man sat behind the steering wheel. He wore dark sunglasses and a baseball cap. The hat was black with orange lettering, likely a San Francisco Giants hat. Mac stopped short at a small patch of dirt just inside the gate to pee. Brian looked out again at the car across the street. The person in the car stared out in his direction.

Mac eyed the white-haired man throw the tennis ball out to the greyhound. The Airedale pulled hard, yanking the leash out of Brian's hand, and bolted for the ball.

"Mac. Mac!" Brian called out. *Damn it.* He rushed back into the park after the dog.

"Maybe you want the ball back?" the white-haired man said, and laughed.

"No, please keep it. My dog has a dozen tennis balls at home. I have a solution. "Hey Mac," Brian shouted out. "Want a treat?" He had a few crumbled dog biscuits in his pocket. The greyhound dropped the ball near his master. Mac snatched it up and brought it back to Brian, who took it and tossed it to the white-haired man. The man smiled.

Brian snatched up the end of the dog leash and fed Mac half a dog biscuit. The Airedale, apparently satisfied, allowed Brian to lead the way out through the gate. The blue Honda was gone. *Was Tim having him tracked as a suspect?*

CHAPTER 10:
"There Is Flattery in Friendship."*

—WILLIAM SHAKESPEARE

BRIAN ARRIVED AT WILDER RANCH PARK AT ELEVEN-FORTY, TWENTY minutes before their agreed meeting time. He was chronically early to appointments. There were no cars except his in the parking lot. Savvy was right. Potential visitors and locals evidently didn't get the word yet that the trails had reopened after the insane fires.

His bike had needed some deep cleaning that morning, but both tires seemed in good shape in terms of air pressure, which was a lucky break, since he hadn't been able to find the tire pump in his garage.

He stepped out of the Jeep Cherokee. The sun was warm but not hot. It was one of those glorious fresh days when you thank God that you live in a Northern California coastal town like Santa Cruz. The smoke, haze, and smell of the ferocious fires that ravaged much of the hills and mountains for well over a month had mostly dissipated, at least in this area. He unloaded his mountain bike onto the dirt lot. Because of the rains in the last week, the edges of the parking lot where the dirt met the bushes and plants were muddy.

---

*   "There is flattery in friendship." Henry V, William Shakespeare, Act 3, Scene 7

His mountain bike was a model voted best of 2010, called the Santa Cruz *Nomad Carbon*, which featured high-quality suspension, chic styling, a signature white leather seat, and a lightweight black carbon frame. The *Nomad Carbon* was popular and had placed Santa Cruz County on the world's mountain-biking map. Brian had purchased it brand-new ten years ago, a few months after his divorce. It had set him back over $7,000, which was an out-of-sight price tag. But he biked at least two or three times a week at that time in his life, favoring solo day trips locally around Santa Cruz and sometimes venturing out to the Monterey Bay. He had needed something to occupy his free time, outside of his work as a police detective, and night school, to get his graduate degree, and had no interest in dating after a tense divorce.

He was not a huge risk-taker when selecting his bike rides, but had developed into a fully capable cyclist, taking on moderate challenges. He had done several of the trails at Wilder Park, but had stayed away from those rated "difficult." Since he hadn't been on the bike for quite a while, he felt anxious, yet energized.

He got on the bike to give it a whirl around the empty dirt parking lot. Savvy wouldn't likely arrive for another fifteen minutes. The cushioned seat felt good under him. He practiced shifting gears, braking, and doing sharp turns. After a few shaky minutes, he settled into a steady rhythm. The light wind and bright sun on his face felt invigorating. He pictured what it would be like mountain-biking with Savvy, the woman who rode a flashy Ducati motorcycle. Was he ready for the risks she might take on the trails?

He saw the red flatbed truck enter the parking lot. It was an older model, a couple of dents on the driver's side door. The "y" in the Toyota logo on the back was rubbed off. A bumper sticker read, **My Other Ride Is a Ducati**. Savvy drove up alongside him, her elbow out the window. She wore black 1950's retro-looking sunglasses, the top corners pointed out on either side of the frames.

"Wanna race?" she teased. She took off the sunglasses, her eyes the same aqua green he'd thought about at least a few times since yesterday. A thin edge of black eyeliner was painted on her lower eyelids.

"Whoa. Some classy mountain bike you've got there," she said. "Already bent on showing me up," she mocked. "We'll see," she teased, and drove off to park the truck.

He could feel his heart thump in his chest like some timorous teenage boy on a first date.

He rode up to her. "I haven't been on this thing for years," he said. "You'll probably kick my ass."

She jumped out of the truck, which she had parked next to his.

"You've got a helmet, right?" she said. "With a bike like that, you're undoubtedly an expert, but ya gotta don the helmet." She shrugged her shoulders. "Personally, I'd rather feel the wind in my hair. But no need for face masks."

"I'll second that," he said.

She looked up at the sky. "God, I love this weather. Nice breeze."

He could distinguish the varied colors in her hair, dark-crimson, orangey-brown, the deep-rust shade on her spiked bangs. Her cropped black T-shirt with white script lettering on the front spelled out *Courage* and stopped an inch above her fitted blue jeans highlighting her hourglass figure. Her wide black leather belt featured an array of tiny crystals embedded in the oval metal buckle.

She opened the latch to the flatbed and took out a beat-up mountain bike. It looked sturdy, but like it had been ridden a thousand times. Dried streaks of mud were splattered across the black frame. Two wide strips of black masking tape covered a partially exposed rip in the leather seat. But both tires looked firm and seemed brand-new.

"Meet my jalopy," she said.

Brian grabbed his helmet and gloves from the back of the Jeep.

"So, here's my proposal. "How about we do the Wilder Circle Loop? Fourteen miles, moderate ride, ocean vistas. Have you done that loop?"

"Yes, a few times, but years ago," he said.

"Good. Have you ever tried the Enchanted Loop? Just an extra little detour off the Wilder Loop, two miles straight downhill. Exhilarating."

Oh God, he thought. Enchanted Loop is rated difficult. He looked away, swallowed hard, and turned back to her. "Nope, haven't done that one."

She laughed. "With that snazzy bike, you could probably do Mount Vesuvius—up and down! Don't worry, I'll take care of you."

As she mounted the bike, he noticed her firm forearms, the definition in the biceps that crept out of her T-shirt, her unblemished skin. He had only seen her with her jacket on the day before.

She squared her shoulders, raised her chin up.

They started up the Wilder Circle Loop, the dirt path clear of debris but with a series of muddy ditches, a byproduct of the recent rains. He was able to maneuver through them, dipping down and hopping up on the front tire. As they gained altitude, the grade of the path steepened. The lapis-blue vista of the ocean came into view. This excursion would be the antidote for his stress about seeing the dead body, the paradox of Consuela's death, the disappointment he felt about his closest friend distrusting him.

Savvy climbed higher, ahead of him, picking up speed, her legs stretched long, pushing hard on the pedals, the trunk of her body lifted up off the seat of the bike—*strong woman, brazen*. He shifted gears to gain momentum, but couldn't keep up with her. She was out of his line of sight. The canopy of trees overhead grew dense, the dirt path veering away from the coastline into shaded forest. The twists and turns more frequent, the potholes riskier. Although rusty, he was holding his own. He felt brawny, alive, connected to the nature around him.

The path shot out from the woods and skewed back to the coastline; the sun bright. Savvy stood next to her bike on the edge of the grassy cliff, her sunglasses and gloves off, a pair of mini pocket binoculars held up to her eyes. She looked out to the stunning Pacific Ocean. The shape of her excited him. Trickles of sweat streamed down his back to the waist of his jeans. Pangs of guilt shot through him, but quickly dissipated once he neared her. He got off his bike, rested his sunglasses and gloves on the seat, and came up next to her.

"You made it," she said, and handed him the binoculars. "A parade of sailboats out there, spectacular," she marveled. "Must be some kind of event."

The binoculars had surprisingly strong magnification. A long necklace of boats, over twenty or thirty of them, their colorful sails out, hulls leaning over to the side, all appeared headed to the mouth of the Santa Cruz Harbor.

She moved behind him, while he gazed through the lens down at the boats. He could feel the heat, her body brushing against him.

"Excellent breeze, happy sailors." she said.

Back at his side, she reached her arm out. Her fingers wrapped around the belt loop on the back of his jeans, like a girlfriend or lover would do. Just like a girlfriend or lover would do.

Her fingertips slowly trailed up the line of his spine to the base of his neck where a few drops of sweat had trickled down from under the back of his bicycle helmet to the start of his T-shirt.

"Hot today, isn't it?" she said.

She moved behind him again, massaged his neck with both of her hands, and whispered. "You're so tight." He lowered the binoculars and closed his eyes as she worked gently around his neck.

"We're having a good time, aren't we? Just friends," she teased.

"Mmm," he mumbled, feeling lost somewhere on the edge of a sensual dream.

Catching himself, he opened his eyes to the scenic view, breathing in the ocean air, taking in the sounds of seabirds and the magnetic touch of a beautiful woman.

Back at his side, she playfully nudged his shoulder. "Ready for something challenging?" she said.

"I think so."

"Then follow me to the Enchanted Loop. It will be fun."

They donned their gear and mounted their bikes.

She made a sharp right on a less-defined dirt path. The shape of her distracted him, as she rode ahead of him, her body leaning into each turn. He didn't want to feel the attraction heating up between them, but he did feel it. He was turning inside out and it was unfamiliar territory.

The dirt path narrowed and started to descend, at first gradually, then sharply. Faster, faster, he went. A steep slope appeared to the right and left of the path. Hairpin turns, one after the other, too frequent for his ability. *A two-mile descent, she had said.* He couldn't spot her anymore in front of him. He didn't know the terrain and was riding too fast to brake. Something dipped beneath him. Bump, bump, dip. His bike swerved, cut sharply to the right, the front tire wobbling out of control, a scrunching sound. He tried to pull to the left. The back wheel came off the ground, jolting him off the bike, into the air. His shoulder hit the dirt. His body slid down the slope. Pebbles, sticks, debris struck his face, his neck, his ears. He closed his eyes.

"Agh." He tumbled head-first, smacking over stones, rocks, debris, his right hip slamming into something hard. His torso twisted, his body rolled, his legs and arms powerless. Time slowed down. He felt the jam of each hard object. The ground flattened out. He had come to a stop. His eyes traveled to the redwood tree some inches away. The pain in his right hip sharpened. He moved his head to look up the slope.

A blurred shape of a person stepped down the hill coming toward him. He thought he heard his mother's voice, "No tears, Brian. No dramatics. No weakness."

"Brian, what happened?" Savvy knelt down in the dirt beside him. He was embarrassed, but angered at the same time. He could see his bike, several feet up the hill, lying on its side. Savvy bent over him. "Can you move your legs? Your arms?" she asked.

He lifted each leg tentatively. He moved each arm up and down, to the left, then right. "I'm good. Ow! Except for my freaking hip," he said and grimaced. "But I can move it." He began to brush the brown tree debris from his shirt and jeans. She put her arm around his waist, then around his torso, just below his shoulder, and gently pulled him up to a sitting position.

"Shit, that hurts," he said and was annoyed at himself. He unbuckled his bike helmet and tossed it down on the ground.

"You're bleeding," she said, "your arm."

He looked down at it. His right elbow was cut. When he raised the arm, red liquid trickled down to his wrist, trailing inside his black leather glove. He hadn't felt the sting of the cut until he looked at it. The skin was scraped off raw, about a half inch wide and five or six inches long, grit embedded. "Nothing's broken," he said. "Small cut and a bruised hip; I'll live."

"It's not a small cut." She examined it more closely. "Looks deep; I've got Band-Aids, rubbing alcohol, and Neosporin in my pack." She pointed at her bike sitting on the path up the hill, and helped brush more debris from his shirt.

"I guess your Cadillac bike wasn't guaranteed protection," she said, her tone matter-of-fact, a sarcastic smirk on her face.

He felt the anger rise from the pit of his stomach. "Fucking hell, Savvy," he exploded. "You knew this trail was difficult. You fucking knew it," he screamed. "You also knew that I wasn't an expert at this."

She seemed perplexed, looked him square in the eyes, bent forward, and kissed him on the lips, her hands cupped around his face, a full-on lingering kiss, an intoxicating, feverish kiss, a kiss that ignited something he thought didn't exist inside him. He pulled her down, kissed her, a fury of kisses, spreading her arms out in the dirt. He kissed her neck, pressed his lips on the bare skin just below her cropped shirt, then back to her lips. She reached down, tugging, tugging, to get the T-shirt out of his jeans, pulling the shirt up high, so they were skin to skin. She moved her hips under him, wrapped one leg around his. Their passion grew more frenzied. His mind jangled. Chaos, Ivy—Ivy sobbing in bed next to him last night.

He sat up in the dirt and looked over at her, taking in all of Savannah Romeo. Her eyes were closed, her arms still outstretched in the dirt, the diamond stud twinkling on the side of her up-turned nose. Her red hair blended with the bronze, orange, rusty hues of the leaves surrounding her. The perfect pale skin of her midriff peeked out above her metal belt buckle. She was a work of art, still a mystery to him, and waiting for his next kiss. A flash of the hand on the bluff swooped through his head. He thought of Consuela, her smile at dinner the night before she left for Mexico, the liquid way she moved when she walked out of the restaurant and disappeared out of his life. He turned away from Savvy.

His eyes glided up to his mountain bike lying on its side on the steep slope. His chest tightened. He knew that it had been the anger, the jagged raw emotion, that led him to lust for a woman he barely knew. Spears of guilt cut through him while at the same time he felt the thick curtain of indifference dissolving inside him. The brief encounter with Savvy had ushered in a kind of physical Intimacy that he could not remember ever feeling before.

Savvy opened her eyes, sat up, and reached out to touch him.

"That was nice," she whispered and smiled at him.

He brushed her cheek with his hand. His bruised hip smarted. Conflicted, without a solution on how to move forward in the next moment, he sat quietly.

She looked down at his arm, and with one finger, traced the line of dried blood from his elbow to his wrist.

"You stay here," she said. "I'll get that First-Aid Kit. Clean it up. Stuff gets embedded."

He nodded and said, "Thanks."

She got up and started back up the hillside, stopping where his bike had landed on the slope.

"Your front tire blew," she yelled down at him, her hands on her hips. "It's shredded. That's what took you out."

Shit. I needed air in those tires. I knew that, he thought. *And I blamed her.*

"It was my fault then," he shouted.

"Hey," she yelled out from her bike. "The First-Aid Kit's not here. It's in my truck. I'll ride back down to get it. Less than half a mile... Just take a few minutes."

With his palms pressed into the ground, he stretched his arms, tried to straighten his wobbly legs, and stood. "I'm up," he shouted and attempted to take a step forward. His hip burned, but he could do it. "I can walk. Savvy, the elbow can wait."

"No, I'll be right back," she said. "It needs a clean out. Trust me." She took off.

The quiet calmed him, the whisper of the light breeze. A flat spikey dark-green leaf fluttered and landed close to him. Something scurried in a tree. The smell of the redwoods, a subtle mild spicy fragrance with earthy undertones, a tinge of sweetness.

He thought of Ivy. *Damn it, I can't do this to her.* He reached into his back pocket for his cell phone to see if Ivy called. *Where's my phone?* He checked the ground around him. Hobbling up the grade of the slope, he stepped sideways, navigating the rocks and debris his body had tumbled over just minutes before, searching for his phone. As he neared his bike, he eyed the deflated front tire, half-shredded, the rim bent, contorted, but still attached to the frame. He scoured the ground around the bike. No phone.

He tried to upright his bike, but it fell over. It was heavy. He tugged it from the dirt and pushed it up the six or seven feet of slope from where it had landed, stopping every foot or so on the way up to rest, his hip aching. Once he made it up to the bike path above, he laid the bike down off to the side. He searched for his phone on and around the path, in his head debriefing how the accident had unfurled, how far downhill he had traveled without breaking a bone.

His phone was lost in the woods.

He sat down in the dirt on the edge of the path, staring downhill, wishing he had Savvy's binoculars to more thoroughly survey the area.

The sound of a bike's tires interrupted the quiet. She came around the turn, up the grade of the narrow path toward him, pumping hard on the pedals, her torso tall, a grin on her face.

"I promised *fast*, right?" She didn't wait for an answer, jumped off the bike, opened the shoulder pouch, and took out a bandage, some white tape, and a small bottle of clear liquid.

"Wow. You made it back up here," she said. "And with your bike, you okay?"

He nodded. "I'm in one piece. Bike's a wreck." She scooted down next to him, held up his arm, and started to dab a wad of cotton wet with alcohol around the cut on his elbow. He gritted his teeth, but didn't utter a sound, as she wiped the wound, taking in a deep breath to avoid screaming out. She added more alcohol and went down his arm swabbing off the dried blood.

She meticulously picked out small bits of pebble and gravel from his abraded skin. The cut was worse—deeper, longer than he had initially thought. The sting was sharp. He appreciated her care and attention. Spikes of her short red hair stuck to her cheek, a few drops of sweat glistened on her forehead. This wild woman he barely knew appeared dedicated to caring for him.

She applied a dab of Neosporin, tore off the white tape with her teeth, positioned the wide bandage on his skin, then crisscrossed three pieces of tape over it. After inspecting her work, she stood up and put the First-Aid Kit in the pack on her bike, sat back down in the dirt next to him, reached out, and curled her fingers around his.

"I think this day will improve," she said and grinned, the diamond stud in her nose twinkling, her dimples deep. He hated himself for having blamed her.

"Yeah," he said, "no doubt, but my damn cell phone is gone. Lost."

"What? No, you didn't lose it." She shook her head. "I found it on the ground in the parking lot next to your Jeep." She took the phone from the back pocket of her jeans.

He narrowed his eyes. "I dropped it in the parking lot?"

"I guess so," she said, and shrugged. "Maybe when you got your helmet and gloves out? I don't know."

"That's great." He took the phone and put his arm around her, pulling her close. "I was an ogre blaming you earlier. I'm so—"

"No apology needed." She kissed him gently, sat back in the dirt, and put her fingers to his lips. "Hey, I'm starved. How about you?"

"Appetite, a universal wolf!"* he said.

"What?"

"Sorry. It's a Shakespeare quote. Habit of mine. Translation: When am I not hungry?"

"Right, you're an English lit professor."

"Adjunct professor."

"Details." She waved her hand in the air. "Mr. Almost-a-Professor, how about we go to the Santa Cruz Wharf, scarf down creamy clam chowder, maybe some calamari?"

"When am I not hungry?" he repeated.

"And when are you not a wolf?" she blurted. He stared at her, a sobered look on his face.

"I'm kidding," she said. "You, my friend, are a closet wolf, but maybe *too much* in the closet."

---

*   "Appetite, a universal wolf." Troilus and Cressida, William Shakespeare, Act I, Scene 3

"Maybe," he said.

"Can you walk your bike down?" she asked.

He stood up, still unsteady, but everything working, and held his hand out to help Savvy to her feet. The hip threw him a jolt.

"Gallant and brave," she remarked. "I'm digging that about you."

"You have an interesting accent," he said. "I can't quite place it. A little bit Eastern European? Or is it my imagination?"

"Really? My mother came here from Finland, a small city near the border to Soviet territory. But I don't speak a second language—only English. I've been here so many years," she said and grinned.

It was an uneventful journey down to the parking lot, both of them walking their bikes. He limped, but as they approached their vehicles, he had acclimated to the dull ache of his hip. He wanted more time with her. The cut on his elbow smarted, but was manageable.

"How about we take one car to the wharf?" she suggested, as she lifted her bike and placed it in the flatbed of her truck. "I'll drive."

"Would you mind if I drove? It'll give me practice with this bum hip."

"Old-fashioned, aren't you? Okay, sure." She locked her bike to the chain in the flatbed, grabbed her leather jacket from inside the truck, and tossed her keys in her shoulder bag.

He loaded his bike in the back of the Jeep Cherokee. They got into his SUV and headed down Mission to Ocean Street. Savvy turned on his radio and moved the dial, searching for something. "There," she said. The music was electronic, up-tempo, loud. She moved her shoulders and upper body to the wild beat.

"My favorite station, you like it?" she asked.

"It's different," he said.

"Synthetic techno pop, Eastern European," she said, her voice raised above the music. "I love this." The beat sounded erratic, frenetic. Too much bass, he thought. But somehow it appealed to him. Her hands were up at her face, her fingers in "V"-shapes, brushing across her eyes, first right and left. It reminded him of the woman in *Pulp Fiction*.

Savvy had told him she was thirty-eight years old. But she seemed younger.

"Do you want to stop at your house and drop off your bike?" she asked, still moving to the beat.

Did she know they were just passing the turn-off from Mission that led to his house?

"Well, we're close by and it's on the way to the wharf."

She stopped dancing and turned the sound down. "That bike you have is worth a bundle. I just thought—"

"Good idea." He turned left up High Street and made a right. He drove around the circular driveway, and pushed the button to open the garage door. Mac came running out to greet them, wagging his tail. "Hey boy," Brian jumped out, the dog excited. Brian bent down to pet him.

Mac barked when he saw someone in the passenger seat of the Jeep. Brian opened the back hatch and lifted the bike out, his hip smarting with pain.

"You need help?" Savvy called from the window.

The dog growled.

"No, it's okay. Hey, Mac, get over here. I've got something for you," Brian shouted from inside the garage. Savvy opened the passenger door and hopped down. She kneeled on the stone driveway near Mac, who still growled, his muscular body swooping down, his tail straight out.

Savvy whispered, "Mac, I like that name. Come, come." She held her hand out. The dog's tail turned to a wag. Puzzled, Brian walked over to them. Savvy was giving the dog a treat.

"Where'd you get those?" he asked.

"From your backseat; you had a bag of dog treats."

He nodded and said, "Right; you're observant."

Mac took the crunchy bone in his teeth and carried it back inside the garage to the rumpled blanket on his dog bed.

"I'll just be a moment," Brian said. "I need to get Mac some fresh water. Put it out in the backyard for him."

Savvy waved. "Bye-bye, Mac."

In a few minutes, Brian came through the front door and down the stone staircase.

"You made a new friend," he said, as he started up the engine. "Sorry, my dog was kind of grouchy at first."

"He was fine. Maybe I can spend an afternoon here with you sometime? Just friends," she said and grinned.

He couldn't pretend to himself that he hadn't imagined the same thing, how they might explore the heat that had surfaced between them in the woods at Wilder Ranch.

He kidded back, "I'm not ruling that out." He smiled.

She turned on the radio and moved to a new techno pop tune.

CHAPTER 11:
"I Get Whipped Like a Dog for Telling the Truth."*
—WILLIAM SHAKESPEARE

THE CACOPHONY OF SOUND FROM THE BARKING SEA LIONS NEAR THE end of the wharf seemed to captivate the tourists. Shared smiles and laughter could be heard as crowds of people, young and old, some face-masked in small family clusters, and others, mostly in their twenties, without masks, were gathered in larger groups. Despite the COVID-19 virus hanging on, people appeared to savor the mild seventy-plus degree temperature of the last precious Sunday in September of 2020.

A few children, their heads bent down over the wood railing, pointed their fingers and screeched happily at more than a dozen noisy sea lions laid out on the wharf's rafters below. Savvy and Brian watched the marine mammals, as they dipped in and out of the water, grunting, hefting their enormous bodies back onto the rafters, shaking the water off their backs, eager to sunbathe.

Brian spotted a young couple leaving a picnic table close by the Dolphin Café take-away window, where he had ordered their seafood a

---

* "I get whipped like a dog for telling the truth." King Lear, William Shakespeare, Act 1, Scene 4

few minutes ago. He took Savvy's hand and led her to one of the few wood picnic tables set outside for casual dining on the wharf.

They sat on the weathered bench, on the same side of the table, facing out to the Santa Cruz Boardwalk Amusement Park, a community jewel positioned above the beach adjacent to the wharf. With the virus still in play, none of the amusement park rides were operating. The Typhoon upside-down experience was fixed in place, the Double-Shot Tower stilled, the roller-coaster had no lightning-speed cars racing through its winding tracks, but the colorful panoramic display of the Amusement Park still gave the impression of family fun and entertainment readied to resume at any time.

Brian saw the man signal to him from the café window and got up from their table to retrieve the food from the counter. He returned with a paper plate piled high with fried calamari, tartar sauce, lemon wedges, and another plate of sourdough bread, then returned a second time with two bowls full of thick white clam chowder. He sat back down beside Savvy.

"Life is good," she said, and brushed his cheek with the palm of her hand. "You're making mine better every minute."

He liked how she made him feel treasured with just a few words and a small gesture.

She slurped down the first spoonful of chowder. "Amazing, but hot. Be careful."

She dipped a small chunk of bread in the soup, blew on it, and popped it into her mouth.

"So, you have a daughter in law school and likely an ex-wife," she said. "And a girlfriend. Anyone else in your life that you're close to?"

"Anyone else?" he responded. "Yes, one more."

"Oh?" she raised her eyebrows. "Who's that?"

"My dog, Mac. I'm probably closer to him than to any human on that list."

She nodded. "Hmm. So, your girlfriend is the only romantic interest in your life right now? Nobody else you feel that way about?"

"And, where are you going with this?" he asked.

"Nowhere special." She shrugged and dipped another piece of sourdough into the soup.

"Tell me about your daughter. I want to know more about her."

"Astrid. Well, she's beautiful...and smart."

"Does she have a boyfriend?"

"Ouch, bad subject. She did. Up until a few days ago, she had a fiancée. I'm having brunch with her tomorrow. She's down in the dumps. They lived together for almost a year."

Savvy placed a hand over his. "I love when you share your life with me."

A seagull landed on the table, darting its head around, ready to snatch up a scrap of bread or calamari. Savvy stood up. "Scat! Shoo." she screamed, and with her shoulder bag, she reached out to flog the gull, swinging the purse back and forth, making contact with the bird's body, before it took off. It screeched and flew off across the water toward the Boardwalk.

"Whoa, you really know how to get rid of varmints," Brian said, surprised at her reaction to the feathered visitor.

Savvy froze, looked over at him, and then sat down beside him. "Oh, that was embarrassing. I-I'm actually afraid of large birds. They scare me. You would think I'd be..." She took a deep breath. "But..." She shrugged, shook her head, and placed her hand on his, clasping his fingers down on the bench between them, like a girlfriend or lover would do, just like a girlfriend or lover would do.

She dipped another piece of bread into the bowl of soup.

He felt the tap on his shoulder.

"Hey man, enjoying your Sunday?" Brian turned to look up. It was Tim, holding a large red plastic cup in his hand. He wore black running shorts, a worn black T-shirt, with the red Santa Cruz surfer logo embossed in the middle, and a black-and-white Oakland Raiders cap. He looked tanned and muscular, except for the slight raised mound of a beer belly.

"Tim." Brian stood up from the bench quickly, which caused a sharp sting to his hip. Savvy stayed seated, a weak smile on her face.

Tim stepped back, keeping some COVID distance between them, as he wasn't wearing a face mask. He peered over at Savvy, back at Brian, his eyes questioning, and took a sip from the cup.

"Is that beer?" Brian asked. "How'd you manage to get that?"

"They love me here, gave me a Bud Light on the sneak over at Gabby's. Police privilege, I guess." He snickered, his eyes fixed on Savvy.

"Oh, sorry," Brian said. "This is Savannah, a friend of mine."

"Hello," she said, her voice subdued, almost shy.

Tim narrowed his eyes and nodded. "Always good to meet one of Brian's friends," he said, raising his cup for a toast. "Anyway," he said, looking back at Brian, "I just finished a run on the cliffs, and came down to the wharf for a quick drink." He gave them a salute. "I'll leave you both to enjoy your evening." He pointed at Brian with his thumb and index finger like it was a handgun. "See you tomorrow morning, pal." He turned to walk away.

"Tim," Brian called out. "I've got that package for you...the dental records, in my car just over there. Tim started back to them. "Want them now instead of tomorrow morning?" Brian asked.

"Yeah, that'd be real good," Tim replied.

Brian glanced over at Savvy. "I'll be right back. Okay for you?"

"Sure," she said. "Nice meeting you, Tim." She waved and popped a piece of fried calamari into her mouth.

When they got to Brian's Jeep, Tim leaned against the door, his arms folded across his chest. "Wow, now that's a choice piece you've got there, pal, young and pretty."

"She's just a friend. And she's not that young, thirty-eight, maybe thirty-nine."

"Just a kid to a fifty-year-old like you." They locked eyes. "Okay, maybe that was out of line." Tim smacked his temple with the edge of his palm and downed the rest of his beer. "Forgive me. So, is your girlfriend, Ivy, out of the picture?"

Brian wanted to slug him, take the empty beer cup and shove it in Tim's mouth. He reached inside the Jeep and handed Tim the oversized manila envelope.

"Here you go," he said curtly. "I better get back to my friend."

Tim slapped the envelope against his hip and looked at it sideways, checking for the dentist's signature. "Hey man, would you mind coming by my office tomorrow morning? I have a few other questions for you."

Brian hesitated, his neck tightening, his hip sore and his elbow stinging. He looked down at the cracked asphalt of the parking lot, the urge to punch Tim still gnawing at him.

"You mind?" Tim pressed him.

Brian turned to walk away. Over his shoulder, he said, "No problem. See you around eight in the morning."

Savvy had finished her clam chowder. A few pieces of calamari were left on the plate in the middle of the table. His soup bowl was half full, but he'd lost his appetite.

"That guy's a trip, isn't he?" she said. Her nose crinkled up like she smelled something bad. "I didn't get a good vibe."

He wanted to tell this woman he hardly knew about his problems, about the strange notes, about Consuela, about his feelings for her bubbling up like a tempest inside him. He sat down on the bench opposite her. The crowds on the wharf had dwindled. The sea lions had silenced. The clanking of kitchenware from the take-away counters indicated that they were starting to close up shop for the night. He recalled that they locked up early on Sunday evenings. He put his head down on the wood table, his face tucked in his hands. Savvy pushed the paper plates aside and reached across the table to stroke his hair. The air was still, the temperature unusually warm for late afternoon on the wharf.

"What's going on?" she whispered.

He lifted his eyes, resting his chin on the back of his hands. "I'm falling apart, accused of something despicable, which I had nothing to do with. I've received threatening emails and texts, impossible to decipher. And I have second thoughts about the woman I thought I loved." He sat up. "I shouldn't be saying any of this to you."

"You can say anything you want to me. Can I stay with you tonight?"

His thoughts tangled.

She came around the table and sat down next to him. They looked out at the shimmering necklace of light that outlined the Boardwalk Amusement Park just across the water. The sun had started to go down. He shook his head.

"Savannah Romeo, what the hell are you doing to me?" He leaned in and kissed her on the lips, his hand slowly brushing down her cheek to her chin. He sat back, annoyed at himself, and stared out. "There isn't anything I'd rather do than be with you tonight, but I have to turn you down, at least for now." His voice trailed.

She touched his hand. "I just want to take care of you," she said.

"You have, already," he said. "You don't know how much you've opened me up. But I need a little more time." He squeezed her hand. "Like you said, I'm an old-fashioned guy."

He got up to gather the paper plates, threw them into the trash bin, and reached for her hand, pulling her up from the bench.

"Come and look at this."

He led her to the other side of the narrow wharf, where a pelican stood very still on the faded white wood railing a few feet away. He edged behind her and wrapped his arms around her shoulders. The sun was setting in the water by the lighthouse, which jutted out on a rocky cliff about a mile away, a sailboat visible in the ocean just below it, the sky, a blend of pastel blues, lilacs, and pinks, the giant orb of burnt-orange gradually headed downward, colors changing by the second. What resembled tiny diamonds in the ocean sparkled on the crest of the silvery waves, where several surfers enjoyed their last ride of the day.

"Stunning," she said, and leaned back into his chest.

"That area over there," he pointed toward the lighthouse, "is one of my favorite hangouts. It's a surfer museum sitting above what is called Steamer's Lane, the best surfing venue in this beach town. Have you been there?"

"No," she said.

"We should go there sometime," he said. "There's a dog park just across the road where I take Mac."

They gazed at the sun dissolving into the sea, his head craned gently into her neck. When she turned her face to kiss his cheek, he could feel the heat of her breath. He closed his eyes and noticed the physical desire pulse through his body. Music...the sound of a radio coming from behind a seafood counter. Workers were cleaning up. The song was *Besame Mucho*, a romantic Spanish ballad.

She turned to face him. He took her in his arms and they began to slow-dance on the blacktop in the twilight, gliding back over to the other side of the wharf, where the lights from the Amusement Park could be seen. With the flair of a professional, she was light on her feet, unusually featherlike in her movements, and twirled three times under his raised arm. She took the lead and seemed to have a knack for making him feel like he was much more than an average dancer. In a few short minutes, the song ended and the radio was shut off.

"You've got skills," he said, pulling her close.

She beamed. "I had many dance lessons—long time ago, and far away."

"No, I mean you're *really* good. The way you move like a swan."

She waved her hand in the air. "Thank you," she said and smiled. "But I never really made it as a professional, though I tried." There was a loud screeching sound. A Stagnaro's Seafood worker was pulling down the corrugated metal door, the fish counter no longer visible to the public. Brian took Savvy's hand, swinging it like he did with his girlfriend in high school. They headed to his vehicle parked a few doors away. Once back in the Jeep, he reached out to buckle her seat belt, and couldn't help but brush her cheek with his lips.

"My heart is ever at your service,"* he said. The Shakespeare quote slipped out. A flash of Consuela's smile flew across his mind. He shut his eyes for a moment, startled at the image, and started the engine. After he paid the attendant at the exit to the wharf, he turned onto River Street, and within a few minutes, hopped onto Highway 1.

The "Hard Knock Life" tune broke their silence. He tapped the button on the steering wheel to take the call, placing the phone in "speaker" mode.

"Hello sweetheart," he said.

"Dad." She sniffled through sobs. "Dad."

"Astrid, what's wrong?"

"I'm so messed up," she cried. "Dennis just phoned me. He wants to come back, said he made a big mistake leaving."

---

* "My heart is ever at your service." Twelfth Night, William Shakespeare, Act I, Scene 2

Brian didn't know how to respond, and with Savvy next to him, he felt self-conscious, awkward. He never liked Dennis, found him to be smug, and too cynical for a man in his mid-twenties, and was happy the guy had broken off the engagement.

Savvy glanced over at him. Eyes wide, she placed her hand to her lips, with a *shh* gesture, and pointed to herself, shaking her head.

"He wants us to get married as soon as possible," Astrid continued. "Can you believe that?" Her voice was strained, high-pitched. "Can I ever trust him again?"

Brian turned off Highway 1 to the right and onto Mission Street, the road that led directly back to Wilder Ranch Park.

"It's a big decision for you," he said softly.

"You'll meet me tomorrow, right Dad? At eleven o'clock at Albie's?"

"Of course," he said, wishing he could come up with something to comfort her.

"Thanks Dad," she said, sniffling. "Are you with Ivy? I know you were spending the weekend. I'm so sorry to interrupt."

The guilt inside him reared up. "Yes, I-I did spend time with Ivy, but she's gone out of town...um...a family issue came up. We'll talk more tomorrow, okay sweetheart?"

"Sure. Love you Dad."

"Good night Asti."

He tapped the button to end the call.

Savvy placed her hand on his pants leg. "Damn! You're quite a dad."

"I didn't know what the hell to say. I was happy they broke up, but she doesn't know that."

"Your daughter confides in you. It was *you* she phoned." Savvy paused. "You know, it's unusual that she didn't call her best girlfriend about this kind of stuff. That's what most young women would do."

"Yeah, well, she used to have a best friend, Consuela. But she died."

He stopped at a red light.

"I'm so sorry. How did she die?" Savvy asked, her tone tender.

He hesitated. His neck cramped. But he wanted to open up. "It was sudden, a plane crash over a year ago, very rough on Astrid. She hasn't really made another close friend since. She has lots of acquaintances but not like Consuela.

"You're sure she's dead?" Savvy asked. "Oh God, please forgive me for prying. That's a terrible thing...I mean, to have your best friend gone...so instantly."

"Yes, it was a plane crash. She's dead."

He reached over for her hand, appreciating the concern, but instead, smacked his elbow into the center console between them. "Ow! Damn." He glanced down at his elbow, which was covered by his thin cotton jacket. I forgot about that." His lips pressed together, his eyes narrowed, embarrassed to express his fragility.

"You're hurt. It's okay to feel pain," she whispered. She stroked his sleeve.

He trusted her. She seemed to welcome him peeling off his armor.

"So, your girlfriend's name is Ivy? Pretty name."

"Yes," he replied.

"And, she's away somewhere right now?"

He turned into Wilder Ranch and headed toward Savvy's red truck, the only vehicle in the parking lot. He pushed the engine button off and looked over at her.

"Yes, my girlfriend had a family emergency. She's away for a few days. I care for her very much. This...this thing you and I have...it's taken me completely off the rails."

"Stop," she said and held up a hand.

"No explanation needed," Savvy shot back. She took her car keys from her purse and held them in her lap, her head down.

"You have my number," she said, looking up at him. "We were destined to meet. I'm not done with you yet, Brian McCallam." Her voice was sultry...silky.

She pecked him on the cheek, dashed out to her truck, revved her engine, and started out of the parking lot. He sat in his Jeep and watched her back light blink and her truck make the left turn onto Mission Street. He had forgotten to ask her where she lived. Was it over the mountain in the Los Gatos area or in Santa Cruz? *Part of the mystique,* he thought. *I'm so fucking screwed up.*

CHAPTER 12:
"Truth's a Dog That Must
to Kennel."*

-WILLIAM SHAKESPEARE

S EPTEMBER 21, 2018: TEARS IN HER EYES, SAD TO HAVE SAID GOODBYE TO her grandmother, her Aunt Marianna, and her best friend, Consuela boarded the Aeromexico Jet with Leonid. The gold chain around his neck caught the light, as he lowered himself into the first-class white leather cabin seat, the sun reaching through the oval airplane window, catching the twinkle in his aqua- green eyes. She was with the man she loved and he was taking her on an adventure.

With only four months into the relationship, she had accepted his proposal to leave California and come live with him in Merida, Mexico, the location of his property development business, agreed to help him build his business into a more sophisticated giant, go head-to-head against his toughest competitors. He had told her that his business was complicated, layered, and that he'd share more about it when they were situated in Mexico. She had tired of the business classes in graduate school and frustrated with the management in the accounting consultant company she worked for in California. They hadn't promoted her and she had been the

---

*   Truth's a dog that must to kennel." King Lear, William Shakespeare, Act I, Scene 4

most qualified for the recently filled Manager position. Mexico would be a refreshing change.

Leonid spread the gray airline blanket across the two seats, which were separated by a narrow console. He slipped his hand under the blanket and ran his left hand under her blue-and-gold linen skirt and up high on her right thigh. With his other hand, he signaled the blonde flight attendant who stood just outside the pilot's cabin. He flicked his wrist to request a drink.

Consuela peered across the aisle to see if other passengers were looking at them. A bald-headed man's eyes were fixed on his laptop screen, and the seat next to him on the aisle opposite Consuela was empty. *Safe*, she thought. She could enjoy Leonid's naughty touch without stares from strangers. The flight attendant approached them. His fingertips stopped where Consuela's panties started, freezing there, as if waiting for clearance. He glanced up at the tall blonde attendant, who didn't seem to notice his clandestine antics.

"And what would you two like before takeoff?" the flight attendant asked in a syrupy voice, her gaze focused on Leonid.

Consuela froze in place, not wanting the woman to realize what was going on.

"Champagne please. We start new life together in Mexico," he said in his broken English and Russian accent. "We want to celebrate whole way." He soared his right hand out in front of him as if gliding into the air, his other hand still hidden under Consuela's skirt.

"Whoosh," he said.

The flight attendant reacted with a high-pitched flirty giggle.

"You got it," she said and smiled, her teeth capped and bleached white. She walked away, swaying her hips down the aisle.

Leonid reached over and nuzzled Consuela's neck, his hand moving again under her skirt. She looked up and saw the salt-and-pepper-haired pilot start his walk down the aisle from the front, greeting first-class passengers. His smile broad, he stopped at each seat and offered a quick "Hello."

Consuela reached under the blanket and took Leonid's hand from beneath her skirt, shook her head, and whispered, "Not now."

The tall lanky pilot stopped by their seats, the last row in the first-class section. Beaming at Consuela who sat on the aisle, he tipped his cap. "You're a celebrity, right?" he said. "I think I've seen you on the screen."

Consuela shook her head.

"Why you ask that?" Leonid popped in.

The man kept his eyes on Consuela. "Pardon me, but Margie, our flight attendant, swears that you're Selena Gomez. I'm so sorry. I don't mean to invade your privacy."

Consuela felt her face flush. "No, I'm not Selena...but please thank her for saying that." It wasn't the first time people had mistaken her for the famous singer-actress.

The pilot nodded. "You're definitely as lovely as Selena. Oh please, forgive me," he caught himself fawning and noticed Leonid's glare. "Welcome aboard," the pilot said. "Have a very pleasant flight, both of you." He grinned, turned away, and rushed back toward the front of the plane, his head down.

"Pompous ass," Leonid commented. He looked out the window, watching the cargo men load bags onto the plane.

"Well, that was flattering," Consuela said, and grinned.

He turned to her. "Look at you, stunning, smart, wizard at accounting and speaking fluent Spanish. You don't even need to talk. People, they fall at your feet."

"You think so?"

"I know so." He took her hand and stroked it, then whispered, "You are going to be huge success and make us both filthy-rich."

After landing in Merida, they went through the immigration and customs process, he, with a Russian passport, and Consuela, with a U.S. passport. Leonid went first and approached the counter. The customs agent tipped his black cap, winked at Leonid, and handed the passport back to him. When Consuela placed her passport on the high counter, the man waved his hand in the air nonchalantly for her to pass through after quickly stamping the passport without asking her any questions.

Leonid spotted the stout man wearing a black fedora and crisp white shirt in the baggage claim area. "*Eduardo, ola,*" he called.

The man rushed over, grabbing a luggage cart, before approaching them. "*Buenos noches, senora,* Leonid."

"Very good," Leonid mumbled. He pointed out the suitcases on the moving belt. Eduardo pulled them off, one by one, onto the cart. They got into a sleek black limo and headed down a long road, which morphed into the quaint streets of Merida, Mexico, pastel-colored buildings everywhere, merchants standing outside with trinkets in hand, outdoor cafés full of people. Leonid pressed the button to open the back windows. The air felt humid, languid, and welcoming on Consuela's skin, which was chilled from the limo's air-conditioning.

Leonid started to point out the notable sights in the city: the massive stone cathedral, the Palace de Gobierno, the Gran Museo Maya, and the main drag called Paseo Montejo. He was an impressive tour guide, knowledgeable, eager, and seemed to take pride in Mexico, the country where he did business and that he called home. The limo stopped at a crosswalk adjacent to a sprawling park. Strings of tiny lights draped across a long row of palm trees on either side of a curvy paved path, where young couples walked, hand-in-hand, and children trailed behind their parents, licking ice cream cones. It was early evening, twilight. The clock on the limo's dashboard read 7:15.

"Tomorrow night, we come here," Leonid said. "See those fancy white stone seats, two chairs connected in the shape of an 'S'?" Eduardo pulled over to the side of the road, along the street, in tune with Leonid's desire to show Consuela the historic park.

She nodded. "Yes, so unusual."

"They call them 'confidant' chairs where lovers kiss, shoulder to shoulder, and share their secrets." He lifted her long curls and kissed the back of her neck.

"Like a fairytale," she said, taking in the dream she felt she was already living with this amazing man.

Eduardo asked, "*Jefe* ("boss"), we go?"

"*Si,* let's get home." They left the park, taking a right at the traffic light. "You will love next stop," Leonid said.

The limo pulled up outside an ornate stone building lit up in soft-blue lights. The sign etched at the top of the white archway flanked by two tall white columns read, "Hotel El Hermoso Palacio." The architecture appeared to be a mix of colonial and Spanish, stones of muted colors, peach, blue, white, and pale-gray. An illuminated lagoon pool meandered off to the right of the archway, disappearing around a bend. A path of gray cobblestones stones between the arch and the lagoon pool led to a fanned white staircase leading up to what looked like the grand entrance of the elegant hotel, the entry doors outlined in bronze.

"Our first two nights will be in luxury," Leonid said. "After that, I will introduce you to Venture Horizons, my real estate business."

He got out of the limo and came around to open her door. He took her hand and kissed it.

Eduardo removed each piece of luggage from the trunk and handed them off to the two porters, who carefully placed them onto a brass cart. Eduardo tipped his cap and headed back behind the wheel of the limo.

Leonid raised his voice, *"Amigo,"* gesturing for his driver to return. Opening his wallet, he thumbed off several bills from a thick wad of cash.

Eduardo's eyes opened wide, his plump cheeks flushed red. *"Mucho gracias,"* he said, beaming, his double chin lowered to his chest, staring at the generous tip.

Leonid tilted his head close to Eduardo's and whispered. "Don't let anyone know I've arrived yet. *Comprendes?*"

"Si. Si." Eduardo nodded and hustled back into the limo.

"You don't want anyone to know you're here?" Consuela asked, lifting her long skirt from the floor, before they started up the marbled stairs leading up to the lobby. Leonid took her hand and held it up in such a way that she felt like a princess returning home to her castle.

"No, I don't want anyone to know," he said. "This is our time alone together, without business interruptions. After these two days, life will get crazy." He grimaced. "For both of us, hard work ahead."

At the top of the stairs, a short man in a double-breasted navy-blue blazer, with brass buttons, approached Leonid. He had a thick black mustache and an unruly head of dark hair. The two men embraced each other. The man stood back, his hands together, as if in prayer, and half-bowed, then scampered behind the Reception Desk. Leonid held up his index finger to the man and led Consuela over to a royal-blue velvet chaise lounge, one of five or six set around the boutique hotel lobby. A gold-rimmed glass coffee table was set in front of each chaise lounge, and the centerpiece on the mirrored glass top was a wide-mouthed light-blue ceramic vase overflowing with deep-blue-tipped dahlias, a shade of dahlia Consuela didn't know existed.

"Have a seat. I'll just be a minute," Leonid said, and walked away. It seemed that once they had touched down in Mexico, he had taken on a more commanding presence, and people seemed to automatically respond to him without much conversation, as if he were their boss. The shift in his demeanor had caught her attention. She had known him to be cocky, sometimes provocative, but this authoritative tone seemed different.

Consuela looked around at her surroundings. The lobby had the feel of a Royal family's living room. Several tall rectangular gold-rimmed mirrors hung on the pale-lilac walls, and colonial white molding embellishments edged the room. There was a huge black iron clock similar to the one in the Musée D'Orsay in Paris and a photograph she had seen many times on the internet set on the wall behind the polished mahogany Reception Desk. A white-and-gray marbled floor sprawled across the lobby to a set of high French doors, where she could see a hint of a beautiful garden of long-necked red and white flowers.

He came toward her, spinning the key ring around his index finger. "Before we go deeper into Yucatan," he said, "we stay in luxury Isabella Suite. Best room in hotel." He pulled her up from the velvet chaise and twirled her around, her long skirt fluttering out, her feet leaving the floor. He set her down, saying, "You are much more beautiful than Selena Gomez."

They entered the tiny elevator and stopped at level 2. The hallway carpet was a midnight-blue, the walls striped wallpaper of light-blues and gold. Once he opened the door to the suite, he swept her up in his arms, carrying her to the king-sized bed. Before he laid her down, she noticed the suitcases already opened and laid out on luggage racks, a bottle of champagne in a silver cooler, two delicate crystal champagne flutes on a small table. He smoothed her long dark curls over the gold-braided maroon satin pillow. She got lost in his aqua-green eyes and in his desire to please her.

Despite her intelligence, her level of education, and her self-confidence, she welcomed this man taking control, his exhilarating touch, his unique style, his Russian flair, taking her to the edge, but always catching her before any part of her was damaged. Although it had been only four whirlwind months since the day they met, she couldn't quite remember how it felt to be without him. In California, before Mexico, he would constantly surprise her, picking her up in a limo on a week night, after a long day of back-to-back grad school classes and her demanding part-time accounting job, whisking her off to a top-rated restaurant, where they'd sip cocktails and talk for hours about their future together.

On their second day in Mexico, they visited the major sights in Merida, swinging hands in the park, exchanging kisses while sitting on the unique 'confidant' stone chairs, savoring ice cream cones, wandering outside the park, through the street market, where he watched her haggle in her perfect Spanish with merchants for peasant blouses and trinkets. He took her on a walk to an expensive jewelry store close to the boat harbor, a location where rich tourists wandered in the late-afternoons looking for gold, emerald, sapphire necklaces or diamond earrings.

"Leonid, what are we doing here?" she asked.

"I want you to have something gorgeous," he said, looking down through the glass counter at the diamond bracelets. "Why you wear that thing on your wrist? You don't take it off even when you sleep."

"My bracelet? It was given to me by two special people."

"Ahh. So, not a man who gave you that? Not a lover? What about that heart in the middle?"

She bit her lip, feeling a bit homesick. "My best friend, Astrid McCallam, you met her—she and her dad, Brian, gave me this a few nights ago, at a farewell dinner they had for me."

"I'll get you something better than that. It's nice, but you need a bracelet more elegant, not such mini diamond in center."

"Leonid," she reached for his hand on the counter, and stroked his wrist, outlining the braided tattoo. "You have a bracelet, one that's very personal to you, like mine is to me. I don't want a replacement. I wouldn't mind a ring or...or something delicate to go around my neck, maybe a small sapphire or ruby on a slim gold chain?"

"*Da,*" he said, hugging her waist, pulling her to him. The shop owner, boasting two gold teeth, approached to assist them. She left the store with a pair of one-carat diamond earrings, surrounded by a slim ring of gold, perfectly complementing her bracelet. She hadn't wanted to take the bracelet off around Leonid for fear he'd find the inscription inside and get upset. She'd seen his jealous side a few times. She thought about the inscription: "Consuela, this heart is always at your service." She knew that Brian had personally arranged the inscription, a Shakespeare quote.

Brian had kissed her that night at the *Il Fornaio* restaurant. It was in the vestibule where there was a coat rack. She had thanked him for the bracelet. She wanted him to kiss her, had fantasized about it each time she was in his presence. Yes, she had fallen in love with Leonid, and was rushing off to Mexico with him, but she couldn't deny the strong attraction she had to her best friend's dad. When she looked up at him in that cramped dimmed restaurant foyer, she invited him, with her eyes closed, her head tilted back, to kiss her. She had willed it to happen. Time seemed to have slowed down for her. His lips were at first hesitant, barely touching hers, then intentional, hungry. She recalled how he clasped her hands on his chest between them as he leaned into her, and then stepped back.

"I'm sorry," he said. "I didn't mean to do that."

"But I did," she said softly, and lowered her eyes. "Please don't apologize. It was meant to happen," she said. "Just once." She had walked away, back to the dinner table, back to the chattering of her grad-school classmates, back to one last toast with her friends. She didn't want to share this private part of her with Leonid, at least not yet.

On the third afternoon in Merida, the driver appeared, but instead of with the black limo, he stood in front of a forest-green Hummer, the largest Jeep she'd ever seen. They had just finished brunch on the terrace overlooking the hotel lagoon.

Leonid helped her into in the backseat of the Hummer and sat next to her. "We go deeper into Yucatan, to my home, a change of pace, but you'll love it."

She nodded, and squeezed his hand.

"You liked this hotel?" he asked, as Eduardo stepped on the gas and drove down the road.

"Leo, it was like a dream for me."

"Good, because I will buy it for you."

"What?"

"*Da,* I have almost enough to purchase it. But, before I do that, you and I will make a lot more money together." He shook his head. "My clients will be enchanted by you."

"How rich are you?" she asked.

"Nothing like what we will be. I will take us to the top and you will help me. You trust me, right?"

She breathed in deeply and let her breath come out slowly, like she did in yoga meditation. Her head was filled with promise. The idea of more adventure skated through her veins. They were headed into the Yucatan. What could be more intriguing?

CHAPTER 13:
"Hell Is Empty
and All the Devils Are Here."*
—WILLIAM SHAKESPEARE

BRIAN PARKED ON THE STREET BY THE SANTA CRUZ POLICE STATION, gave Mac a bone before he left the Jeep, and put his face mask on, as he entered the one-story brick building. Six chrome chairs cushioned with black vinyl, three on each side, lined the walls, before you got to the Reception Desk. There were usually people waiting to be seen filling out paperwork.

He was greeted by a blond-haired young man who looked like a surfer wearing a dark- blue police uniform. The welcome desk was now equipped with a clear plexiglass partition that featured a small rectangular opening centered on its bottom edge. The place felt more like a bank than a police station. The man's nameplate was "Calhoun." Brian didn't recognize him.

Calhoun looked up. "Can I help you, sir?"

"Brian McCallam, here to see Tim Carrick."

"You reporting an incident, sir? Then, you'll need to first complete a form." Calhoun reached for a pink printed slip of paper from a metal tray.

---

*   "Hell is empty and all the devils are here." *The Tempest,* William Shakespeare, Scene I, Act 2

"That won't be necessary," Brian responded. "Carrick's expecting me."

Calhoun hesitated, and then nodded. "Uh...sure, it'll be a minute. The waiting area is right there." He gestured to the set of chairs behind Brian.

"Thanks." Brian didn't move to take a seat.

Calhoun disappeared into an alcove behind Reception. Brian couldn't quite make out the words he said into the phone. When he returned, he asked Brian to sign the visitor log. Brian noticed how the young officer shot him a curious glare as he scrawled his initials and entry time into the log. Calhoun buzzed the entry door. Plexiglass partitions were everywhere separating the gray Formica-topped desks, with three rows of four or five investigators, and Police Department officers, with their heads down, all wearing face masks, the protocol in an open workspace during the COVID-19 pandemic. Brian felt the eyes on him, as he walked through to the back office, where Tim sat as the lead investigator. He recognized a few of the officers, but they didn't offer him any shout-out. The exception was when he got to Lydia, the station's administrative supervisor. She sat at her desk outside Tim's office and looked up to give Brian a wink. He could see her eyes crease with warmth and knew she was smiling at him under her mask.

"He's waiting for you," she said.

"Thanks Lydia. Good to see you."

She gave him a nod and a thumbs-up.

The centerpiece in Tim's office was a huge black desk, covered with piles of manila file folders, loose typewritten papers, scribbled notes in black felt-tip pen scattered, a blank yellow pad, several stray pens, a laptop, two Starbuck's coffee cups, an open white paper bag with a half-eaten toasted sandwich set on top, and another unopened paper bag sitting beside it. Even with his promotion to lead investigator, Tim hadn't modernized his way of working.

"Hey man," Tim said, looking up at Brian. "Have a seat." Tim gestured to one of the green faux leather chairs opposite his desk. "You can take off the mask. We're more than six feet away. I'm not wearing mine."

Brian stuffed his face mask in his sweatshirt pocket. "I can't stay too long. I've got Mac in the car and I'm headed over the hill."

"Can you believe it's fucking October already?" Tim responded, and took a sip of his coffee.

"Time flies, even when you're *not* having fun," Brian replied.

"Bravo." Tim applauded. "You've become a real jokester. Must be the young woman you're hanging with lately."

"Can we just get to it?" Brian snapped. "Do you have the test results on the dental records yet?"

"Whoa. You really are a kidder. I just handed them to the lab early this morning. They don't work that fast. Sit down, man."

Brian was annoyed, but sat himself carefully in the chair, avoiding a sharp pain in his hip, and instead hit his injured elbow on the wooden armrest. Despite the thick sweatshirt, he felt the sting of the cut.

"So, why am I here?" Brian asked.

Tim opened a desk drawer and reached inside, taking out a clear plastic evidence bag about eight-by-ten inches in size. He pushed away some files and placed the evidence bag on the desk. He looked down at it, shook his head, and then held the bag up in the air. "Look familiar?" Tim asked.

Brian recognized what was inside the bag, the gold bangle bracelet with the twinkling diamond set on a small raised heart in its center. His head throbbed.

"It's a bracelet," Brian said, all he could muster.

Tim gave him a slow nod, and set the bag on the desk. "There's an inscription on the bracelet." With his fingers, Tim turned the bracelet inside the bag to read the inscription. "My heart is ever at your service."* He raised his shoulders with an emphatic shrug. "I was curious and did some research. Guess what I found. Take a close look at it." Tim gestured for Brian to pick it up.

Brian swallowed hard, picked up the bag, and stared at it, knowing what was coming. He placed it back down on the table.

"Turns out it's a fucking Shakespeare quote," Tim said, his voice cold.

---

*   "My heart is ever at your service." Twelfth Night, William Shakespeare, Act I, Scene 2

Brian's mouth went dry.

"And you're the Shakespeare professor."

Brian reached up to rub the back of his neck. "It was Consuela's brace-let. We gave it to her before she left for Mexico."

"We?" Tim asked, raising his voice.

"Yes, Astrid, my daughter, and I. It was our parting gift for Consuela."

"Shall I read you your Miranda Rights?"

"I fucking know that anything I say may be held against me. I have nothing to hide. Just go ahead with your questions."

Tim paused, tapped two fingers on his lips. His voice lower, his tone less accusatory.

"So, you claim the dead woman on the bluff is not Consuela because Consuela died in a plane crash over a year ago. Yet, the dead girl found a couple of days ago was wearing Consuela's bracelet on her wrist." He scrunched up his lips and shook his head. "Doesn't add up."

"I know it doesn't."

"You can see why I'm confused, right?" Tim leaned back in the squeaky chair. "Please, explain it to me." The tension in his voice had returned.

"I can't," Brian blurted.

"You can't or you won't?" Tim leaned forward. "I'm positive you know more than you're saying.

"Are you holding me? Am I under arrest?" Brian demanded, his anger rising.

He wanted to protest, scream at Tim, make him see that something obtuse, unexplained, must have happened for the dead woman he found on the bluff to have been in possession of Consuela's bracelet. But he kept his mouth shut. He wanted the interaction with Tim to end so he could go figure out this nightmare for himself.

Tim pushed back on the chair, the creak louder. He clasped his hands in front of his chest. "You can go," he said.

"I can go?"

"No lab results yet from the dental records. So, you're free to leave."

Brian stood and glared at Tim. He knew that look on his ex-partner's face, the expression he'd get when he was going down one lane in one direction and headed straight for a perp's ass. Only this time it was *his* ass.

He had planned to tell Tim about the cryptic Shakespeare messages he was getting on his computer and cell phone, but he just wanted to get out of there. He turned to go.

"Wait," Tim said. "You're not going off on any trip with your new friend in the next few days, are you?"

"No. And fuck you."

Tim stood from the chair and held out an unopened small white paper bag. "Here, give this to Mac. Melted ham and cheese croissant. He'll love it."

Brian didn't reach for the bag.

"This is my fucking job," Tim said in a lowered voice. "You know that." He came around the desk and held the bag out close to Brian, who took it, left the office, and slammed the door behind him.

CHAPTER 14:
"All the World's a Stage, and All the Men and Women Merely Players."*

—WILLIAM SHAKESPEARE

SEPTEMBER 24, 2018: CONSUELA'S LIFE OPENED UP WHEN SHE FELL IN love with Leonid. Having left California, their first two days together in the provincial city of Merida bolstered her enthusiasm for the next phase of the thrilling ride.

She recalled Leonid telling her that the ranch sprawled across seven miles on the edge of the Yucatan jungle. She was eager to officially begin her new life with him. The Hummer made a sharp turn to the right and approached an elaborate wrought-iron arch, with its curvy lettering at the top: *RANCHO VENTURE HORIZONS*. A beautifully crafted horse's head in the same black iron flanked each side of the words.

Once the Hummer passed through the archway, within about thirty feet, they stopped in front of a chain-linked fence, topped with barbed wire, which seemed to go on for miles and likely surrounded the whole property.

---

*   "All the world's a stage, and all the men and women merely players." *As You Like It*, William Shakespeare, Act 2, Scene 7

She spotted three men standing by the gate, one unlocking it, each man dressed in army camouflage clothing, and with large guns slung across their shoulders, what looked to Consuela like automatic weapons. She felt a stone lodge in her chest. Her head flooded with thoughts of violence. She wasn't expecting the first sight of his home to generate the feeling that she was about to enter a prison.

Leonid pressed his hand down on the leather car seat, his fingers touching hers. "There are predators, bad people out there with blood in their eyes," he said. "Defense system works—nobody dare invade my home or my business."

Leonid waved to one of the men.

"And now I have something most precious to protect. *You,*" he said, and squeezed her hand.

Once the gate was opened, Eduardo drove them down a long, dusty narrow road leading to a sprawling three-story Spanish-style white-stucco mansion sitting at the top of the hill. A few smaller buildings of the same architectural style sat off to the left, lower on the hillside, and what looked like a large garage further off in the distance. She turned her head. There were pastures and wood fencing enclosing a paddock. A cowboy walked a horse around in a circle. A gray barn sat beyond the paddock, where a man wearing a broad-brimmed hat, which cast a shadow across his face, hauled a bale of hay out of the back of a flatbed truck.

As the Hummer climbed the hill to the mansion and swooped around the paved circular driveway, she noticed the spires of black wrought iron over the six front windows. A black lacquered lion-head door knocker was centered on each of the two side-by-side high-arched red-painted doors.

"Eduardo," Leonid said, "*Por favor,* take us to my fountain first."

"You have a fountain?" she asked.

"*Da.* Most-prized treasure on property, a replica of one from Mother Russia."

Still reeling from the sight of the armed men and the barbed-wire fence, Consuela sat quietly.

Yellow poppies lined the narrow road. She peered out the window. In about a quarter of a mile, a white-stone alabaster fountain came into view, its centerpiece in the shape of a beautiful vase. A wide fan of water shot up from the top of the vase, dropping into two tiers below. The bottom tier featured four stone lion's heads, a stream of water spurting out of each open mouth, into a circular pool of crystal-clear water. Small stone flowerpots filled with bright red flowers were set every so often on the curves of the pool's two-foot wall. Maybe begonias, Consuela thought.

When the Hummer came to a stop just before the stone pavers that surrounded the fountain, Leonid rushed out and came around to open her door. He took her hand to help her step off the vehicle's running board and led her close to the fountain. The sound of the rushing water eased her anxiety.

"Designed exactly same as garden fountain at St. Catherine's Palace," he said, "near my childhood home in St. Petersburg."

"This is enchanting," she said.

"I show you something else," he said. "You sit here." He gestured with his hand and a bow for her to sit down on the ledge of the stone pool.

Eduardo drove the Hummer away, off to the left, and stayed in the SUV.

"Now, I hope you will enjoy," Leonid said.

He stepped in front of her, a few feet away, in his black T-shirt, tan chinos, and black sneakers, his legs together, his toes pointed out to the sides, one hand arched above his head and the other rounded in front of his chest. He raised one leg off the ground and swooped it around, performing a *tour jete,* which she recognized from her dance classes as a young girl. He twirled around, his head following the rest of his body in perfect harmony, over a dozen times, circling around the fountain's pool, occasionally pausing to do a *jete* to the right and then to the left. She craned her head, turning her body, to watch him. His jumps and turns were impeccably clean, the choreography simple but elegant. There was no musical accompaniment, but she could tell that he had some classical piece in his mind based on his head movements and the almost sweet expression on his face.

The sound of the falling water blended well with his dance. She pressed her hands to her heart, in awe of his talent. Once he circled back to her, he performed a final grand *tour jete,* ending down on one knee in front of her, his head bowed, a red flower he had picked held up in one hand.

She took the flower from him, and smiled.

"You've got incredible talent." Why aren't you still dancing? Or...are you?"

He stood up, took her hand, and pulled her up from the stone ledge. They started to walk arm-in-arm around the magnificent stone fountain.

"No, I gave that up," he said. "I had a dance partner, my sister. But we didn't make it to professional."

"How's that possible," she asked, "with your level of talent?"

"Very competitive in Russia." He jerked his head, a disgusted look on his face. "Ruthless people. Those dancers...they look harmless. But they can kill with their shenanigans, cheat like crazy, sabotage their foes without guilt. But I got even." There was a chill in his voice.

"You got even?"

He raised his eyebrows and wiped the beads of sweat from his forehead. "I came here to Mexico, started my business, made a lot of money, and then to top off, I found you, my greatest accomplishment, never for me to be lonely again." He patted her hand.

Her heart warmed from his words, but she felt a tinge of fear as to what those words really meant.

"Come, we go to house. You meet my staff."

Two men wearing cowboy hats opened the red lacquered front doors to the mansion. Leonid waved his hand politely for her to enter before him. She saw the highest archways of polished teak wood she had ever seen inside a house.

"Oh my God," she whispered to herself, dazzled by the sight.

Inserted between the archways were exquisitely designed stained-glass windows seven or eight feet in width and what seemed like twenty feet or more from the ceiling down to the parquet wood floor of the huge entryway, four astonishing works of art. The scenes on each window were of two dancers. She walked over to one of the windows and touched the glass, a ribbon of light catching her gold bangle, the colors running over the bracelet and across her wrist. She looked up and stepped back. The stained-glass artwork was of a young couple, dressed in red and black, wrapped around each other in a sensual tango, the woman's shapely leg hiked up the man's black pant leg. She turned to gaze up at the second window, which featured the same couple dressed in ballet leotards, the woman in pale-pink wearing a tiara, the man in gray, both with their toes pointed out to the side, their legs muscled and firm. She came up close to the glass, ran her finger down the raised dark lead between the panes, and marveled at the intricate crafting it took to create such things. The third colorful glass panel was of the man and woman holding gold tambourines, dressed in matching red, blue, and yellow calypso costumes, both wearing red stacked heel ankle boots. The fourth window dazzled her even more than the other three, the woman dressed in an elegant royal-blue flowing ball gown, her head back, the chiffon of her dress sweeping the floor, the man in a traditional tuxedo, except for the royal-blue cummerbund and matching bow tie, the pair engaged in a classic waltz.

Her singular focus on the stained glass was interrupted by the clattering of heavy footsteps. Several men dressed alike rushed from another place in the mansion into the massive entryway, which was more like the lobby of a hotel. The men formed two rows in a semicircle around Consuela and Leonid. As they gathered, the men placed their arms stiffly at their sides, their eyes straight ahead, their wide-brimmed hats held in one hand. Each man wore a white short-sleeved shirt, black jeans, and brown cowboy boots. Consuela noticed that there were no women in the group of maybe fifteen men. One stout short man with a scraggly beard stood out in front facing the rest, the only one wearing a black shirt.

She looked up at the ceiling where a breathtaking crystal chandelier hung. Dozens of long narrow prisms dangled at various lengths, catching the hues and light from the towering stained-glass windows. Leonid clapped his hands twice, which took her gaze from the chandelier back to the men in front of them.

She moved away from Leonid up to the third step of the grand winding staircase, the stairs carpeted in a royal-blue. She rested one hand on the black iron railing. She could feel the thump of her heart in her chest.

"I am home," Leonid declared, looking out at the men. "Sanchez, request each *hombre* to give update."

Sanchez shouted, *"Informar!"* He pointed to a plump man who stood at one end of the first row.

"Domenico, *informar!"* Sanchez instructed.

Consuela listened as he went down the first, and then the second, row, instructing each man to give their individual report. They each spoke in short Spanish phrases, which Sanchez translated into English for Leonid. Consuela understood every word they spoke. They all talked about shipments that they had completed to Saudi Arabia, the U.K., Greece, Iran, Japan, and Korea, giving specific dates in the last four weeks, and whether each shipment was performed late or on time. She was puzzled because the updates seemed to have little to do with the real estate development business, the business she had come to help Leonid take to the next level.

Occasionally, Leonid grimaced and yelled back at a man, demanding more information. He ruefully questioned any bad news about missed dates or shipments, Sanchez translating their words into English for his boss.

Each man referred to their shipments in quantities of hundreds and with what seemed to be model numbers like K-309's, Z-2450's, T-450's, and R-604's. She was puzzled by it all but impressed with the efficient reporting process and use of concise language to communicate the important information.

With one man, Leonid seemed especially annoyed. "Stupid one, make it happen tomorrow!"

"Estupida. Haz que suceda manana!" Sanchez translated back to the *hombre.*

The man nodded nervously, his head bobbing up and down.

After the last man, tall, his face a long oval with a full black beard, finished his update, Leonid walked slowly across the large space, his hands clasped behind his back. He came up very close to the bearded man, as if sniffing him, and then said something in his ear. Consuela thought she noticed the man tremble. Leonid turned and walked slowly back to where she stood on the staircase. He placed his arm around her shoulder and looked out at the men.

"Some progress made while I was away," he said. "But not enough! No more deadlines to be missed. Punishment will be harsh." He paused and surveyed the group of men with his eyes, gradually turning his head from right to left and back again. "Any questions?"

After Sanchez translated, there was a long silence.

"*Jefe,* should I dismiss them?" Sanchez asked.

"One minute," Leonid said. "I have announcement." He raised Consuela's hand up high in the air. This is my princess, the woman I love," he said. "Do not disappoint her any time, in any way."

Sanchez said the same in Spanish. Some of the men smiled; some made brief comments among themselves. One of the men yelled, *"Bueno."*

"She is American," Leonid continued, "but she speaks fluent *Espanol.*" He let out a guttural laugh, a laugh she hadn't heard from him before. "Be on your toes," he shouted, "even what you say under breath," he warned, and hugged her waist.

Sanchez translated. Some men nodded. Others showed no reaction. Sanchez glanced over at Leonid, who waved the back of his hand a few times as if shooing away a fly."

"Terminado," Sanchez called out. Some of the men clamored out the front door, while others scattered elsewhere inside the mansion.

Once they were gone, Consuela walked around the spacious entryway to take a closer look at each of the four stained-glass panels. Reaching up, she traced the lead between the panes of two glass pieces. She looked up at the man's face on the glass, and then at the man's face on the other three windows. She realized that the male dancer depicted on each one was Leonid, slender, yet strong, confident, yet seductive, and that the woman he danced with had the same striking aqua-green eyes as her partner's.

The front door to the mansion opened. A husky brown shaggy dog scampered inside and bolted straight over to his master. Leonid's dimpled smile replaced the commanding scowl he had worn a few moments before.

"Smudge!" Leonid shouted with joy, and slid down to the parquet floor, rolling around with the dog, whose long curly tail vociferously wagged.

"Your dog is here?" Consuela placed her hands to her heart. "I thought you found a home for him with a family in California."

"No, no, I could not leave best friend," Leonid said, and sat up on the floor. The dog sprawled out next to him, his tail whipping back and forth.

She felt happy that Leonid was so attached to Smudge. She had given Paisley, her little white terrier, to her closest friend, Astrid, before leaving California. Why hadn't Leonid offered to get Paisley to Mexico along with Smudge? The thought sent a wave of melancholy through her body.

Leonid reached up and playfully tugged at her skirt, coaxing her onto the floor next to him. "Smudge, he missed you, too." She bent down near him. "We have family reunion," he said, leaning into her. The dog licked her arm.

She managed a half-smile, and stood up.

"You maybe want me to arrange your dog come too?" he asked.

"I didn't know we could do that without a very lengthy quarantine," she said. "I thought that's what you told me."

"I'm big man here. I could make it happen if you want."

"Let me think about it," she said, knowing that Astrid had already fallen in love with Paisley.

"Anything you like," he said, nuzzling Smudge.

"Leonid, what were those men reporting on? It didn't sound like anything to do with real estate development."

He waved his hand in the air. "Just business—let's not talk of business until morning. Then I show you everything. *Da?*"

His pushing it off troubled her, yet she was hopeful about her new life in Mexico. She watched as Leonid chased Smudge around the entryway, and couldn't help but smile.

She looked up at the stained-glass panel where the beautiful couple was in the tango hold.

Leonid came up next to her. "You like them?"

"That dancer is you," she said.

He nodded. "Guilty."

"And the woman is your sister?"

"*Da.* Sabrina, beautiful sister."

"You mentioned her earlier at the fountain. She has stunning eyes, like you. Where is she now?"

He pressed his lips together, his eyes narrowed. "I'm not sure, but she will let me know. Maybe you meet her sometime."

He took Consuela in his arms, dancing her across the parquet floor, from one end of the expansive grand entryway to the other. Smudge lay down near the front door.

"It's like a cathedral in here," she said, as they danced. "Beautiful!"

"Nothing compared to you," he said softly.

CHAPTER 15:
"I Would Not Wish Any Companion in the World but You."*

-WILLIAM SHAKESPEARE

S EPTEMBER 24, 2018: HER FIRST NIGHT AT THE RANCH WAS WRAPPED IN luxury. The master bedroom was furnished in Baroque-period antiques. Her two suitcases were open and laid out on racks. Leonid left her to change her clothes. She put on a red skirt and black peasant blouse and a wide multicolored beaded belt, one that she bought at the marketplace in Merida.

Dinner was in a beautiful high-ceilinged dining room, the walls painted in a deep-red cherry with contemporary prints of black-and-white Don Quixote drawings. Leonid pulled out her chair and seated her at the long heavy oak table, which appeared to seat a dozen guests. The high-backed, black leather-covered chairs were comfortable and exquisite. An oval wrought-iron chandelier holding over a dozen iron-encased candlesticks hung above them and ran the length of the dining-room table. Two thin Mexican men, both under five-foot-five inches, wearing matching white shirts, black pants, a string tie, and black boots, served them without speaking a word.

---

*   "I would not wish any companion in the world but you." *The Tempest*, William Shakespeare, Act 3, Scene 1

Leonid nodded or shook his head when he was being served and said "*Da*, or "No," to the various dishes. Mole chicken enchiladas, Mexican rice, fried plaintains, and salad were offered. She felt ravenous, even though they had eaten very well over the last two days in Merida. She responded to the servants with "*Si, gracias*" to every dish. She smiled, as they moved around her, hoping to engage them, but both men seemed to avoid making eye contact with her and didn't converse. Consuela was curious about the lack of any women in the house.

Leonid talked about the ranch, the kinds of stallions he had, the number of buildings on the property, and promised to give her a grand tour the next day. The bearded servant gathered away the plates, while the other brought out a frost-covered metal container.

"*Ochen' khorosho,*" Leonid shouted when he saw the container. "Very good. Vanilla ice cream from Russia." The bearded one nodded, but made no eye contact.

"*Si, jefe.*"

"From Russia?" she asked.

"*Da*. My chef, a magician. I've been wanting this for long time. Only thing good in Russia, except for this." The bald-headed man put down a fancy crystal bottle of vodka, with the label, Chopin Family Reserve Vodka.

"We must celebrate being home." The man poured the clear liquid into two small chilled glasses. "First time we have vodka together. You must slug it back fast. *Da.*"

She giggled. "Okay," she said and downed the icy smooth, bitter-tasting liquid, and quickly felt a hot fire inside her chest.

He reached over and skipped his fingers down her bare arm. "We take rest to bedroom."

Leonid picked up the bottle, threw the red cloth napkin on the table, and led her up the grand staircase.

He opened the door to the master bedroom. Two heavy mahogany dressers, a mirrored armoire, a king-sized sleigh bed in the same Baroque style, antique pole lamps, with rippled ivory cut glass shades. The lights were dimmed and the sheets folded down at the corners. A landscaped watercolor painting, an aerial view of what looked like Leonid's ranch, hung above the headboard. He led her to the armoire, had her face the full-length mirror, and stood behind her. His beguiling smile, his eyes an even deeper green in the dim light, her skin reacting to his fingers sliding down her back, he slowly unzipped her dress.

She stood there in her black-lace bra and matching panties, as he smiled into the mirror and sprinkled kisses on each of her bare shoulders. He rested his hands on her hips. "Look at us. We make beautiful couple. Don't we?"

She nodded.

"Let's mark this first night in new home with special lovemaking," he said.

He kicked off his shoes, lifted her up in his arms, and on his toes, he moved like a dancer across the room to the king-sized bed. He placed her on her knees atop the gold-and-blue tapestried comforter. Curling his hands under her arms, he edged her gently up against the mahogany headboard, her back against it. They embraced one another, their kisses deep and long. He placed her arms out to rest on the top edge of the curve of the dark wood, ran his fingers down past her belly button, and pulled down her black lace panties. Her head swam. Her surrender to this man seemed to come naturally. He loved her, worshipped her. It was like the dream she had when she was a young girl. His self-confidence, the exotic everything about him, she could not get enough. To feel like this, to feel like this every night.

When she opened her eyes the next morning to the daylight creeping in through the sheer voile curtain on the arched window, Leonid wasn't there. The door opened. He carried a silver tray, topped with a steaming plate of something Mexican and a small silver coffeepot and flowered coffee cup.

"Good morning. You eat, dress. Then, we go to work," he said.

"Yes, good morning," she sang out, excited to get her new life started.

She poured some coffee and nibbled on the tortilla and eggs.

"I'll be downstairs waiting," he said. "Wear whatever you like, very informal." He pecked her on the cheek and left.

He stopped talking to Sanchez when he saw her at the foot of the staircase. He took her hand and led her out of the mansion to a beautifully decorated electric golf cart, a red-fabric- covered awning above the two seats, the seat cushions, a black-and-red flowered pattern, covered in clear plastic; the body of the golf cart was painted in shiny black with touches of small red embossed roses on the black floor mats.

"Get in," he said. "We go to your new office in style."

"Oh my God," she said and smiled. "Precious transportation."

When he opened the door to the small white stucco building about a seven-minute ride from the main house, she felt her body unexpectedly stiffen. Sanchez, the man instructing the men to report out yesterday, was standing just inside the door to greet them.

"Sanchez!" Leonid said. "I'll be about thirty minutes here. Bring Javier over to meet my fiancée."

"*Si jefe*. I will get him," Sanchez said, and left

"I call this place office cottage," Leonid said.

"Who is Javier?" she asked.

"He's man designated to your every need, whatever you want, anything you need. He is tough. Protect me in past and will do same for you."

She couldn't argue with that. But why was so much protection necessary?

The office cottage was tastefully decorated. A large "U"-shaped oak desk and swivel oak chair sat in the middle of the room. There was a studded brown leather loveseat against a window to the left of the front door. She liked the deep color of the burgundy carpeting that covered the entire space and the white eyelet curtains on the two rectangular windows to the right, where you could see the horse paddock from afar. She looked over at the oak desk that was piled high with several stacks of manila file folders full of paperwork, a slate-gray laptop and a printer beside it. She walked around and peeked at the bathroom off to the left corner of the room, beautifully done with traditionally designed tiled Mexican accents on the counters and around the vanity mirror.

"And look," he said, leading her to the kitchen, "a full pot of coffee already brewing." He opened the fridge. "Plenty snacks, water, and food if you get hungry."

With its tiled countertops crafted in the traditional Mexican style, it was beautifully done. She glanced at the gray stainless-steel appliances, which included a fridge, microwave, dishwasher, and a two-basin sink. A small, white, distressed, wooden dining-room table, with four matching chairs, topped with embroidered cushions, was set off to the right side of the kitchen near another lace-curtained window. A large blue ceramic bowl of fruit was set on the dining-room table. It was an entirely comfortable space, but for some reason, her skin tingled, her hands felt moist, almost clammy. Maybe it was the tall piles of files on the desk or the look on Sanchez's face before he left to get Javier.

Leonid moved close to her, his arm around her shoulder. "Let's go over files. More boxes in the storage room." He pointed to an alcove off to the side of the kitchen. "Many more in there. Five years of boxes. I'm sorry," he said, and hung his head.

"I guess I have my work cut out for me," she said, and grinned. "I can handle it."

As he went through the folders on the desk, numerous transactions of antique furniture and properties, each one with a name at the top, he'd stop and ask if she had any questions before he moved on. Although the files were mixed together, it looked like there were two separate businesses. She could set up the books for each one, but it would entail a lot of work. When he led her back to the storage room and pointed out a pile of more than twenty-five or maybe thirty cardboard boxes full of file folders, she gasped.

"Leonid, this will take me months, if not a year." She shook her head and shrugged. "But then you'll have a decent accounting system. That will be good." She had no idea how he even reconciled his taxes like this, was able to track receivables or decipher profit margin. She'd figure it out. This, after all, was her area of expertise.

"This is private space for you," he said. "Javier will be outside whole time with electric vehicle, waiting upon you, take you anywhere on ranch or get whatever you need."

"And you?" she asked.

"Me, I sell properties, do business deals, manage men."

"Of course, I understand," she said. "But I-I thought we'd be working together."

"We will. At night, two, maybe three times a week, I invite clients to ranch or we go out, have nice dinners with them. Together, we will host. Most business happens at night in Mexico."

He brushed her cheek. His green eyes sparkled, as he leaned her against the kitchen counter.

"One thing about office cottage," he said, "bad reception."

"That's not good," she said, and grimaced. "But I probably won't need the internet to set up the accounting system. All on Excel, Word. You have those programs on the laptop?"

"*Da,* all basic programs. Let me know if you need other one. We get installed." He took a small object from his pocket. "I give you beeper. You beep me anytime, send message. Internet people come next week. Do hook-ups, get internet."

He held up the black beeper, showed her the LED screen, where she would text and the buttons to use to "beep" him on '699' and another number, '698' for Javier, who would be just outside. Her palm felt moist, as she clutched the plastic device.

Sanchez came through the front door. Behind him was a short handlebar-mustached man. She recognized him from the group of men who reported out the day before. He looked rugged, weathered, about forty or forty-five years old, with a sizeable beer belly.

"Javier," Leonid greeted him with a handshake. "Take care of her. Whatever she wants." Sanchez said some words in Spanish to Javier, who nodded, one hand in his pocket, the other holding his sombrero by his side.

Consuela settled into her life on the ranch. The days were long for the next several months. She worked alone, but enjoyed the progress she made, the rhythm she got into, the feeling of achievement, and the high praise from Leonid. Javier got her everything she needed whenever she asked.

Many nights were filled with clients, usually real estate investors or wealthy antique collectors. Leonid and Consuela hosted lavish dinners at home and out at restaurants in Merida. He had extraordinary coastal properties on the Mexican Riviera, which he touted for large price tags, while also importing and exporting antiques from and to many exotic areas of the world. He played many roles as distributor, marketer, influencer, and deal-maker.

Both sides of the *Venture Horizons* business reaped hefty profits and it showed on the accounting books. She was impressed with Leonid's flair for business and the charisma he showed with clients. But there were some clients, those from Saudi Arabia and Central America, who didn't seem to be visiting for antiques or real estate. He introduced them to her as friends he knew from previous dealings outside of his current business ventures.

They drank a lot, socialized as a prominent Merida couple, which included large parties and events around the city at high-end venues. With her fluency in Spanish and her elegant eveningwear, formal dresses and gowns that Leonid had custom-designed for her, the clients, both men and women, flocked to her. Though the women she met didn't seek her out as a personal friend, most were fascinated by Leonid. His aqua-green eyes and saucy nonchalant attitude seemed to mesmerize and feed into their attraction to him. But she never noticed him giving any woman a second look, attentive to only her wherever they went.

One night, five months into her life in Mexico, Leonid presented her with a pear-shaped yellow diamond ring. It was after dessert at a romantic coastal restaurant just north of Merida, after a client had left the venue, drunk on whiskey, and happy to have made a good deal with Leonid, or so he had thought. Once the client was gone from the table, Leonid joked about how he had sold the huge property way beyond his expectations. He appreciated how she had dazzled the stubborn client, influenced the man to take the deal. Leonid bent down on one knee and presented her with the two-carat ring. She was startled and cried with joy, thankful to have the life she was living.

She was Leonid's fiancée, a powerful magnet for him, time after time helped him close challenging real estate sales, and pricey antique deals with prospects that otherwise would resist the outrageous price tags. She became more and more creative, discovered little things about the male clients, complimented them, fed their ego, and invited them to envision their life once they owned the new property or spectacular antique featured by her fiancée. She evolved, became a master seductress, realizing the very potential that Leonid had spotted in her from the start. She wasn't quite aware, but she had done the same even with Leonid. She was his treasure, his star acquisition.

His boundless energy amazed her. He made love to her every night, whispering his praise for her financial acumen, her array of talents, her beauty. He'd describe their eventual life together on some far-away Malaysian island, retired young, and filthy-rich. She'd fall asleep in his arms listening to him.

Some weekends, he'd take her to the Merida coast and rent a private yacht. They'd snorkel in the turquoise waters, drink champagne, entwined on the deck of the boat, and fall asleep under the stars. She'd bring along a volume of Shakespeare's plays and read to herself, while Leonid fished off the back of the boat, his favorite way to relax after a loaded workweek.

The months flew by. She managed to call her grandmother every few weeks, connected with her Aunt Marianna every few months, and spoke with Astrid, her closest friend in California, every other month, checking on Paisley, but never suggested that she should ship the dog to Mexico. Astrid was engaged, living with her fiancée, and seemed very attached to the little dog.

Sometimes in the office cottage, where Consuela spent her workdays, she'd have lunch brought to her by servants and read bits of Shakespeare's plays. She'd curl up in the cozy velvet armchair she had Javier find for her, and think about Brian, Astrid's father, the college teacher for whom she had developed a crush. She often thought about the afternoon she spent with him at his home in Santa Cruz, where she recited Katherine's final speech from *Taming of the Shrew*. She remembered the way his eyes lit up as she moved across the room, dramatizing the scene. What if she had kissed him then? What if she had crossed the river of no return with her closest friend's father? Would he have allowed her to seduce him? Sitting at her desk, at the Venture Horizons Ranch, she'd look down at the gold bangle still on her wrist. Sometimes she'd slide the bracelet off her wrist and read the inscription, say it aloud: "This heart is ever at your service." She knew it was only a silly crush for a man she thought of as a literary god. She loved Leonid, but in a much different way.

She'd ask Javier to foray out to find books for her in Merida's numerous bookstores. She was surprised at his success and started a collection, filling a tall bookcase on the free wall in the office cottage with several of Shakespeare's plays, biographies of his life, and critiques of his writings.

Although Javier was committed to Leonid, she had created a strong bond with the short stubby man with the bushy handlebar mustache. He was, no doubt, a tough guy who would protect his boss no matter what and presented himself with a bully exterior, a holstered gun always attached to his belt, a sour expression on his face, the look in his eyes fierce. But she caught him blush more than a few times. He seemed delighted when she'd invite him to have coffee. He'd lower his head shyly, his sombrero in his hand, as he sat on the leather sofa ready to listen. She'd read him snippets of a sonnet or scene from a play. She'd get lost in the poetry of the words, pace the cottage space, and often just about perform for him. He'd smile, even on occasion applaud. Javier was the closest thing to a friend during those months on the ranch. She felt their mutual respect for one another grow each day, yet she was troubled that he followed her everywhere she went outside the office cottage. Even when she thought she was alone in the garden or out on a solo walk around the property or when she'd sit on a fence and watch the cowboys in the horse paddock, she'd turn her head, and there was Javier, peeking from behind a wall or alcove. He'd act as if he had accidentally come upon her. He always spoke to her politely and formally addressed her as Senora Petrovsky, even though she was not a relative of Leonid's.

At the end of the workday on their rides in the fancy cart back to the mansion each day before sunset, Javier would ask her how her day went. He seemed to want to hear her talk, admired her ability to speak fluent Spanish but with an American twist to her words and phrases. Occasionally, he'd ask her if she wanted to accompany him to Merida to hunt down books. But with so much work to do setting up the accounting system and entering the hundreds and hundreds of transactions, she would decline his invitations, thinking that once she got caught up, she'd accept his offer.

Consuela became accustomed to having servants. Her acceptance of that extravagance surprised her. The ranch hands and servants were polite and good to her. She felt privileged to have their care, but also found herself becoming dependent, almost addicted to them giving her anything she wanted. She got used to the two halves of her life: the solitude of the daytime hours and the socially packed nightlife with Leonid and his wealthy clients.

CHAPTER 16:

"Affection Is a Coal That Must Be Cooled. Else Suffer'd It Will Set the Heart on Fire."*

—WILLIAM SHAKESPEARE

W HEN BRIAN EXITED THE POLICE STATION, HE WAS STILL FUMING from his conversation with Tim. Mac 's head was half out the open back window of the Jeep, waiting for his return. Reaching inside through the opening, he stroked his dog's head. "Sorry Mac, that took longer than I thought. That guy's a real bastard."

He pressed his key fob to open the door and let the dog out. "Yeah, have a pee right here." Brian led Mac over to a patch of dirt under a tree on the station's lawn. He tossed down the contents of the white paper bag Tim had given him. "Here boy, ham-and-cheese croissant from one of your fans."

Mac wasted no time and started to take the sandwich apart with his teeth. Brian's cell phone chimed a greeting he had for incoming calls from Ivy. How would he sound to her after what happened with Savvy?

---

* "Affection is a coal that must be cooled. Else suffer'd it will set the heart on fire." Venus and Adonis, William Shakespeare, stanza 65, line 1387

"Ivy. How's everything going?"

"Not so good."

"You're okay?"

"I hope so." Her voice was shaky, the soothing effect he usually got from her absent. "I-I just found out that my Carl has COVID-19. So now he's got brain cancer, and the virus, on top of it."

As usual, he felt at a loss for words when someone needed him. "You must be overwhelmed."

He could hear her voice crack. "I was exposed," she said.

"Oh no," Brian said. "I'm sorry." He took a deep breath and looked down at Mac, who had finished the croissant and licked the grass for crumbs. He led the dog back to the Jeep while he listened to Ivy.

"Becky and the kids are here with me," she said. "We're all being tested later this morning. Then, we'll need to quarantine at Carl's place. He's in the hospital, but not doing too badly, so far avoiding the ICU. And the silver lining is that he's agreed to the brain surgery once the virus leaves him."

"That is one piece of good news," Brian said. "But does this mean that I won't see you for a while?"

He wanted to tell her that he loved her, but it was everything he was questioning. Another part of him wanted to tell her about his accident, the intense interaction he just had with Tim, and come clean about his indiscretion with Savvy. Share his struggle, his guilt, lay it out on the table.

"I'll be here with Becky and the girls, checking on Carl each day," she said. "Probably ten days, maybe fourteen." He could hear her deep sigh. "Depends on the test results and how Carl is doing."

Mac jumped up into the Jeep and then quickly into the backseat. Brian slid in behind the wheel.

"Can I do anything to help?" he asked. "At your house?"

"Oh, I can't think of what. Wait. This is a strange request, but can you pick a bunch of lemons off the tree in my back garden? It's way overloaded. Otherwise, the birds will just get them. Make a mess and waste my treasured Meyer lemons."

"Yeah, sure, I can do that. How about I give them to Astrid? Her fiancée called and wants her back."

"Oh," Ivy said. "I don't think I knew that."

"Maybe she can rustle-up some lemon meringue pie." He chuckled. "Yeah, she can make up her mind about him while chowing down on *lemon* pie."

Ivy burst out laughing.

"It's a metaphor. You know I think the guy's a lemon," he said.

"Well, I hope she doesn't make the connection." Ivy's tone had returned to her more usual positivity.

"I'm on my way over the hill to have brunch with her right now. I'll get her the lemons in a few days."

He started up the engine, and stopped at the traffic light. An elderly couple, holding hands, wearing face masks, crossed the street in front of him.

"I'll be in touch," Ivy said, her voice tired.

"I miss you, he said. "Let me know how those COVID tests turn out. My fingers are crossed."

"Thanks. I miss you too," she said. "Goodbye love."

His eyes moistened.

He drove down Ocean Street and hooked onto Highway 17, headed over the mountain to Santa Clara County. He turned on his favorite radio station. He enjoyed the classic rock music and the amusing commentary from the morning host. Bon Jovi's *Livin' On A Prayer* started to play. The music seemed to loosen up his neck, ease the dull ache from his injured hip.

He wanted to forget the strained morning interaction with Tim at the station, put the bad news from Ivy in the background, get the image of the moving hand on the bluff out of his head. How could it have been Consuela? Impossible.

He sang out the words, an attempt to wipe it all out of his mind. He looked forward to brunch with Astrid, hoped she'd fill the troubled space he found himself in with her chatter about law school or her runaway fiancée. He yearned for his life to return to "normal," without the bloody COVID virus, without the jittery butterflies he had in the physical presence of Savvy Romeo, return to a time when he was not being accused of murder.

"Whoa, we're halfway there," he sang out as he climbed the mountain in the Jeep Cherokee. The peeling bark of the madrones gave way to the majestic redwoods on either side of the winding twenty-six-mile highway, also known as Blood Alley, the most treacherous two-lane road in all of California. The concrete divider separating traffic from head-on collisions was built finally by the state only a few years before. It could be a wicked ride for anyone in the rain or fog, but on that sunny autumn day, the twists and turns felt exhilarating to him. It was good to be out on a drive after a long COVID-19 hiatus. He pressed the button to open the windows and turned the radio up. Mac jumped from the back into the front passenger seat and stuck his snout out the window, as Brian shot into the fast lane, to overtake a slow 18-wheeler.

Another 80's hit blasted out from the radio, Pat Benatar's *Hit Me With Your Best Shot*. As he approached the perilous Laurel Curve, and started downhill, a yellow Corvette cut him off. He pressed his foot on the brake to slow down, but something was wrong. *Shit*. The brakes failed. Bewildered, he put his foot down harder. He pumped them. Nothing. He pushed the pedal to the floor and leaned back. His body stiffened. Nothing! "Fuck."

He swerved to the right to get out of the fast lane, barely missing the green truck in front of him. The truck accelerated and jutted into the fast lane to the left. *Thank God*. His speedometer read 76 mph. He needed to do something bold. *Fuck, what?*

The steep curve north of Summit Road—a semi-truck was ahead of him, burning its brakes. He smelled the fluid and saw the smoke. If he could just make it around that next turn before hitting the semi, maybe he could somehow peel off onto the shoulder.

"Shit, hold on Mac," he shouted.

He tried pumping the brakes again. Zero. "Get around the semi, get around the semi," he told himself. The needle edged to 80 mph. He zigged to the left and zagged to the right, his tires screeching. The Jeep seemed to wobble. Louder screeching. He could feel Mac's eyes on him, smell the ham-and-cheese croissant on the dog's breath. He yanked up on the emergency brake and turned the wheel hard all the way to the right. He was off the asphalt, the gravel scattering, smacking his right cheek from across the passenger seat through the open window. He heard the brush rip up. Branches hit the windshield. *Fuck*. He couldn't see. Mac howled. They hit some massive bump and the Jeep tilted, slid slightly downhill, and collided with what sounded like thick brush. The image of Consuela's beautiful face swept through his mind. Her cheeks were flushed. More grit sprayed his face. A hard jolt and he was thrown forward. He reacted quickly, and crossed his arms in front of his head. The airbag exploded. He heard metal crunch. Mac was silent. Quiet. Darkness.

His face was buried in the gray pillow. Distant voices told him he was alive. Mac whimpered. Brian looked down in the small space to the right beneath the pillow and could see his dog move around on the floor mat. *Thank God.* The airbag hadn't deployed on the passenger side. He pulled his arm out and reached inside his jacket pocket. Clutching his car key, he sprung open the two-inch Swiss Army knife, and plunged it into the airbag. He heard the hiss as the bag slowly began to deflate. Two outstretched hands reached through the window and pulled away the deflating airbag. Brian saw light and felt relieved.

"Mac, buddy," he said. "You all right?"

The dog jumped up from the mat onto the passenger seat.

"Hey," a voice from outside called. "Hello, hello." The teenager stuck his head inside. He had stringy hair, a collection of nasty pimples, and large brown eyes. He pulled the door open.

"Can you move?" the boy asked.

"I think so," Brian answered.

The passenger door opened.

Mac jumped over Brian and belted out the door, colliding with the teen.

"Whoa. Cool dog, man." As the teen helped Brian out of the vehicle, he could see Mac already sprawled out in the brush, panting. His legs were unsteady as he stepped onto a jumble of tree branches and shrubs of manzanita bushes. His right foot faltered. He stumbled, but managed to stand up. He tested his legs, moving one knee up and down, and then the other.

"Hey, thanks," he said to the teen who wore a black Grateful Dead T-shirt.

"You want me to call an ambulance?" the boy asked. They heard a police siren.

"I think I'm okay. Nothing seems broken."

Brian looked up by the road and realized the Jeep hadn't slid very far off the flat shoulder, maybe a couple of feet, if that. The thick foliage had stopped him. A highway patrolman stepped down the slope toward them.

"Whoever was in the accident, you might want to sit on the ground," the officer called out. "Never know—could be a bad injury."

"It was me." Brian raised his hand. "This guy here came to my rescue. I'm okay." His hip smarted, but other than that, and his cut elbow, there didn't seem to be any other injury.

The officer took down the information, asked to see his license, filled out a sheet of paper on his clipboard, and suggested that Brian thank the higher spirit.

"A good tow truck will get you out of that mess. No problem," the officer said. He got back in his patrol car and took off. The teen named Jeff left in his pickup truck, but not before Brian got the boy's contact info. He wanted to make an effort to thank him more appropriately later.

Brian phoned Zeke's Towing and Repair, a shop he knew in Los Gatos, had used over the years, owned by a Santa Clara High School classmate and star football player. Zeke answered and offered to come out himself since the crash occurred only four or five miles away on the mountain highway.

In Zeke's truck, Brian held the hefty Airedale in his lap. He told Zeke the story of what happened on the hill.

"So, your brakes suddenly failed?" the broad-shouldered two-hundred-thirty-pound Zeke asked.

"Apparently. Guess I was lucky to walk away."

"And the repair needed doesn't look too bad." Zeke shrugged. "Really, just your bumper...oh, and the brakes." He laughed. "Yeah," Zeke added, "we'll see what that's about."

"I was on my way to have brunch with my daughter. I was supposed to be there at eleven. I better call her." Brian took out his cell phone and felt the paper face mask in his pocket. He pulled out the mask and put it on, noticing that Zeke wasn't wearing one.

Zeke waved his hand in the air. "Don't worry about the mask. I got results from the anti-body test a month ago. Evidently, I had the COVID awhile back and didn't even know it. So, you're safe, buddy."

Brian nodded and put the face mask back in his pocket.

"I could do your brake repair today," Zeke said, "and you could borrow my jalopy Ford loaner. Runs good. Then, you could make that eleven o'clock brunch with your daughter. Slow day for me, anyway."

"I appreciate it, man. I'll pay you for the loaner."

"Nah. You left the police force and you're a college teacher now, aren't you?"

"Yeah."

"Hey, we need our teachers and you guys don't make all that much money. Loaner's on me."

"You're a great guy, Zeke, always have been. Thanks." Mac scooted down onto the floor mat, releasing his full weight from Brian.

"Beautiful mutt," Zeke commented.

"Yeah, my best friend."

"There's an auto body shop next door to my place, Benny's. I could inquire how much your Jeep's body repair would cost you. I'll get you a deal. Just your bumper and maybe some dent damage on the passenger door."

"You're golden in my book, Zeke." Brian smiled and reached down to nuzzle his dog, grateful neither of them were hurt badly.

CHAPTER 17:
"Though She Be but Little
She Is Fierce."*

—WILLIAM SHAKESPEARE

A STRID WAS OVERPROTECTIVE WHEN IT CAME TO PAISLEY, THE SEV-en-pound white terrier, whose tiny snout peeked out of the harnessed doggie carrier in the passenger seat. Paisley's furry little head strained to look out the rolled-down window of the Toyota Prius. It was nine-thirty in the morning, still enough time to stop at the University bookstore to snag that textbook, the last one Astrid needed for the semester, before meeting her dad at Albie's Café.

"Come on, Paisley, you're coming with."

She hitched the rhinestone-studded pink leash to Paisley's collar, un-harnessed the carrier, and placed the dog in her lap.

"You're as pretty as your mama, aren't you?"

She nuzzled the dog and thought of Consuela who had left Paisley in her charge two years ago, before she ran off to Mexico with Leonid. When Consuela's plane crashed twelve months ago on her flight back to visit her ailing grandmother, Astrid was devastated. She had trouble sleeping for weeks and had to get sleep medication to take her through the rough

---

* "Though she be but little she is fierce." *A Midsummer Night's Dream*, William Shakespeare, Act 3, Scene 2

period. A year had gone by, but she still mourned her friend's death every day. Sometimes she would just gaze at little Paisley and think of the good times she had with Consuela, whether hanging out on a Sunday binge-watching a Netflix series, or even when quizzing each other for an upcoming exam, while devouring a quart of ice cream. They had been like sisters, Consuela sensationally beautiful, into books, and a math whiz, and Astrid into fashion, yet with her head savoring politics and constitutional law.

After she managed to park close to the quad, where the bookstore sat on SCU's campus, Astrid put on her face mask, passed through the bookstore's metal detector, and headed straight for the law book section. Although she was sure that dogs were not permitted in the university store, she knew the student cashiers wouldn't confront her, since they hadn't before. With classes starting up that week, there were several customers in a frenzy to purchase school supplies and pricey textbooks. Santa Clara University, set in the heart of Silicon Valley, was a serious institution, full of students with ambition, brains, and the drive to excel.

"Damn it," she muttered under her breath. The *National Security Law, 7th Edition* textbook was sold out. The space on the shelf was bare where the tiny clip-on indicator noted the book title, along with the price tag of $286. *Crap. How the hell can I read three chapters by Wednesday's first class?* There was no online version available. She had searched for hours on the internet.

She turned to the bookshop employee stacking a shelf behind her. Paisley settled down on the tiled floor at her feet.

"Excuse me," Astrid said, "but any chance you have some copies of the *National Security Law, 7th Edition* in the stock room? This shelf's empty."

The disheveled long-haired teenager wore a royal-blue SCU face mask. He shot her a resentful look.

"There were two on the shelf thirty minutes ago. I know because I stocked them. Looks like they're gone now. May be another week before more come in."

He turned and walked away, smacking the empty cardboard box with his free hand as if it were a drum.

It was going to be one hell of a semester. She took out her phone—9:55, plenty of time left to look for a new laptop bag, which she badly needed. Albie's was only 10 minutes away from campus. She walked two aisles over, and from a large array of shapes and sizes, she selected a dark-gray suede high-tech-looking shoulder bag from the rack. After coaxing Paisley up from the floor, she headed to the cashier.

Astrid stopped on the embossed blue circle on the floor, each spot the required 6 feet apart, to ensure the required social distancing. She was just two away in line from the cashier. The petite young woman standing on the spot in front of her wore a black leather jacket and a black wool cap embellished with tiny white pearls, the cap covering her hair. Astrid noticed that she was holding two heavy textbooks in her arms. When the woman reached down into her shoulder bag, Astrid noticed the gold-lettered title on the burgundy-covered textbook, *National Security Law, 7th Edition.*

"Excuse me," Astrid said. "May I ask you something?" The woman looked up. Her eyes were a sea-foam green color, which dominated her rosy cherub-shaped face.

She flashed a smile and nodded.

"That's the exact textbook I'm trying to hunt down, the burgundy one you're holding." Paisley started to circle Astrid's legs, the dog wrapping the leash around her ankles. She reached down and untangled the leash, patted Paisley's head, and looked back at the pretty woman.

"Did you happen to see a second one of those on the bookshelf?" Astrid asked. "The stock guy told me there were two there thirty minutes ago." She stopped herself. "Oh God, I'm so sorry. Obviously, they're both gone."

"Sorry," the woman responded. "Looks like I got last one. Cute dog. Boy or girl?" The woman had a thick accent that sounded Eastern European.

"A female," Astrid said. "Her name's Paisley."

The cashier called out, "Next."

The young woman gave Astrid a quick wave, winked, and moved to the counter, where Astrid noticed she pulled out four one-hundred-dollar bills to pay for the two hefty books. Astrid regretted having asked her about the textbook since it was clear that the woman was just about to purchase it. *Maybe she's in my Wednesday class. She seems nice.*

Astrid reached down to calm Paisley, the dog still circling her feet. "Next," the cashier called out. When she looked up, she saw that the woman in the leather jacket and pearl-decorated cap was gone.

Astrid paid, left the bookstore, and noticed the coffee wagon just outside. She needed a latte and there was still plenty of time before meeting Dad at eleven. She ordered a vanilla latte, found a stone table on the quad, sat, and removed her face mask to sip the foamy latte. God, *I'm so sick of these face masks,* she thought. She set down her new computer bag on the bench by her side, plunked little Paisley on her lap, and gave the dog some deserved attention after the good behavior in the bookstore.

"May I join you?" a female voice asked.

It was the pretty woman from the bookstore. She recognized the ruddy cheeks, the stunning eyes, the unusual wool cap, and the sultry voice.

"Of course," Astrid said, and smiled.

"Thank you," the woman said. She put her books down on the stone tabletop. "So, you need textbook for law class?"

"Yes. But I'll figure out something or otherwise just look stupid in the first session. It's okay. It's happened before."

They both laughed.

"How about you take this one?"

"But *you* need it...don't you?" Astrid replied.

"I have other one, same one."

Astrid frowned, not quite understanding why the woman would have two of the same textbook."

"I'm picky student. I have used one at home. Previous book owner marked up whole thing with messy notes in thick blue pen. Very distracting, but no big deal. I can sell you this one for same price as inside the store."

"No, I couldn't do that," Astrid said. "You should have a clean copy for yourself."

"Hmmm." She nodded. "I have idea. How about I sell you the used one if you don't care about mark-ups? For...say forty dollars. You can pick it up from my house. You know what, I'll give to you free."

"For free? No."

"I'm wealthy exchange student. Free book for you. No problem."

"You're sure?"

The woman pressed her lips together and nodded.

"I live not far in Rose Garden area. Five minutes in car. You come by tomorrow afternoon? At two o'clock?"

"Yes, I can come. Wow. I really appreciate this. It will still give me time to read the first three chapters tomorrow night."

The woman reached into her jacket pocket and took out a pen and a small slip of lined yellow paper. She wrote something quickly. Astrid sipped the rest of her latte.

"*Da,* here's address. Come around back of pale-yellow house. I rent garden cottage. Sorry, but I must go now." She stood up. "Appointment." She bent down to pet Paisley and then picked up her two heavy books. "See you tomorrow."

Astrid waved, feeling like the day had turned lucky for her.

Just a few steps away, the woman pivoted, and said, "Ah, one request."

"Yes?" Astrid replied.

"I love dog but please don't bring tomorrow. I have anxious cat." She shrugged.

"No problem," Astrid said.

The woman grinned, turned, and rushed away.

Astrid hugged Paisley and looked down at the yellow piece of paper.

"615 Primrose Court, Santa Clara"

Oh God, I didn't even ask her name.

CHAPTER 18:
"There Is No Darkness but Ignorance"*
—WILLIAM SHAKESPEARE

SEPTEMBER 24, 2019: IT HAD BEEN TWELVE MONTHS SINCE SHE ARRIVED at Venture Horizons Ranch. Consuela felt restless. She needed a long break, maybe return to California or take a trip to Europe, and had mentioned it a few times to Leonid. How could she complain about the fairytale life she was leading? Leonid would comfort her, distract her with gifts, lovemaking, and special weekends. He taught her how to ride a horse, and she fell in love with the sport. They took long rides often near the beach and it was glorious, and where she felt closest to Leonid. As they approached a full year living in the Yucatan, she finally let the idea of leaving Mexico fall away.

The internet never got fixed in the office cottage, although men visited several times to try to set it up. Leonid chalked it up to bad reception in general on the ranch. Because Consuela worked so diligently during the day, she hadn't missed it. In the evenings, Leonid encouraged her to use his cell phone in the main house, which seemed to be reliable, and invited her to call her relatives and friends in California. But over the

---

*   "There is no darkness but ignorance." *Twelfth Night*, William Shakespeare, Act 4, Scene 2

months she gradually lost the drive to continuously connect with the life she left behind.

She enjoyed the work and had organized and entered all the data from the piles of files on the desk and from all thirty or more boxes in the storage room. It had taken an entire year to do all the work. There were solid accounting practices being applied and the business strengthened, transparent, with profits rocketing. Leonid would net at least $150 million for year end. The system she had created was humming, the big job done, and now it would merely be processing the monthly accounting entries and reconciliations, and report to Leonid on the sum of the assets, liabilities, and profit margin. She would now be able to foray out into the field and assist Leonid with marketing and sales.

She entered the storage room to check if she missed any loose files, maybe some strays on the white shelving. Consuela was a careful accountant, which meant that she persevered to ensure all data was captured when it came to business transactions. She noticed an indent in the wall by a shelf in the back of the storage area, behind an assortment of cleaning supplies. She pushed away some plastic bottles of *Fabulosa*, a popular cleaner, and saw a door about three feet high and two feet wide inserted into the wall. A small keyhole was set in the middle of the door. She tried to pry the door open with her fingertips but it was locked. She stared at the unusually shaped keyhole, which likely needed an old-fashioned long-necked key. She searched the shelf area, but found no key. She went back to the desk and checked inside the top drawer and then in every drawer. No key. She'd ask Leonid about it that night. Were there more files in the locked cabinet? Files she needed to reconcile?

They were going out to dinner with a client that evening and she'd have to rush to get ready. She'd take a quick shower, pin up her hair, and wear the black sequined cocktail dress. The client was Massimo from Iran, a man she had met a few times before. She felt jittery when she was around him. There was something unsavory about him. She went back to the storage room and arranged the bottles of cleaner and supplies on the shelf, placing them back in place. Using her beeper, she summoned Javier to take her back to the house. Dinner played out as she had anticipated.

Massimo seemed slimier than usual. He reached behind her to touch her bare back a few times. He brushed her hand on the table when picking up his glass. She drank more than she should, gradually scooting her chair further and further from his spidery touch. Leonid didn't seem to notice any of it. He talked on and on about the year's business success and how Massimo was an important part of it all.

When Leonid invited Massimo back to the ranch for after-dinner drinks and cigars, Consuela cringed inside. Once at home and settled in the sitting room by the fireplace, she tugged at Leonid's sleeve.

"Can we talk in private?" she asked. Leonid seemed puzzled but followed her to the kitchen. She told him she had a headache likely a migraine coming on and needed to get some sleep. He held her close, then kissed the top of her head.

"You work so hard. Go, get some sleep," he said.

She said good night to Massimo, apologizing for having a bad headache, while Leonid poured two glasses of his special vodka.

Alone in the bedroom, she undressed. She switched off the antique lamps and tiptoed over to the armoire to retrieve the flashlight from the back of the top shelf, planning to read some Shakespeare under the sheets, since she wasn't really tired. If Leonid walked by the bedroom to use an upstairs restroom, he'd think she was asleep.

When she picked up the flashlight, she saw the metal key taped to the back shelf of the armoire. She plucked the key from the shelf and removed the tape. It was an unusual long- necked shape and maybe fit the door in the office cottage storeroom. Something told her not to mention it to Leonid before she checked to see what was locked inside that cabinet. She had too much sangria at dinner, which had somewhat reduced the anxiety she usually experienced when interacting with Massimo. Tipsy, she tucked the key into the pocket of her lilac cardigan hanging in the closet. She placed the flashlight back on the shelf, deciding not to read, but instead close her eyes, rush through the night, and try the key out first thing in the morning. A creepy chill ran through her body.

She heard Leonid's footsteps on the staircase and then the squeak of the bedroom door; her eyes half-opened. She heard him fumble to peel off his clothes and stumble to get out of his dress pants. He threw each item on the floor and got into bed next to her.

He whispered, "Your head still ache?"

"It feels better now," she whispered.

"Massimo knew you faked it," he said. His head on the pillow, he stared up at the ceiling. "You did same prank before, pretended headache. Massimo remembers. He mentioned it. You pissed him off."

"But—"

"You don't want to piss off best client, do you?"

"No, I—"

Leonid turned to her. He took one of her long curls in hand and gently twisted the hair around his index finger.

"We have dinner with him again Friday. You must give him extra attention." He reached under the sheet and stroked her between her thighs, softening his voice. "Please my love. I make millions from his business."

"But what business does he give you?" she asked. "I haven't entered anything in the accounting books under Massimo Hosseini."

Leonid pulled his hand away.

"He uses other name for business," Leonid said sharply. "You shouldn't ask stupid question. And by the way, I saw inscription on precious gold bracelet, from some man in love with you."

The room was dark, but she could sense his eyes slicing into her. It was the first time she felt threatened by him. He's very drunk, she told herself.

"The bracelet was from my friend, Astrid McCallam, and her dad, Brian. I told you."

He laughed. "It was from a man who was in love with you. The dad? *Da,* you are a bad girl."

"Don't be ridiculous," she said.

He kissed her lips hard.

"Too much vodka for me," he said, and sank back on his pillow, turning away from her.

I've angered him, she thought, *the way his workers sometimes do.*

When he made love to her early the next morning before the sun came up, the touch of his tongue inside her blended with the dream she was in.

She was flying over an ocean, lifted by beautiful white angel wings, which she could flex with ease, whip past airplanes in the sky, slow down and glide with the clouds. Her journey across the sky landed her in a field full of tall yellow flowers, the orgasm he gave coming together in one euphoric crescendo. Her eyes were closed, as Leonid moved his head back onto his pillow and clung to her.

"I'm lucky man to have you," he whispered. "I will never forget again."

When she entered the office cottage that morning, her bag full of files with this month's business transactions, her plan was to do the accounting entries and close the books for the month of September, 2019. She made some coffee in the cottage kitchen and turned on her laptop.

She took the key out of the pocket of her cardigan and stared at it, her hands shaking. She lowered her coffee mug, but it slipped out of her hand and smashed onto the mahogany surface, breaking into pieces. The brown liquid splashed onto the laptop screen, spread quickly under the black keyboard, and ran off the side of the desk onto the carpet.

"Damn it," she yelled out. A knock at the cottage door. "Damn," she muttered to herself. The door opened. It was Javier, her designated helper.

"*Que pasa, senora?* I hear scream." She quickly stuffed the key back into her pocket.

"*Si, si. No problema,*" she said, and picked up the broken pieces of the coffee mug, held them out to show him, then rushed to the sink to grab the roll of paper towels.

"Ahh," he said. "*Estas bien?*"

"*Si, gracias,*" Consuela said, and nodded, as she wiped up the spill. She looked up and waved for him to go.

The door closed behind him. She then tossed the shards of the mug and soaked paper towels into the trash bin. Her nerves were frayed. Her mind churned with guilt. The glimpse she got last night of the venom Leonid could bestow frightened the hell out of her and was the reason she had decided not to ask him about the locked cabinet.

She went into the storage room. Pushing aside several bottles of cleaning supplies on the shelf, she slid the long-necked key into the key hole of the cabinet, realizing it was a good fit. Inside was a tall stack of manila folders; each looked to be full of paper. She reached in and pulled out the stack. A few bottles of cleaner toppled over. The folders scattered to the tiled floor; some slid under the shelving.

As she knelt down, she noticed colored photos peeking out of one manila folder. She pulled out a photograph. It was an eight-by-ten of a large gun, what looked like a machine gun or some type of automatic weapon. There were more photos, guns with long barrels, others with short narrow ones, different colors, shapes, and sizes. Her head felt light. Her tearful eyes blurred the shape of the gun in the photograph. Fear and anger bubbled inside her. She wiped her eyes with the sleeve of her cardigan and refocused. Each photo had an alpha numeric caption at the bottom below the image: "K-309," "Z-2450," "R-604," "T-450." They didn't sound like names of guns she'd heard of, but they did sound like the numbers the men had reported out on that first day when she arrived at the ranch.

She opened one of the files and thumbed through the paperwork. Names of countries, names of people, invoices with price tags like $126,000 and $290,000. She noticed that on the front of each file, at the top, a name was scrawled in black felt-tip pen. She sat down cross-legged and hunted for a folder that maybe had Massimo Hosseini's name. She had a gut feeling, and he had seemed slimy enough to be in the gun business. She spotted Hosseini and opened the file. More invoices: "$485,000," "$409,000," "$329,000." Her stomach cramped.

This gun thing was bigger than any of his property or import/export ventures. There were about a dozen invoices in the folder. She looked at each one, and after a quick calculation in her head, the lot for Hosseini alone added up to more than $4 million.

"Oh God," she screamed. She heard the creak of the front door. She hurriedly started to stuff paper back inside folders. He came through the storage room door and looked down at her, his mouth open.

"*Senora!*" Javier shot her a look more like a stern parent than a ranch hand. He shook his head, his lips pressed together. He placed his hands firmly on his hips, and warned, "*Una mala situación.*"

She ignored his disapproval and continued opening files and looking at gun photos. Javier stood over her, watching, shaking his head, and occasionally said, *"Senora! No buena."*

She heard the front door to the cottage open, and close again. Leonid bolted in and stood behind Javier. A fierce fire ignited in his aqua-green eyes. His eyes darted from right to left and back. His face darkened.

"Javier, leave! Out!" Leonid shouted.

As Javier scrambled out of the storage room, she noticed his hands tremble. His hat fell onto the floor and he bumbled to pick it up.

"Si, Jefe. I go," Javier said, and ran out.

Leonid got down on the floor next to Consuela. He hurriedly gathered up the folders and started to sort paperwork and photographs back into individual files. He attempted to organize them and placed one file atop another. Still on her knees, she plucked two of the loose photos from the floor. Her throat strained to get words out.

"Leonid, what are these photos?"

He shook his head. "Nothing. Just storing files for a friend," he said, his voice hollow. "Nothing to do with me."

"Storing files for a friend? What are you talking about?"

He stopped sorting. His eyes narrowed.

"You're lying," she said. "You think I'm just some stupid American woman. This gun thing is obviously another business you're in. One you did not tell me about."

He grabbed the photos from her, and pulled her up, pressing her back against the white shelving. He threw the photos in his hand on the floor. His breath felt hot on her forehead, his voice chilling, a growl. "It's none of your fucking business. My business. Only *my* business!" Fury burned in his eyes; the eyes she had thought so magical. He let her go and stepped away, leaned back against the opposite wall, his ankles crossed, his arms folded in front of his chest, a soured look on his face.

"What made you go into my private locked cabinet? What?" He barked.

"What made *you* put barbed wire on the fence around your whole property?" she snapped back.

"Protection," he shouted. "Protection from bad people, much worse than me."

Their eyes locked for what seemed like minutes. It was their first real conflict.

Her body was an empty shell, her thoughts racing in all directions, the walls of the small storage room closing in. Alone, she felt alone, powerless and trapped.

He looked down at his feet, his head in his hands. He straightened, cleared his throat, stared at the floor and spoke in a hushed tone, "Sorry I react in such bad way. You pin me down with accusations." He looked up at her. "Of course, I know you are smart, high intelligence. I would never think anything else about you."

She struggled with what to say, what not to say.

He moved to her, took her hand in his, tracing his fingers over her pear-shaped engagement ring. "I'm not going to be in gun business anymore. I have plan to get out."

"Do you?" she said, her words flat.

"Yes, one year more and we have enough money to leave all this. Retire on private island in Malaysia. I already have location picked out." He grinned. "No more business deals. No more dinners with greedy fools. Fully enjoy life."

"I-I can't talk about this now," she said, pulling her hand away. Her head pounded.

"You were right about one thing," he said, with a smirk on his face.

"I was? What's that?" she asked.

"Massimo, he's kingpin of gun-running business. We are partners." Leonid leaned back and sighed. "Big mistake. The things he does would horrify you, even me. He has no respect for human life."

Leonid kneeled down and picked up the stack of folders, stood up, and placed them back inside the wall cabinet, locked the door, and put the key in the pocket of his chinos.

He moved close to her and gently placed his hands on her shoulders.

"You have good instincts," he said.

"Not that good." She looked away.

"I was coming to see you here this afternoon anyway? Do you know why?"

He shrugged. "Unusual for me to visit you during day."

She shook her head. "Why?"

"To tell you that your Aunt Marianna phoned from California."

"What?"

"*Da,* your grandmother is in hospital. Maybe stroke."

"Oh God."

"I told your aunt you'd phone her back before dinner. Come, we go to house now."

"Um, I-I need to do a few things on the laptop to close out the month. You go. I'll be right there."

She was falling apart; the beat of her heart thumped inside her head. She needed to be alone even for a few minutes, wrestle with what to do next. The spell he had on her was broken.

"What you saw in that cabinet, you didn't see," he said.

"Of course." She nodded.

"I'll send Javier back for you," he said, kissed her on the cheek, and left.

She came out of the storage room and sank into the loveseat, placing her head down between her knees. She could feel the bile rise up into her throat. She bolted into the bathroom and threw up in the toilet, stifling her muffled screams in case he was still outside the front door. He sickened her, but she could not let him know. *How will I manage to fake it long enough to escape him?*

CHAPTER 19:
"The Sins of the Father Are to Be Laid Upon the Children."*

-WILLIAM SHAKESPEARE

ASTRID FELT A SLIGHT CHILL IN THE AIR AS SHE ENTERED THE OUTDOOR patio at Albie's. September had brought cool temperatures with the recent rains, but that morning the sunshine was brilliant, a pleasant sixty-eight degrees, except for a wind gust every now and then. Rain was predicted but hadn't yet materialized. Since there was no inside seating permitted during this phase of the pandemic, the patio was busy. The hostess led her to a table in the far corner, where she placed Paisley's plastic dog bowl down on the cement and asked the husky waiter for some water.

Her phone buzzed. A text from Dennis:

Call me.

She decided not to respond to her ex-fiancée. It was after eleven. Her dad was late, which was unusual for him.

Mac scampered ahead of Brian, pulling hard to the table, where Astrid sat, her small terrier under the table lapping up water from a bowl. She noticed her dad limping and was concerned about what looked like a cut

---

*   "The sins of the father are to be laid upon the children." *Merchant of Venice*, William Shakespeare, Act 3, Scene 5

on his forehead. She wanted to hug him, but with the virus still in full throttle, they elbowed each other hello.

"Dad, it's good to see you."

"I am so tired of these damn things," he complained, as he removed the face mask and stuffed it in his pocket. "How the hell did you snag this big table?"

"Strings," she said. "I know how to pull them." She shook her head. "I think the host didn't want the dog near the other patrons. And now, his worst nightmare, two dogs at one table." She shrugged and looked down at Paisley and Mac, both sprawled out, side by side, on the gray cement, like brother and sister.

Brian looked down and grinned.

"Dad, are you limping?"

He took a seat across the table.

"Are you bleeding?" she asked.

He reached his fingers to his temple, felt along the raised lesion, and picked up the paper napkin to dab his forehead.

"I had a car accident coming over the mountain."

"What?"

"Yeah, Jeep's at the repair shop. Got a loaner so I could meet you."

He didn't want to tell her about the mountain bike accident the day before.

"It's only a scratch, and my hip aches a bit. Other than that, I escaped injury." He looked down at the menu to review the omelet choices, his fingers tapping on the glass table top.

She glanced down at his nervous fingers. "What's going on?" she asked.

He placed his hands in his lap, out of sight.

"My life has suddenly become complicated," he said.

"You were with Ivy this weekend, right?" Astrid asked.

He nodded. "We had a great evening together. She's off on a trip now. Family issues. Long story."

The waiter approached and turned over their two empty mugs. "Coffee?" he asked.

They both nodded.

"Need more time to decide?"

"Yes, thank you," Astrid replied.

"Back in a few," he said, and left.

She poured some cream in her coffee. "Do you love her?"

"Wow, you know how to intimidate your dates," Brian said, with a smirk on his face. "Funny you asked because I've been thinking a lot about that."

"Why don't you just pop the question?" she said. "It's been what, four years since you started dating?"

He took a sip of coffee. "Not so simple," he said, pressing his lips together. "I-I met someone else recently and..." The woman at the table across from them shot him a disapproving look.

"Dad? I don't remember when you've ever shared your love life with me."

"Well, you asked." He shrugged. "I'm trying out some new behavior. Opening up more to those close to me."

"Hmm, I'm loving this new side of you." She sat back in her chair. "So, you're going to cool it down with Ivy?"

"I have strong feelings for her and I don't want us to end. She doesn't know about this other woman. It's all very new."

He closed his eyes for a moment. "Frankly, as I listen to myself, I seem to be getting in touch with how I really feel."

She reached across the table for his hand.

"This is so nice...you and me talking like this." Her eyes teared up.

The server approached. "Ready?"

"Veggie omelet for me," Astrid said. "Rye toast."

Brian put his hand up to his forehead to hide the cut.

"Eggs Benedict for me."

The server poured more coffee and left.

"What about you?" Brian asked. "You taking Dennis back?"

"I made my decision this morning." She bit her lip. "And, I've decided against it."

Brian leaned back, impressed to hear the assertive clarity in her words.

"This last week, being alone in the apartment," she continued, "I realized that I like the solitude, the freedom. You know, I've never lived alone. Always with roommates and then a fiancée."

Brian wanted to jump up and pull her to him, proud to hear her make the call. He didn't like Dennis anyway, and whether good or bad, Astrid reminded him that he, too, had coveted his freedom. Since the divorce from Astrid's mother, ten years before, he had savored the privilege of answering to nobody.

"If there be truth in sight, you are my daughter," he said, and raised his hand in the air.

She rolled her eyes. "Shakespeare, right?"

"Yes, my favorite quote from *As You Like It*."*

He leaned forward, his elbows on the table. "But I think I'm changing," he said, his expression more serious. "I'm realizing that I actually *need* someone to love, not just on weekends. Break out of my cocoon, open up to love, to commitment. I didn't think I wanted that but recently my life has been upended."

"Is it your health?" she asked.

"No."

"What is it then? Why the sudden course change?"

"Because," he said, "I don't want to end up living my life alone."

His cell phone buzzed. It was Tim. Brian's face soured.

"Take the call if you need to," she said.

He nodded.

"Brian here," he answered.

"Dental records showed the dead body on the bluff is not Consuela Rae Malecon," Tim announced. "But that bracelet, it's Consuela's, isn't it?"

"Yes, it was hers," Brian replied. "You already know that."

"So, the question is, how in the bloody hell did it get there?" Tim pressed. "At least your fingerprints are not anywhere on that woman's body."

"My fingerprints?"

Astrid's eyes opened wide.

"I got your prints off the plastic evidence bag," Tim said. "Remember, you picked it up in my office. Hey, I could have gotten them from your employee record, but when you touched the bag, too convenient."

"What a fucking great investigator you are," Brian sneered back. A woman at an adjacent table stared at him.

---

* "If there be truth in sight, you are my daughter." *As You Like It*, William Shakespeare, Act 5, Scene 4

Astrid's eyes narrowed. She hadn't heard a swear word out of her dad's mouth in a long time.

"We just need to put the pieces together," Tim said. "I'm not accusing you, but the coincidences are still baffling. Well, hang in there, buddy."

"Yeah, thanks," Brian murmured. "Sounds to me like I'm still in your crosshairs." Mac squirmed at his side, stood up on his haunches, his paws resting on Brian's knees.

"I'll be in touch," Tim said, and disconnected.

Brian stroked Mac's head and gently nudged him back down on the ground next to Paisley. "Some kind of friend I've got there. Sorry, Asti, please excuse my French."

"Dad, what the hell's going on? Tell me," she insisted. The woman looked over at them again.

His phone vibrated.

"Sorry Asti. Car repair shop. I need to look at this." She nodded.

Someone fiddled with your brakes. Brake line badly damaged. Repair complete. Benny's Body Shop will take another couple of hours. Good pricing—$350 from me. Body repair is $300. Let me know if okay.

Brian tapped in his response:

Go ahead with Benny's. Thanks for all your help, man.

He put the phone back in his pocket.

"What?" Astrid shook her head.

He decided to be transparent with his daughter. In a hushed voice, he spilled out a list of events that had exploded his life: the body he found on the bluff, the mysterious Shakespeare quotes on his computer and phone, his friend, Tim, at the police department questioning him.

Astrid gasped as she listened to his list of horrors. He left out that his brakes had been purposely tampered with.

"You didn't touch your food," he said. "Come on, you need the energy for your first class today."

"Dad, I'm having a hard time catching my breath."

He felt a weight lifted from his shoulders. Except, he still held the most important information back from her, details she would definitely want to know.

He stared down at the Eggs Benedict. He had taken only one bite.

"Asti, there's more."

"More?"

"The young woman's body on the bluff that Mac found? The police were convinced it was Consuela's."

"What? She died a year ago in the plane crash."

The waiter approached, but walked past them, when he saw they were deep in conversation.

Brian nodded. "I know."

"That's insane," she said, pushing her plate to the side, her fork dropping down off the table, clinking on the cement. Mac licked the downed fork before Astrid could bend to pick it up. The woman close by gave them another hard look.

"You remember the bracelet we gave Consuela at her going-away dinner?" he asked.

"The bangle with the little diamond? Of course, I do."

He swallowed hard. "I had a special inscription done for her inside the bracelet. I don't think you ever knew about that."

She picked up Paisley from the cement and held the little dog in her lap. She stared at him for a moment.

"Consuela showed me the inscription later that night," she said. "I-I was puzzled. But she was so excited about it, I mean, when she read the Shakespeare quote, she was floating on a cloud. I pretended I knew the inscription was there and that I had planned it with you. Otherwise—"

"Otherwise, it would look like I was enamored with her," he finished her sentence.

"She had a crush on you too. I knew you had a thing for her. How could I not see it? Your eyes lit up whenever she was around."

"I didn't realize that."

"Honestly, after we'd spend a weekend at your place, she couldn't wait to see you again. I chalked it up to a schoolgirl crush."

A tear escaped his eye and ran down his cheek.

"Dad, you don't need to feel guilty. You're human. She was beautiful, a stunning twenty-four-year-old woman, who happened to be my friend."

"Your closest friend," he said.

Astrid nuzzled Paisley, took a treat from her purse, and fed it to the dog.

Brian wiped his eyes, feeling the bond deepen between them.

"That was Tim on the phone letting me know that finally they've figured out that the dead body is not Consuela's."

"Wait," she said. "How the hell did a dead woman on a bluff in Santa Cruz get Consuela's bracelet?"

"The million-dollar question," Brian replied, "the million-dollar question."

CHAPTER 20:
"In Time We Hate That Which We Often Fear."*

−WILLIAM SHAKESPEARE

SEPTEMBER 25, 2019: CONSUELA SAT IN THE ELECTRIC CART NEXT TO Javier who drove in silence. It was a seven-minute ride from the office cottage back to the mansion. The air was thick, the humidity stifling, typical for late-September in the Yucatan. It had rained several inches the night before and the vehicle was barely able to dodge the marshy puddles that would appear quickly on a ranch surrounded by dirt. The smell of the horse manure overwhelmed her.

Still trembling from the intense exchange with Leonid in the storage room, the ranch seemed more like her jail than her home. She glanced over at Javier and was puzzled to see tears trail down his cheeks, his lips tightly pressed together, his bushy eyebrows furrowed.

"Javier! *Que pasa?*"

He shook his head.

"*Que es mi culpa,*" he murmured.

Why would he say it's his fault?

---

* "In time we hate that which we often fear." *Antony and Cleopatra*, William Shakespeare, Act I, Scene 3

"Detente por un momento," she said, and pointed to the right. They were about to pass another cottage where business guests occasionally stayed, but not too often, since it was downwind from the largest barn on the property. When the humidity was high, and the air still, the stench was overpowering.

Javier veered the vehicle off the road and stopped behind the white stucco cottage. He wiped his eyes with his shirt sleeve.

Head down, he spoke softly, confessing that he had notified Leonid that something was going wrong at the office cottage. When he saw that she had unlocked Leonid's secret cabinet, he had pressed the red button on his beeper, signaling his boss to come quickly.

"Me gustas." Javier spoke, looking down at his lap.

She reached out to touch his sleeve, moved by the sincerity in his words. "I like you too," she said.

He spilled a river of rushed words in Spanish, explaining how he had always protected his *jefe,* even did grim dirty work for him. He was only following instructions that if anyone got into that cabinet, Leonid should be notified immediately. When he saw the fury in Leonid's eyes in the storage room, Javier had instantly felt remorse for having betrayed the woman he had come to greatly admire. He looked up at her and asked her if Leonid had ever been violent with her.

"No." Consuela shook her head.

He told her how he feared that Leonid might do something bad to her, that he shouldn't dare give her such a warning, but he cared for her, had enjoyed the adventure of searching the shops in Merida for her books on Shakespeare, had savored the moments when she read aloud to him in the late afternoons.

"Lo siento mucho," he whispered. He tented his hands together for forgiveness, his eyes red and wet.

She tapped his sleeve. *"Estare bien."* "I will be fine;" she repeated the words in her head.

She pulled out a flowered handkerchief from her purse and held it out to him. Javier took it and wiped his eyes, then placed the cloth on the center console between them.

He started up the vehicle, turned onto the narrow dirt road, and headed to the mansion. When they arrived, she picked up the handkerchief and pressed it into the palm of his hand.

She told him to keep it to remember their friendship. Her grandmother was ill in the hospital in California and she would likely leave Mexico, not sure if she would ever return to the ranch. She asked him not to share their conversation with Leonid or with anyone else.

"*Si,*" he said, his brown eyes warm and sweet. "*Ten ciudado. Por favor.*"

She pressed his hand and assured him that she would indeed promise to be careful.

When she opened the front door to the mansion, Leonid was in the foyer looking up at one of his prized stained-glass panels, the one with him dancing the tango with his sister. His hands were in the pockets of his black sweatpants and he rocked back on the heels of his black sneakers.

"Come here," he said. "I want to show you something."

"Oh Leonid, I-I need to phone my Aunt Marianna as soon as possible."

He nodded, still looking up.

"You see our eyes on this panel?" he asked, "how we look so determined?"

A shiver ran through her body.

"Yes, I see that," she replied.

"We had single focus, obsessed with being best dancers in all Russia. Sabrina and Leonid, the greatest brother-and-sister dance team in whole country," he shouted, his arms out. His words echoed in the spacious high-ceilinged foyer.

"Leonid, I need to phone my aunt right now," she said, flustered with whatever distraction he was constructing.

He turned to her and took her hand. "I want to be best husband for you. Six months since engagement. We planned to marry by end of year."

Her mind flooded with excuses to end the conversation. Her skin crawled. She said nothing.

Smiling, he said, "I can see us on wedding day." He pulled her close. "Stunning bride and groom."

She wriggled free from his embrace.

He let go of her hand and stepped away from her, seeming to have come out of his reverie.

He waved his hand in the air. "Go, phone your aunt," he said. "Use land line. My cell not good for long distance and yours we know barely works anywhere on ranch.

"Yes, I'll phone upstairs in the sitting room."

Relieved, Consuela started up the staircase. She looked back at him. His eyes were on the stained-glass, a smirk on his face. She hoped he wouldn't follow her.

She sprinted up the stairs, opened the door to the sitting room, picked up the handset on the gold-leaf table, and tapped in the numbers. Aunt Marianna picked up after two rings. She sounded tired and tearful. They exchanged words on how good it was to hear each other's voice.

"I am afraid to tell you this," Marianna said, "but I think your grandmother is dying." There was a long silence. "She's had a stroke. Her right side is paralyzed from head to toe. She's not breathing well either. Oh, father in heaven."

"My God. When did this happen?" Consuela asked.

"Two days ago. No warning signs. I waited to see if it was short-term." Marianna broke into tears. "I-I wasn't going to phone you if—"

"Auntie, I must come home."

"It would be good if you could, dear one."

"I'll look into flights and keep you posted."

"You, my sweet niece, and my mother are all I have left in this world."

"I love you Auntie," Consuela whispered.

"And I love you. Good night."

Her aunt disconnected. Consuela heard a second click on the other end of the phone. *Nothing I do is private. Nothing.* She hung up, and paced the room to gather her thoughts. Leonid opened the door. She cringed at the sight of him.

"How did it go?" he asked.

"Can we sit and talk?" she said, and gestured to the black velvet sofa opposite the marble fireplace. The sitting room was her favorite space in the mansion. She often used it as an escape to read her books.

He pulled her down on the plush cushions, his eyes wide and playful. She felt cornered, her breathing labored. He seemed devoid of any empathy or concern.

"You know I want to marry you," she said gently. "But first I must go home, see my grandmother. She may not make it."

"But you can't go," he insisted.

"Why not?"

"Because I need you. Important clients expect to see you this week, and next week. They come to see such beautiful face...visit with you. I—"

"Leonid, the accounting books are done, all set up. I even closed the third quarter. You don't need me to make deals with your clients."

"What do you mean? I count on you."

"Look, September is a perfect time for me to take a break. My grandmother is dying." Her mind raced. *Why do I need to convince him?* Her back stiffened.

"*Da,* but we must arrange wedding. I want it special."

"You can do a lot while I'm gone," she said, intent to sound lighthearted. "Hire a wedding planner. I'll catch up as soon as I return."

She stood from the sofa, and erupted. "You must let me go."

He got up and folded his arms across his chest.

"For a week," he said. "*Da.* Then you're back and we marry before end of year."

She nodded. He clapped his hands together twice.

"I will arrange charter flight to California," he said. "Day after tomorrow."

"That would be great." She softened and moved close to him. "Thank you." She stood on her tiptoes and kissed him lightly on the lips. "I love you," she said.

He brushed her cheek with the palm of his hand. "I remind you again, my love. You must not speak of what you saw in storage room. To nobody, wherever you are."

"I already promised you that. You can trust me."

He grinned. "I know."

The hours ticked by slowly over the next forty-eight hours. When he'd come up behind her to squeeze her, when he'd touch her arm at dinner to tell her a joke, when he'd wrap his legs around hers in bed, her stomach turned. She dreaded each moment when they were in the same room. The trip to California could not happen soon enough. It would be her escape.

The only way out was to trick him, keep her cool, and smile. When he introduced her to the young big-haired male wedding planner, who wore a suit to meet with them, as if he were running off to a wedding right after their meeting, she feigned interest in the details of the ceremony, the array of wedding cake flavors and fillings, the choice of table settings, how and where the reception would be organized on the ranch property. Leonid preferred to have both the ceremony and reception by the fountain, where he had danced for her on the first day she arrived. She nodded enthusiastically in agreement.

"We invite at least one hundred people, maybe more," Leonid declared. "I have many I want to include, clients, restaurant owners, friends."

But there was a look in Leonid's eyes that didn't ring true. She couldn't pin down what it was. Was he faking it like she was? Did he see the same disconnect in her eyes?

She packed lightly, careful to gather clothes and toiletries enough to last only a week. She threw crumbs to lead him to believe that her departure would be brief, maybe five or six days. She even reminded him to have all the transaction folders on her desk in the cottage while she was gone, so that she'd enter them immediately upon her return. No sale would be missed on the property or the import-export side of the business.

She anticipated that he would make love to her the night before she left. It would be a test, she knew. Her only way to hide her disgust when he touched her was to drink as much vodka after dinner as possible, consume more alcohol than when Massimo, the gun client, would touch her bare back at dinner. She was packed, her suitcase by the bedroom door, her clothes for the trip laid out on the loveseat, a black short-sleeved button-down cashmere sweater, gray jeans, her red ankle boots, and red jacket ready to slip on in the morning before departing for the airport. On the bedside table, she placed her gold bangle bracelet, so she wouldn't forget to put it on.

The three full glasses of neat Russian vodka she drank after dinner felt like fire in her belly, her head fuzzy, her mouth dry, her five senses dull to Leonid's touch on her breasts, her hips, her thighs. Her heart was closed.

She despised him, couldn't wait to be released from his hold. The question snaking through her mind as he made love to her with a fervor like no other night was whether he had any idea of what was going on in her head.

To her surprise, Leonid did not escort her to the airport. Instead, Sanchez was waiting for her sitting in a black limo outside the mansion's front door. Javier lifted her suitcase into the trunk, his head down, careful not to make eye contact with her, after his confession two days before. Pretending to make sure her suitcase was well-placed inside the trunk, she touched Javier's hand and whispered, *"Gracias mi amigo. Gracias."*

Leonid stood talking to one of his men near the front door of the mansion, wearing his black fleece sweats, the same casual outfit he often wore around the house before getting into bed. He nodded to the worker, shooed him to go, and moved close to the limo. He pulled her to him.

"I won't sleep well again until you return to me," he whispered.

Her head ached. The nausea from the vodka hangover overwhelmed her.

"I put you on small elite charter flight. Probably less than ten travelers on board. I wish you smooth air, relaxation, and good food," he said, playing with one of her dark curls. "I think you drink too much last night. First time I see you like that." He shook his head.

"I-I guess I was anxious about my trip," she replied. "Being far away from you."

He beamed. His aqua-green eyes opened wide. He brushed his hand through her hair and slid his palm gently down her cheek to the base of her neck. Her stomach turned.

He stepped back, and from his sweat pants pocket, pulled out some paperwork. She felt her eyelid quiver.

"Be safe," he said. "Your flight will return in five days from San Francisco, same charter plane. Here, your tickets," he said, and handed them to her. "You have your passport?" She felt relieved. For a moment, she thought he was coming with her.

"Yes, it's in my purse," she smiled.

She reached her hand to his lips. "I'll miss your kisses," she said, turned away, and slipped into the back of the limo. He closed her door, bent down, and peered through the glass to gaze at her, then blew her a final kiss.

Sanchez started up the limo. Javier stood behind Leonid and waved. She could see that he was biting his lip. She turned, looked straight ahead, drew in a long breath, and let the air out slowly, feeling one step closer to freedom.

It was ten in the morning. The Merida airport was bustling. Screaming children, the ticket counter with long lines, seniors on scooters, suitcases loaded on carts, their noisy wheels rumbling across the tiled airport floor. Sanchez pulled her suitcase to a check-in counter. "Contour Air Charters," the sign said.

"*Senora,* I just got text. You must check in for this flight here, and then a motorized cart will take you to private terminal for boarding." He pointed to the cart waiting for her once she checked in.

"I go now. *Si?*" he said, his eyes cold and resting on something behind her. She knew that Sanchez, Leonid's right-hand man, had never warmed to her. Thank goodness it was Javier who had been by her side each day instead of this beast. Her head pounded.

She nodded. "*Si,* Sanchez. *Gracias.*"

He turned away and disappeared into the frenzied crowd.

The dark-haired ticket attendant who wore thick black eyeliner that went beyond her eyes and curled upward, smiled at Consuela. She quickly proceeded with the check-in process, glanced at Consuela's passport, ticketed her herringbone black-and-white suitcase, and slid it on the floor to the bulky man in uniform who placed the bag onto the moving conveyer belt. The attendant handed her back her boarding pass and passport. The man waiting in the motorized cart signaled to her. In Spanish, she told him that she needed to use the restroom first. He pointed just around the corner. She nodded and told him she'd be right back.

She was woozy, her stomach unsettled, and needed to throw up. She regretted having the coffee earlier that morning, but she had hoped it would help her sober up, get her back to feeling at least physically normal.

Consuela rushed around the corner, pushing past strollers and luggage carts, to get to the restroom, the bile rising up in her throat.

She turned to see a line of several women outside the restroom. A baby screeched in a small woman's arms. The man driving the cart had followed her. He could see that she was in dire need, her hand pressed over her mouth. He told her there was another small restroom, difficult for most travelers to spot. He pointed to a gray nondescript door tucked between two souvenir kiosks.

"*Gracias,*" she said.

She opened the heavy metal door. There were two stalls inside. Nobody was in there. She could lock the door behind her, but was panicked she'd puke on her clothes if she took the time. Desperate, she pushed open a stall door, kneeled down, raised the toilet seat, and heaved. The bile came up through her throat, and out of her mouth, the lumpy liquid splashing into and outside the toilet onto the wall. The pasty mess dripped from her lips, the taste sour. On the white tiled floor, she had dropped her passport, boarding pass, and black shoulder bag. She heaved again, this time the liquid looser and more than before. She pulled on the toilet paper roll, ripped off a wad of tissue, and wiped her mouth, her head leaning on the porcelain base of the toilet. She heard the door lock. Someone pushed into her stall coming up behind her. She felt the kick of a shoe on her back. Another hard kick on her thigh. Another one. Her hair was grabbed, her head pulled back. She tried to fight off the hands, twisted around to face the attacker, desperate to whip out of the hold. She looked up to see a woman, maybe in her late-twenties. She wore a green sweatshirt, the hood pulled over her head, two long black braids stuck out. Her teeth were bared, her expression fierce.

The woman pulled hard on Consuela's hair with one hand and with the other reached into a black vinyl bag. She took out a large gray rock. Her eyes were brown, large, dark circles puffed out beneath them. She plunged the rock down, aimed at Consuela's head. Determined to yank herself away, Consuela grabbed at the woman's wrist. But the rock came down again. She fell back, she was dizzy; the cut stung. She closed her eyes, as the rock came down a third time, but only clipped the side of her head.

She feigned unconsciousness, pretended to go limp. No way to fight back.

The woman tapped her shoulder for a reaction. Consuela kept her eyes shut, her body still. The woman let her go.

She could hear her move around quickly, felt her pull off her red jacket, tug at her ankle boots, remove each one and toss it aside. She tried not to stiffen up. She felt the woman's rough fingers go to her wrist and unhinge the gold bangle bracelet gifted to her by Astrid and Brian. *"No!"* Consuela screamed inside her head. *"Shut up,"* she told herself. *"She's going to kill you if you move."* A yank on her left ring finger. The woman slipped off the two-carat engagement ring, the only thing Consuela didn't care if she lost.

The attacker unbuttoned her cashmere sweater and brutally jerked her arms out of each sleeve, yanking the garment out from under her. Consuela felt the cold tile on her skin, but stayed focused on making no intentional movement. She kept her eyes closed and heard the sound of the woman's shoes being tossed on the floor, then the zip of boots, Consuela's red ankle boots with the tassels, the tiny clinking of the metal buttons on her cashmere sweater being buttoned up and the snap of her gold bangle bracelet re-clasped. Something was thrown on top of her body. It was heavy and felt like clothing, then the clacking of the restroom door being unlocked and slammed shut. Silence. Consuela waited for a few minutes before she moved or made a sound.

She opened her eyes, but still remained still. A dark-green item of clothing lay on her chest, the attacker's sweatshirt. She pushed it away and reached up to feel the gash in her forehead. Her fingers came back bloody. She tried to sit up. The side of her head felt bruised, but when she checked for blood, there was none. Her upper-thigh, where the attacker repeatedly kicked her, ached. She was still in her own jeans, but her sweater, purse, boots, passport, boarding pass, and jewelry were gone.

She grabbed the green hooded sweatshirt left by the attacker, which smelled like stale smoke. She pulled it on over her head, reached for more toilet paper, wiped her mouth, and threw the wad into the toilet. The attacker had left a pair of scuffed, black leather, low-heeled shoes behind. Both lay only inches away. She reached out for them. When she went to try the shoe on her right foot, she winced from the sharp pain in her thigh from the attacker's hard kicks. She squeezed both feet into the scuffed shoes, which were one size too small, but she could wear them. She stood up, came out of the bathroom stall, went to the sink, and splashed water on her face. "Ouch." In the mirror, the image of her gashed forehead and the attacker's clothes on her damaged body made her cringe. Tears spilled from her eyes. With a wet paper towel, she dabbed the cut on her head and pressed down on it, hoping to stop the blood from flowing. *I survived.* Her mascara had smeared. Her hair was matted, clumped with what felt like remnants of vomit from earlier. She splashed her face again, wiped the black splotches below her eyes, and wet the tips of her long dark hair to get the sticky dried vomit out.

She dabbed her forehead one more time, pushed a clean paper towel into the sweatshirt pocket, opened the entry door, and left the restroom. She looked for the man in the motorized cart and was not surprised that he was nowhere to be seen. Had he been in on the attack?

She felt at something in the back pocket of her jeans. "Thank God," she muttered. Her cell phone was still there, where she had put it this morning. *Should I dare to use it?* She was petrified that he was tracking her. Although baffled and confused, one thing was clear. She had to get away. The attack was arranged, pre-mediated. She was set up, sure of it. *Did he mean to have me killed?*

CHAPTER 21:
"A Friend Should Bear His Friend's Infirmities."*
—WILLIAM SHAKESPEARE

REALITY SUNK IN WHEN BRIAN WALKED INTO ZEKE'S GARAGE AND SAW the worried expression on the gray-bearded mechanic's face.

"You know I remember you as the nicest kid in high school, always with a good word," he said, and wiped his hands with the dirty rage. "It's hard to imagine someone wanting to hurt you, man. You got enemies?"

Mac settled down in the back corner of the garage near Zeke's electric heater. The weather had changed, the temperature dropping to a cool sixty degrees, with a threat of rain, and Brian knew that Mac was likely feeling it in his hips.

"My dog's got arthritis. Bad before it rains, Brian said, and leaned against Zeke's supply cabinet. "So, tell me about my brakes."

"Your brake line was badly damaged. Looks like sabotage, but I can't be sure." Zeke picked up what looked like a log book. "I checked my records and see I did a complete brake job on this Jeep less than a year ago. Taking it apart today, I swear the damage looks to be intentional."

He shook his head. "It's not from normal wear and tear, no way."

---

*   "A friend should bear his friend's infirmities." Julius Caesar, William Shakespeare, Act 4, Scene 3

Brian let the stone settle in his gut for the first time. He had been convinced he was being framed for murder, but not the *target* of murder. The Shakespeare quotes on email and text, where they veiled death threats?

"Somebody wants me dead," Brian said, staring outside the garage, wondering if he was being watched.

"What?" Zeke said, as he stroked his beard. "Did I hear you right?"

"Fool me once, shame on you; fool me twice, shame on me." Brian spit the words out. His neck ached. "Guess I better keep my eyes open, huh?" he said, a smirk on his face, in an effort to make light of it.

After he paid with his credit card, he turned to Zeke and said, "That was probably just some kind of dopey prank. Thanks for everything today, man."

"You stay safe," Zeke said.

On the drive back over the mountain, he put the heater on for Mac. The dog curled up on the passenger seat. As he approached the summit, the light drizzle turned to a steady rain.

He turned on the radio to NPR and listened to an update on the global pandemic. The commentator reported that instead of turning the corner on the virus at the end of a dismal September, 2020, statistics on lives lost were increasing in several countries, including the United States.

He thought of Ivy and would phone her as soon as he got home. Her voice would calm his nerves. He wanted to see her. Talking with Astrid at brunch, opening up on his feelings had ignited his true emotions of love for Ivy.

The call came in. For a moment, he thought it was Ivy. He pushed the button for speaker mode.

"Brian here," he answered.

"McCallam, where you at?" Tim said.

"Why? You got more taunting up your sleeve today?" Brian replied. "I'm driving back over the hill from the valley."

"Let's meet," Tim said. "I've got some news about the girl on the bluff."

All the injured places on Brian's body ached. "Okay, I'll head to your office when I get to Santa Cruz."

"No," Tim said. "Let's meet off the record."

"Where?" Brian asked, annoyed at the thought.

"In the middle of a pandemic and it's fucking raining," Tim said. "Um, how about Jay's Deli at Rio Del Mar Beach? They has some picnic tables outside with big umbrellas."

"Sure," Brian said, "lattes and a friendly chat, just what I need today."

"It's two-thirty. How about three-fifteen?"

"Yeah. Can't wait," Brian said, and disconnected.

He hoped he wouldn't blow up again with Tim. The rest of the thirty-minute drive allowed him to process the day, realizing he had less concern for his own safety than he had for Tim believing he was guilty of murder.

Tim sat at a table under a red umbrella. The deli was just across from the entrance to the beach where the rumbling waves crashed against the shoreline. Brian could see the back of Tim's head from the street where he parked the Jeep. He leashed Mac and let him out of the vehicle. The Airedale pulled him over to a patch of grass before they walked over to the deli's deck and get out of the rain.

"Hey Mac," Tim reached out to pet the dog. Mac wagged his tail, crept under the wood table, and sat down in the protected dry spot.

Tim placed a bottle of Michelob in front of Brian. "Only thing they had, but I got a big table, so we can socially distance," he said and grinned. "Not that I'm paying much attention to that pandemic crap." Tim took out a cigarette and lit it. "Yup, back to my fucking bad habits again." He took a puff and sipped his beer.

"No smoking here," Brian said.

"Nobody's here and we're outside," Tim said, and shrugged.

"By the way," Tim added, they're closing Rosie McDougal's Pub, a Santa Cruz icon no more to be. I had dinner last night with Rebecca, you know, the hostess you thought I should have kept dating. She told me the place was closing its door for good."

"Why do you fucking do that?" Brian soured. "Start off with some flimsy small talk before getting to the point. I'm not some perp off the street. I'm onto your antics."

Tim took the last sip of beer, and smacked the empty bottle down on the table. He bit his lip. "Maybe it's another one of my bad habits. Look,

I need to ask you a couple more questions," he said, and leaned forward. "Might be uncomfortable, hence, my awkward foreplay."

"What questions?"

"Before I get to that," Tim said, "there's good news. The dead woman on the bluff was not Consuela Rae Malecon. It was someone else by the name of Cora Morales."

"You already told me that on the phone," Brian said.

"Yeah, so, back to my questions, where did Consuela go off to live in Mexico?" Tim asked.

Somewhere in the Yucatan, I told you before. Near a town called Merida. Why?"

"Bingo! Well," Tim said, "turns out Cora had a sister, Anna Morales, who was in a Merida prison for grand larceny and credit card fraud. She escaped prison two days before that plane crashed a year ago where supposedly Consuela was killed. Anna Morales got on the flight that day instead of Consuela. And Cora, Anna's sister, came to California later on a different flight."

"Damn," Brian muttered.

Tim nodded. "Dental records based on the remains just confirmed it was, indeed, Anna Morales on that bluff.

"Consuela wasn't on that plane," Brian said, shaking his head, processing the new facts.

Tim narrowed his eyes. "Cora Morales, the dead girl, had Consuela's driver's license, credit cards, her shoes, her gold bracelet – all of it."

"And?"

"And, so another coincidence," Tim said, "another fly in the ointment. Did you know this Cora Morales?"

"Fuck you," Brian said, tugged on Mac's leash, and stood up. "Thanks for the shitty beer, pal."

"Look man, I'm guessing you didn't know her. But I had to fucking ask."

"Never heard of her."

"Good. Relax. I want you to help me sort this out. You were good at investigations; dare I say talented. And, whether you want to be or not, somehow, you're entangled in this shit."

Brian sat down. "A backhanded compliment. Finally," he said, downed his beer.

"Then, what the hell happened to Consuela?" Brian asked. "She didn't die on the bluff a few days ago, and she didn't die a year ago in the plane crash. That means she's alive."

"Fucking jigsaw puzzle," Tim said, and blew cigarette smoke in the air.

She's alive, Brian repeated to himself in his head. *Alive.*

Brian turned and stared out at the waves across the road and wondered where Consuela was, if she was still alive. A gust of wind swooped up the paper napkins from the table. He reached down to retrieve them.

"Someone wants me dead," Brian spit out the words. "My brakes were tampered with, caused me an accident on the mountain."

Tim grimaced. "Oh?"

"And, I'm receiving strange texts and emails in Shakespeare speak. They go nowhere when I try to see who sent them."

Tim lit another cigarette.

"Wow," he said.

Brian leaned back in the chair. "Someone came to my house and left a scrawled not in my backyard. I'm sure those notes are connected to the failed brakes."

"Anything else? Tim asked.

"Yeah, you suck as a friend," Brian said.

They locked eyes and both burst out laughing.

"True, I suck." Tim pushed the butt of the cigarette into his empty beer bottle.

"Let me do some research," Tim said. "There's some link with the Morales sisters, and your friend, Consuela. Maybe she was helping them." He shrugged. "I have a call with Merida's Chief of Police in an hour. Turns out one of my guys knows him."

Brian's phone buzzed. "It's Ivy; I'd like to call her back. She's having a rough time."

Tim stood and tossed his beer bottle into the bin. "Sure. Phone you later, mate. Look, I never really thought—"

"Hey, let's leave that dynamic buried. Shall we? Brian shot back and turned to walk away.

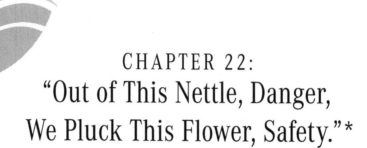

CHAPTER 22:
"Out of This Nettle, Danger, We Pluck This Flower, Safety."*
—WILLIAM SHAKESPEARE

SEPTEMBER 25, 2019: CONSUELA HAD NO IDEA WHAT TO DO, WHO TO contact, where to hide from him. She looked up at the clock on the wall, 12:06. The plane she was supposed to be on was scheduled to take off in twenty-four minutes. If Leonid didn't intend to have her killed, what was it he meant to have happen to her? The woman who robbed and beat her, took her boarding pass and passport, was either on the Contour Air Charter flight pretending to be her or else she was commiserating with Leonid on success at *almost* killing her, ensuring she didn't board the airplane.

Maybe Leonid's plan was to watch to see what Consuela would do next. *Would I come back to the ranch to get help? Or, would I try to get away?* Yet something about the whole thing didn't add up. Consuela had the gift of seeing the logic in situations, figuring out the most difficult puzzles, breaking down the sum of the parts to see the individual pieces, and vice-versa. If she was supposed to have been murdered, it was odd that the attacker didn't check to make sure their victim had stopped breathing.

---

*   "Out of this nettle, danger, we pluck this flower, safety." Henry IV, Part I, William Shakespeare, Act 2, Scene 3

She moved through the crowd in the international terminal. Or, could it possibly have been a random crime? Unlikely, but possible, she thought. Speculation ate at her. All she had left was her cell phone. And the airport had Wi-Fi. She sat down on a black metal bench. She couldn't go through security without a passport and boarding pass. Feeling threads of dried blood on her face from the gash on her forehead, she reached inside the sweatshirt pocket for the paper towel. She dabbed at the cut. The towel showed blotches of blood, but a least the cut wasn't gushing. She pressed the towel to the gash, her head down, trying to be small, blend in. People rushed by, dragging suitcases. She was intent to hold back her tears. She looked up. Off to the left, she spotted a Starbuck's kiosk. She could see some travelers standing in a queue, others sitting at small, round, elevated tables on tall stools, drinking coffee, their carry-on bags next to them.

I have the app, she thought. She remembered that she had at least $75 left on her Starbuck's card from a year ago, before she left for Mexico. She turned on her iPhone. It was fully charged, but she'd have to be careful, because she had no charger with her now. It was in her stolen purse. After linking with the Wi-Fi, she opened the Starbuck's app. The balance on her card was $92.71. It was the only good thing that had happened since arriving at the airport. She walked up to the Starbuck's counter, aware that her thigh must be turning black-and-blue because It ached like hell. The attacker had no mercy when she kicked her so violently.

She noticed that the Starbuck's sign indicated that the special of the day was Pumpkin Spice Latte, available for a limited time.

Barely holding her head up, she said, "Pumpkin Spice Latte, *por favor*." She tapped her phone on the monitor and saw that it deducted $5.50 from her balance.

"*Gracias,*" she said to the cashier.

She moved away and stood near the end of the counter where the barista made the coffees.

"Pumpkin Spice," he yelled out. When she reached for the coffee cup, he looked up at her and stared at her forehead.

Damn it, he can see the blood. She rushed over to a free table and sat on the tall stool. The first sip soothed her nerves. The sweet pumpkin cinnamon flavor reminded her that she was alive and things could still taste good.

An older couple sat a table close by. The woman smiled at her. They both appeared to be in their late-sixties, on vacation, and held hands across the small round tabletop. The woman had a salt-and-pepper cropped haircut and dancing blue eyes and a light-blue shawl around her shoulders. She was animated and chatted nonstop to the white-haired man who wore a navy-blue lightweight sport jacket and had a rosebud in his lapel. They were well-dressed and appeared to be American, perhaps flying home. Consuela took more sips of the latte. The woman hopped off the elevated stool and approached Consuela's table.

"Dear, you head looks to be bleeding. Are you okay? Can I offer you a Band-Aid?" she said in a Southern accent. I have several in my carryon, a whole kit, even a cloth bandage perhaps?"

Consuela's eyes filled with tears. "Oh God, I'm still bleeding?" she said.

The woman nodded. She opened her white leather purse. "Here's a mirror for you." The woman with the sparkling eyes handed her a small mirrored compact.

"Take a look," the woman said.

Consuela gazed at her damaged forehead. A narrow trickle of blood had traveled from the gash down to her eyebrow and one had settled just above the bridge of her nose. She hadn't felt it. The woman handed her a couple of tissues. Tears trailed down Consuela's face. Her head was swimming. She felt dizzy.

"It's nothing some alcohol and a clean bandage won't mend," the woman said, touched Consuela's hand, and glanced over at her husband. "Honey, hand me my carry-on, would you?"

"Is the girl hurt?" he said, his nose scrunching up. "Did someone hit her?"

"My name is Gail Carlisle and that's my nosey husband, Bill," the woman said, shaking her head. She patted Consuela's arm. "And you are?"

She hesitated for a moment. "Consuela."

Gail took out a wipe from a small plastic pack and gently dabbed the cut on Consuela's forehead. She gritted her teeth at the touch of the wipe.

"Thank you for being so kind."

Bill came over to the table. "I didn't mean to pry or assume anything," he said, apologizing. "But maybe we should get you medical attention."

"No, no thank you." Consuela pleaded with her eyes.

"Okay, dear," Gail said, and took out a plastic bag full of Band-Aids. She pulled out a thicker packet and ripped it open, exposing a white fabric bandage. "This'll do it," she said. She held up a small roll of white tape and fixed the bandage in place on Consuela's forehead.

"There! You look better already."

Gail stuffed the wipes and bag of Band-Aids back in her herringbone travel bag and placed the bag on the one empty stool. She reached for Consuela's hand. "How can we help you, dear?" she asked. Bill stood close by and looked at her, his eyebrows raised.

Consuela fumbled. She closed her eyes, then opened them, and peered into Gail's peaceful eyes.

"I'm...I'm escaping a bad situation. A man...a powerful nasty man. And on top of that, I was just mugged in the restroom." She stopped talking and started to cry, turning her head away.

"Please. We want to help," Gail said and nodded to her husband. He nodded back.

"My passport was stolen, and my boarding pass; my purse is gone, too, everything but my cell phone." She held it up from the table. "I was supposed to get on a plane to San Francisco. I-I think maybe this man, my supposed fiancée, had done this to me."

Gail frowned.

"I need to hide out. I think he wants me dead."

Consuela stepped off the stool. "I-I need to go. I've said too much."

"Nonsense," Gail said. "Stay with us a bit longer. Please, dear. I can see desperation in your eyes. Your sincerity is obvious."

She settled back onto the stool.

"Bill and I spent a week in Merida, where we honeymooned a long time ago."

"We had to come back," Bill added.

"And glad we did. Then we spent another week at a private house on the coast in Soliman Bay, a gorgeous place about four hours away by car." Consuela started to relax, listening to the energetic woman's Southern drawl.

"My niece and her husband, Bridgett and Greg, and their little boy Antonio, are there in Soliman Bay. We were supposed to stay in that incredible house at least a few months."

"It was more like a mansion," Bill said. "Very private."

"But our daughter Tyra, is having a C-section later this week," Gail continued, "so we're going back to South Carolina three weeks early. The birth wasn't supposed to happen for another month, but there are some complications."

Consuela listened feeling like an archangel had appeared out of nowhere.

"Maybe you can stay with Bridgett and Greg for a while," Gail offered.

"I don't know," Consuela replied. "I'd be too much trouble for them, I don't—"

"My dear, it's a huge house on its own slice of beach, and there's a private entrance where we stayed downstairs. Even with a small kitchenette. Dear, you can stay there for a month or more. We already paid for it and we'll be with our new grandchild in South Carolina. Not coming back here."

Consuela was speechless, conflicted.

"Please," Gail said, "let an old couple with a heart come to your rescue."

Bill smiled. Consuela felt grateful. May she could accept their offer, have a place to figure out an alternative escape plan, somehow get a replacement passport. She nodded in response.

"Perfect!" Gail exclaimed. "Excuse me for a moment, dear. I'll phone Bridgett on her cell. They were going to have lunch in Merida after they dropped us off here." She took out her cell phone and walked away.

Bill engaged with Consuela and talked about their week in Merida, how they enjoyed the sights, especially the marketplace, the churches, and the romantic stone chairs in the park, the same seats that Leonid had shown her, where they had kissed. Gail was quick on the phone. She came back to the table, smiling.

"It's all set. They will be here in forty minutes. We'll introduce y'all. Our plane doesn't leave for another few hours. We can't go through security yet anyway."

Bill rolled his eyes. "She's a worry wart, wants to arrive at the airport at least three or four hours before takeoff, every trip we take." He grinned "But I still love the woman." He patted his wife's hand.

They heard shouts coming from behind the Starbuck's counter. It was the barista and cashier.

The barista yelled out something in Spanish. Bill and Gail looked puzzled. Consuela whispered, "I speak Spanish. He says there's been an airplane accident, a crash!"

Consuela listened for more. The cashier was on the phone. Everyone around the Starbuck's area froze in place, waiting for more information.

The cashier spoke out in a loud voice.

Consuela translated, "He said the plane took off about fifteen minutes ago from this airport."

"What airline?" a traveler at a table came off his stool and shouted back.

The cashier spoke into the phone repeating the question in Spanish. When he yelled out the answer, "Contour Airlines, Flight 428," Consuela dropped her head in her hands, closed her eyes, barely able to catch her breath.

"Oh God," she raised her head from the table and cried, "Oh God."

"Are you okay, dear?" Gail asked.

"That was the flight I was supposed to be on," Consuela said. A shudder went through her bones like an electric shock. "He meant to kill me."

CHAPTER 23:
"Better a Witty Fool Than a Foolish Wit."*
–WILLIAM SHAKESPEARE

ASTRID PULLED UP TO 615 PRIMROSE PLACE, A PALE-YELLOW STUCCO one-story house, the front garden overgrown with wildflowers. She noticed the two picture windows that seemed to lack blinds or curtains. Beyond the windows inside the house, she could see an empty living room, no furniture. The Russian woman said she lived in a cottage in the back. Something nagged at her about the vacant house. Maybe it was between renters since there was no "FOR SALE" sign on the lawn.

She opened the side gate to the back and almost collided with the pretty young woman from the bookstore who wore black jeans and a cropped black T-shirt, the word *Courage* in curly white lettering splashed across the front, a rhinestone embellished metal buckle at her waist.

"Hello Astrid. You found me," the woman said in a thick Russian accent.

"I feel so foolish, but I didn't even ask your name yesterday," Astrid said. "I guess I told you mine though."

"You are not fool. Law school make brain fuzzy." She grinned and pointed to her head. Astrid let out a giggle. She liked the woman's sense

---

*   "Better a witty fool than a foolish wit," *Twelfth Night*, William Shakespeare, Act I, Scene 5 of humor and admired her daring spikey red haircut, a stunning complement to her light-green eyes.

"Sabrina, remember? I thought I told you at coffee place. Maybe not. No matter. Would you mind driving your car through gate to back and park next to red truck? We will have nice visit."

"I-I parked on the street. My car should be okay there," Astrid replied.

"Sorry, but they get ready to sell front house. Many people come look. Snobby realtor, fussy about parking."

"Okay. Sure."

"Plenty of room next to truck," Sabrina said, and smiled.

Astrid left to move her car. She noticed several vehicles parked along the tree-lined street, but also at least a few open spots not far away. But since her new friend insisted that she park in the back, it was not a problem.

Sabrina stood waiting at the front door of the cottage. As Astrid got closer, she saw the tiny diamond sparkle at the side of Sabrina's upturned nose. This woman has style she thought, kind of a Gothic earthy look to her.

"I make Russian tea. Please come in," she said, and eased the door open.

The furniture in the low-ceiled studio was a potpourri of what looked like second-hand items. An overstuffed faded navy-blue sofa, which was likely a roll-out bed, an old-fashioned high-back cane rocking chair, a chipped dark-brown wood coffee table, and two pole lamps. The woman told her that she was a wealthy exchange student, but the furniture didn't match that picture. She heard the blue enamel kettle on the stove in the small kitchenette begin to hiss, white vapor rising from its spout. A shrill whistle followed.

"Please sit," Sabrina said. "I get tea for us. Take off face mask. We stay six-feet distance. *Da*?"

Astrid put down her backpack near the sofa, stuffed the face mask in the front pocket, and sat down in the cane rocking chair. She wanted to try it out. She was thinking of adding one to her living room.

"You like rocker." Sabrina grinned, and stood in the kitchenette, pouring the boiling water into a small flowered teapot.

"You seem nervous," Sabrina said, as she laid out some cookies on a small plate. "New law school semester is stressful."

"Agreed. And, I just made a big decision about a boyfriend, well, my fiancée, I mean my ex-fiancée... Oh God." She rocked back and forth, enjoying the motion and the sound of the cane squeak on the wood floor. "Never mind. Too complicated to focus on. My attention needs to be on academics. A lot of reading for me tonight."

"*Da*, me also." Sabrina carried out a metal tray with two mismatched ceramic mugs and a plate of thin round chocolate wafers. She placed it down on the coffee table.

"I like your rhinestone belt buckle," she said.

"I like your turquoise Ugg boots. Will have to get a pair for winter months."

Astrid playfully kicked her feet up in the air, leaning back on the rocker. "Yes, they are comfortable."

"I hope you like special Russian tea." Sabrina said, and handed Astrid a full mug.

"Thank you. So, I guess we're in the same class – National Security Law?"

"*Da*." Sabrina nodded.

"I hear this professor is tough," Astrid said, and took the first sip of the hot tea. The weather had turned chilly that afternoon, and she welcomed the silky warm liquid trailing down her throat into her chest.

"I hear same thing," Sabrina replied, "but teaching method is very good. He has excellent reputation."

Astrid took a long drink of the tea. "He?" Astrid asked. "Actually, the professor is a female, Dr. Loretta Harwood, a nationally renowned expert in National Security Law. Didn't you know that?"

"Oh *da,* I mix up sometimes. Male. Female." Sabrina cleared her throat and waved her hand in the air. "I am anxious for semester. I don't know if I'm smart enough to do more law school. My English, not so good."

"Nonsense. You seem to have plenty of grit and smarts," Astrid replied.

The tea had a strong spicy cinnamon flavor but was slightly bitter. She drank it down and nibbled on a chocolate cookie, as Sabrina chatted about the house in front being empty, which made her a little concerned living alone on the big property.

Once she finished her last sips of tea, Astrid leaned forward in the rocker to place the empty mug on the metal tray. Her head felt heavy. Her foot faltered on the wood floor. The mug clinked the edge of the tray and she lost her grip. Sabrina jumped up and caught the mug before it hit the table.

"Come, get off silly rocker." Sabrina gestured with her hand. "Makes me dizzy too. Sit here on comfortable sofa."

"Oh God, I guess I'm more stressed than I thought." Her skin felt clammy. She pushed her hair back from her forehead.

"Plenty of room here." Sabrina patted the dark-blue cushion on the sofa and stood up, lifting the tray of mugs. "I clean up," she said. "Then we get textbook for you. In box, back of truck. I forget to bring inside."

Astrid moved to the sofa. She felt relaxed around her new friend, and thought maybe she'd spill her fiancée story to get a second opinion. She hadn't gotten close to any female since Consuela's death. The girlfriend she had gone off to Napa with for the weekend had bored Astrid with her gossipy chatter about other law school students. She sat back and closed her eyes, listening to Sabrina wash up the dishes. She looked up when Sabrina sat down on the other end of the sofa.

"Did you say you have a cat?" Astrid asked, as she looked around the studio for signs of a feline. *No water or food bowl. No cat toys.* What's your cat's name?"

"Petrovsky. Out all last night. Has not returned. I am worried." Sabrina's eyes followed Astrid's across the room.

"Ahh, I moved cat food and water outside."

"Yes, cats sing to their own tune, don't they?" Astrid smiled.

"*Da*. I think time now to get you textbook." Sabrina stood up. "No cost for you, as I say yesterday."

"I'm happy to pay you."

Sabrina shook her head and grinned. When she opened the front door, a gust of wind blew in from outside. Astrid grabbed her backpack. As she stood up from the sofa, her left knee buckled. She pressed her hand down on the coffee table to help steady herself.

"Wow. When I get home, I'll need a nap before all that reading. I didn't sleep well last night. A lot on my mind."

"You're okay. Just a little tired. *Da*?"

"Yes, I'm fine." she lied. Her head pounded.

Sabrina held the door open. The truck's flatbed was open. Astrid glimpsed up at a large cardboard box in the corner set just below the back window of the driver's cabin.

"You see cardboard box?" Sabrina pointed. "Oh, I think I hear cat. I need to catch him. Can you grab textbook from box?"

"Um, sure, I think so. Please, go after your cat."

Sabrina turned away. Astrid awkwardly hiked herself up into the open flatbed and moved to the box. She looked inside at what seemed to be a set of jumper cables. She bent down and pulled them aside to look for the book underneath. Her head clouded. Her sight blurred. An overwhelming dizziness swept through her. She slipped down, her ear brushing the stiff cardboard edge. She landed on the floor of the flatbed, the metal cold on the side of her head. Her arms tingled and started to numb-up. Her legs felt like lead. A hand reached down and pressed something over her mouth.

Sabrina hovered over her, a roll of masking tape in her hand.

"You look same as pathetic daddy." Sabrina said, with a smirk on her face. "Weak, naïve, hopeless."

Astrid tried to move her hand to her mouth to pull off the tape, but she didn't have the strength. Her hands were yanked together in front of her. The tape was wrapped tightly and cut into her wrists. Her thoughts darkened. Dizziness overwhelmed her. *She knows my dad. And he is her enemy.*

Astrid squinted, the world around her slipping away. The letters of the word *Courage* on Sabrina's black T-shirt morphed into a white blob. Sabrina's red hair became a ball of fire, her eyes like the pins of two darts. Her head seemed became two swirling heads, then four heads. Astrid could barely make out the woman's form as the shape jumped down from the back of the flatbed.

Why? Astrid kept asking herself, *why?* She felt the weight of the heavy fabric thrown down on top of her. An image flashed through her mind: her dad reading her favorite book to her when she was a little girl, both of them cozied up on the floor pillow, sharing an Almond Joy. She could hear the rustle of the candy bar's paper wrapper, as she peeled it down and pulled off a piece of coconut chocolate to give to Daddy. She could see his face smiling down at her. Everything went black.

CHAPTER 24:
"A Ministering Angel Shall My Sister Be."*

—WILLIAM SHAKESPEARE

SABRINA SLAMMED THE BACK OF THE FLATBED SHUT. SHE HURRIED IN-side the cottage. She tapped the button on her cell phone for contacts and clicked on Leonid's name. Fed up with taking orders from her brother, she waited impatiently for him to answer.

"Is it over?" he growled.

"I'm working on it." She didn't want to tell him she had already killed one woman in Santa Cruz, someone she had mistaken for Consuela.

"I want bitch dead," he said. "Hiding out for months in Mexico. But I know she in California now. You find her?"

"No. But she's here. I saw her. She was in car watching him from street at dog park. But drove off too quickly."

"So, she hasn't gone to lover boy yet? Just watches him? I know she will," Leonid sneered. "She knows too much. Must die."

"I thought you were in such love with sweet Consuela. Now can't wait for her to die. Fickle fool you are."

---

* "A ministering angel shall my sister be." Hamlet, William Shakespeare, Act I, Scene 3

"She's in love with fucking McCallam. I remember the look in her eyes before she left."

"She hasn't made contact yet. I've been close with Brian."

"You use fake American accent around him?" Leonid asked. "He could be onto you."

"He is *not* onto me."

"*Da*, you studied English hard. So, you fucking him?"

"Don't get personal, Leonid. You are brother, not keeper."

"I sent one of my *hombres* to California to do job instead of lovesick sister."

"Shut up. I can do job."

"I text you photo of my *hombre*. Should be there by now. How could I believe you kill bitch if you spend time fucking the man she loves?"

"Because I have valuable insurance—his daughter, she's out cold in back of my truck. McCallam will trade Consuela for her. I am sure of it. I know him."

"So, you *are* fucking him."

"Get off that. Listen. Once I kill your discarded Consuela, I want to cash out my thirty percent of gun business. You promised."

"Yes, I told you it was deal! Don't ask me second time," he said dismissively. "You don't trust own brother. Tell me, what will you do after you get big chunk of money?"

"Go back to Russia. Try dancing again."

He cackled, a deep gravelly cackle that trailed on.

"I must go," she said. "And do your fucking dirty work."

When Sabrina backed her truck out of the driveway, the mustached man in the rented Ford Escape followed close behind. He had been ordered to kill. Tears ran down his face. He had never disobeyed a command from his *jefe*. He took the handkerchief from his pocket and dabbed at his eyes.

CHAPTER 25:
"Things Sweet Prove in Digestion Sour."*
—WILLIAM SHAKESPEARE

IT WAS LATE AFTERNOON WHEN BRIAN OPENED HIS FRONT DOOR. THE conversation with Tim had eased his jitters, but the brake incident nagged at him. Somebody was likely watching, the same jerk sending the Shakespeare messages. He climbed the staircase and looked out the front window in the living room and down at the Jeep.

He decided to phone Ivy, but it went straight to voicemail. "Please call me," he said. "I need to talk. Miss you."

He'd take Mac for a walk on the bluff and watch the sun go down, gather his thoughts, phone Ivy again, tell her he was driving up to Sebastopol, persuade her to meet with him, even if six feet apart on a park bench. Now that Tim had taken the heat off, he needed to share everything with her. For the first time, and not in the midst of having sex, he wanted to tell her that he loved her. And if she'd have him, planning a wedding would make him a happy man.

He also had to set things straight with Savvy. Maybe in person. Maybe not. Connecting with Ivy was more important to him.

---

*   "Things sweet prove in digestion sour." Richard II, William Shakespeare, Act I, Scene 3

The start of the new semester was only eight days away. Checking his lesson plans for his two Shakespeare courses, making sure all the pre-work was posted on the university website for his students were tasks he hadn't done yet. He'd do that later in the evening before turning in for bed.

He opened his neglected mail, mostly junk, waited for Mac to lap down half a bowl of water and gobble up some dog food, and grabbed the leash for their walk across the road.

"Hey Mac, let's get the longer leash."

He had left it out on the back patio deck that morning. He went downstairs and opened the sliding-glass door in the spare bedroom to the backyard to pick up the leash from the bench. The wind had kicked up, and with the smattering of gray clouds, the sunset would likely be terrific on the bluff.

As he bent down to attach the leash to Mac's collar, it struck him that his neck pain was gone. He turned his head to the right and left a few times. No indication of an ache. It had loosened up, a good sign, both physically and emotionally.

A woman stood in his garden, her back to him. She turned to face him. Her dark hair was cut in a page-boy bob, her long curls gone. Her saucer brown eyes stared at him. She wore a black-and-white herringbone jacket, blue jeans, a white knitted scarf, and a black wool cap.

"Brian," she whispered, and walked up the deck stairs.

He sat on the bench. Mac went running over to her, the long leash flapping behind him. She smiled, knelt down, and nuzzled the Airedale.

"Consuela!" he said.

"I'm sorry to shock you." She sat in the lawn chair across from him. Mac followed her. "I've been back in California for a few days," she said softly.

"Oh my God. You are alive. Does Astrid know?" His eyes brimmed with tears. "She didn't say anything. I just saw her today," he said, shaking his head.

"Astrid has no idea. I've been hiding out for months in Mexico and flew into California just a few days ago. It was me at the dog park watching you from the blue Honda. I'm being hunted by a dangerous man."

"Hunted?"

"The man I went with to Mexico, Leonid Petrovsky, my fiancée. He's very bad. He owns a real estate development firm, but he's also a gun smuggler. I found out. He wants me dead."

Mac jumped on the bench and set his snout on Brian's lap.

She spilled the events of the past year, her opulent lifestyle, finding the files and photos of Leonid's gun business, her attempt to get away, how she was violently mugged in the airport restroom, the news of the airplane she was supposed to be on crashing minutes after takeoff, and her hiding out for months in a small town in Mexico afraid to make a move.

"Remember the inscription on the gold bangle?" she said. "My heart is ever at your service?"*

He nodded.

"It was me that sent you the Shakespeare quotes. It was my lame way to connect. I didn't want to place you in danger. But I wanted to give you a clue that I was alive. It was stupid."

He listened and thought how lovely she was, except the playful light in her eyes had dimmed.

"So, that's what *'Death is a great disguiser'*** meant," he said. "You were alive."

"I knew that Leonid would figure out that I wasn't dead and chase after me," she said. "He knew about the bracelet and that it came from you. He knows your name," she cried. "I-I never meant for you to get caught up in this." She bowed her head and pulled on the two ends of her white scarf.

"Well, you got your Shakespeare quotes down." He grinned. He sat quietly for a few minutes.

"You should have contacted me a year ago when you were in trouble," he said.

"I know." She sighed. "I need your help now. Does the inscription on the bracelet stand? Do you still care about me?"

---

*   "My heart is ever at your service." *Twelfth Night*, William Shakespeare, Act
     1, Scene 2

**   "Death is a great disguiser." *Measure for Measure*, William Shakespeare, Act
     4, Scene 2

He felt the blush warm his face. "Consuela," he whispered. "I'll help you in every way I can." Like Astrid, he'd do everything he could to protect her. "You were like another daughter to me," he said.

She put her hand to her mouth. "Please forgive me asking you if you still care, I didn't mean, oh God, you must have someone special in your life. I-I—"

"I do," he said. "And I'm about to propose to her."

She hesitated. "I'm happy for you."

The phone buzzed. He pulled it from his jacket pocket. Savvy's number. "No worry," he said, looking up at Consuela. "I'll call her back later." He placed the phone on the glass-topped table.

"Your girlfriend?" she asked.

"No, just an acquaintance."

Consuela paced the deck. The dog's eyes followed her.

"I don't know what to do," she said. "I'm scared out of my mind." She turned to him.

His phone buzzed again. Consuela sat on the lawn chair. "Take the call," she said.

He nodded. "Hello."

"Are you home?" Savvy asked. "I've got some Chinese take-away, and I'm here on Mission just a few streets away. I want to see you."

"Um, sorry, that's not going to work right now. I have a close friend of my daughter's visiting. She needs my help."

"Oh, I don't want to intrude," Savvy replied. "I understand. But how will I eat all this food by myself?" She teased. "It is a shame though."

"I'm sorry. I've got to go," he said, and disconnected.

He looked over at Consuela who stood, her back to him, looking out at the garden.

"I'm going to call Tim Carrick, my police detective friend," he said. "Before I do that, I have some news I need to share with you. It may shake you, but you need to know."

She turned to him and bit her lip.

He spoke gently. "A young woman was found dead on a bluff here in Santa Cruz just a few days ago." He pointed over at Mac. "Actually, Mac spotted her body. The police identified the dead woman as you!"

"Me?" She started to pace; her hands clasped to her forehead.

"Yes," he said, "and she had your identification, some of your clothing, and she was wearing your gold bracelet."

Consuela stepped down from the deck onto the grass, and looked out at the tea roses. He grew silent, knowing that she needed to process the startling information.

Mac went to her, his tail wagging. He nudged the yellow tennis ball that had been left on the grass. Consuela picked up the ball and tossed it onto the deck. She came up the stairs and leaned against the wood latticed railing across from Brian.

"Was the dead woman wearing red leather ankle boots?" she asked.

"Yes, she was."

She rolled her eyes. "So, I guess you thought I died twice. And how could that be?"

He nodded and decided not to share that he was the one accused of Consuela's death the second time around.

"That must have been the woman who mugged me in the airport restroom a year ago," she said.

"Mugged. Yes, Tim and I figured it was something like that but weren't sure. It was likely the mugger's sister who actually got on the flight in a hurry to leave Mexico."

"The attacker's sister?"

"Yes, she had just escaped from a Merida prison," he said. "She gave her sister the boarding pass. But she kept your handbag, your ID, your red boots, your jacket, and the gold bangle, and then got on another flight to California herself, later that day.

"And likely she has my diamond engagement ring," Consuela added.

"The police didn't recover any diamond ring that I know of," he said.

She pursed her lips as she pieced together the sequence of events. Leonid must have thought it was *her* on the chartered flight a year ago and had orchestrated the mechanical failure to down the plane without any idea that she'd been mugged in the restroom, and not make it on the flight.

Consuela pulled off her wool hat and threw it down on the table. She paced the deck again and ran her fingers nervously through her dark hair.

"Oh God," she said. "May I use your bathroom? I need to splash some water on my face."

"Sure," he said. "I'll show you where it is."

She held her hand out. "I-I need a few minutes alone."

He nodded. "Through the bedroom and to the left."

"Yes, I remember."

She walked through the sliding door's entry and disappeared through the bedroom doorway.

I shouldn't have told her about the body on the bluff. It was too much for her.

He had planned to call Ivy back, but that would have to wait. It was Tim he needed to connect with, and fast. He picked up the phone to press on Tim's number. As he listened for the ring, he noticed the weather had turned blustery. The wind flapped the fabric of the large patio umbrella.

He heard the metal clank of hardware on the side gate. Savvy came up the steps to the deck, a large brown paper bag in her hands. She stood there in her black leather biker jacket, the same T-shirt she had worn at Wilder Ranch, the rhinestone-studded belt buckle at her waist.

"Hello," she said, her voice sultry. "I couldn't leave Santa Cruz without dropping this off." She placed the brown bag of Chinese food on the table in front of him. He could smell the sweet-and-sour sauce.

"Savvy!"

"Your friend hasn't already left, has she? There's enough here for both of you."

"N-no. Listen, this is not a good time for a visit. Can I call you later?"

Her bottom lip pushed out like a disappointed child. She tilted her head and shrugged her shoulders. "But I wanted to meet her," she said, and frowned.

Brian felt the irritation grow inside him.

"Not problem," she said.

He thought he noticed an accent and broken English. She turned to leave. He listened for the latch on the gate but didn't hear it. He heard the sound of the screen door. Consuela walked out onto the deck.

"You feeling better?" he asked. As he picked up his cell phone to call Tim, he saw Savvy rush up the stairs back onto the deck, a small black pistol in her hand.

"Put phone down," Savvy commanded. "Move hand slowly to table," she said, the gun pointed at him. She glanced over at Consuela.

"You, sit down in chair," she said.

Consuela recognized the aqua-green eyes and red hair from the stained-glass panels at Leonid's ranch. *His Russian sister, here to kill me.*

Brian's eyes narrowed. "Who are you?"

"Sabrina," she said. "Not your sexy little Savannah Romeo."

Mac scampered onto the deck from the garden. Sabrina pulled out something from the brown paper bag sitting on the table. It was a large rib of meat soaked in sauce.

She opened the screen door and threw the rib inside onto the carpet.

"Mac, fetch!" she shouted.

Mac dashed inside after the rib. Sabrina snapped the screen door shut.

"Who the hell are you?" Brian demanded.

"Stupid man," Sabrina snarled. "Was too easy to fool you."

"She's Leonid's sister, and here to kill me," Consuela said.

His eyes darted from Consuela back to Sabrina, Savvy, whoever she was. "The police are right behind you," he said.

"You lie. I hear your conversation over fence."

Sabrina spit on the deck at Consuela's feet. "I killed wrong woman on bluff. This time, I take more care." She aimed the gun at Consuela. "But not here."

The Russian glared at Brian.

"I'm taking her. First," she looked down at Brian on the bench, "put hands out in front of you." She pulled out a pair of handcuffs from her jacket, grabbed one of his hands, attached the cuff to his wrist, and then to the deck's wood railing. He heard the metal click.

"Fuck you. You won't get far," he said.

Consuela froze in the chair, shaking her head, her hands over her mouth.

Sabrina hovered over Brian.

"Do you think I really wanted romance with you?" she said. "By the way, do you know where precious daughter is at moment?"

"Fucking bitch." Brian looked up to see a cocky expression on her face.

"You think I might know where she is?" the Russian teased, and laughed.

Consuela rose from the chair, caught Brian's eyes for a split-second, and pushed the patio umbrella on top of Sabrina. The metal pole hit the Russian's head. She went down. The gun escaped her hand and slid across the wood deck. She scrambled and managed to stand up.

With his free hand, Brian reached out to grab Sabrina's arm. She kicked her leg high, her boot striking him in the groin. He fell back. She moved quickly and kneeled on the bench above him. She smashed her fist into his stomach. He yanked on the handcuff that attached him to the railing. Her elbow sprang up, clocking him under the chin. He fell back on the bench, reeling in pain, his head smacking into the pole of the umbrella. He saw Consuela pick up the lawn chair and hold it out, ready to heave it. Sabrina turned, and with a high kick to the chair, it went back, toppled Consuela to the deck floor, the lawn chair falling on top of her.

Mac barked furiously, growled, and pawed at the screen door from inside the house. Consuela pushed the chair off her body. She eyed the handgun on the deck and reached for it. She pointed the gun at Sabrina, who bolted down the deck stairs. They heard the clank of the gate's latch and then a car engine start. Brian opened his eyes, his neck strained from the kicks and the jolt backward. His head throbbed.

"She's got Astrid," he said. "Bitch!"

Consuela bent down and yanked at the handcuff that attached him to the deck's railing.

"The bitch has the key," he mumbled.

He looked over at Consuela, her eyes teared up, the same beautiful girl who had pranced across his living room less than eighteen months ago reciting the monologue from *The Taming of the Shrew*. She had fallen in love with the wrong man, became entangled with the dark side, the same bottom-feeder world Brian had escaped from years ago when he left the police department. That same seedy world of criminals and murderers had returned to haunt him and ruin his life.

"Fuck," he screamed.

Mac yelped. The dog had clawed a small hole in the screen door. Consuela slid the door open. The Airedale scrambled over to Brian, who was bent over on the bench, his right hand cuffed.

"Can you get the electric saw?" he asked. "In the garage, bottom shelf behind the lawn mower. The plug on the wall is just inside the door. You can cut right through this damn thing." Consuela nodded and headed inside.

Consuela returned, and without words, she plugged in the saw, moved close to Brian, and with both hands, lifted the orange tool and turned on the switch. A ray of sunlight glimmered off the jagged edge of the metal saw. He had to save Astrid without giving up Consuela. Mac hated the buzzing sound and darted under the patio deck.

Brian slid the handcuffs off the wood slat of the cut railing. The handcuffs dangled from his left wrist.

"Can you steady the saw and cut through this?" He pointed to the narrow middle section of the handcuffs.

"I think so." She bit her lip and steadied the tool in both hands. After a short buzz, one metal cuff dropped to the deck, leaving the other around one wrist.

"Good work." He took the tool from her and laid it on the deck.

He looked down at the table where the umbrella pole lay across the shattered glass top and onto the bench. "My fucking phone! Gone," he said, and stood up.

Consuela stood up and looked around. "She dropped it." Consuela bent down by the deck stairs, picked up the phone, and handed it to Brian.

"There's a text from her," he said. He read it aloud:

"Bring Consuela to lighthouse, you know the one, 8:00 tonight. Meet me at bottom in museum. No police or precious Astrid dead. NO TRICKS."

"Turn me over to her," Consuela said, her voice firm. "That woman is here to kill me. You need to get Astrid back." She handed him the phone.

He tapped on Tim's number.

"What are you doing?" Consuela said sharply.

"Calling my police friend."

"No," she pleaded. "This is my fault. I am your collateral. I'm begging you, no police."

"You're not going anywhere near that woman again." He glared at her.

She touched his sleeve. Tears streaked down her face. She looked broken. "You heard Sabrina," she said. "Are you willing to risk the police getting involved? These people are murderers. We can't lose Astrid."

He felt light-headed. He reached up to the back of his neck, puzzled that it was the only part of his body not in pain. Consuela stepped back, picked up the tossed lawn chair, and sat down. "I don't know what I'm saying," she said. "I'm just scared." She held her hand to her temple, shaking her head. "But please, no police."

She had a point, he thought, *any sign of police could instantly end Astrid's life.*

The time on his phone read "6:15." He looked up at the sky. Dark-gray clouds had crept in from the ocean over Santa Cruz. The sun was low in the sky and due to set in about forty minutes. It would be pitch-black at eight.

His phone buzzed. A text from Tim:

Don't trust anyone, it said.

"Got it," he tapped in response. Tim must know something big. Brian hesitated, then added more words to his return text:

In danger, meet me at the Surfer Museum Lighthouse at 7:00 p.m. Leonid Petrosky, a Russian in Merida, Mexico is behind this.

"I have her pistol," Consuela said. She picked it up from the deck.

She gazed down at the pistol in her hand, held it away from her, like it was someone she never wanted to meet.

He re-focused on the text, back-spaced, and erased most of his message, leaving only two words in response to Tim: *Got it.* He slipped the phone into his jacket pocket.

"When we get to the lighthouse," Consuela said, the pistol in her hand. "I'll spring out of your car and put the gun on her."

For a second, her words amused him. Although she had blossomed into a more-mature woman in her mid-twenties and had been through her own hell, she remained incredibly naïve.

"Yeah," he said. "But I'm just not sure that bitch won't have some surprise up her sleeve. Something we can't anticipate."

Consuela burst into tears. He moved to her, the handcuffs hanging on his right hand. He took the fringed end of her white woolen scarf and wiped her eyes.

"We'll drive to the lighthouse," he said "You'll stay in the Jeep with the gun. She's going to need to see you there, but you won't get out of the Jeep. I have a plan."

"Do you know how to use a gun?" he asked. She shook her head.

"Let me show you because you may be faced with the choice of whether to pull the trigger or not."

He examined the handgun. It was a Beretta 92F, a semi-automatic pistol, nine-millimeter. The range was about a hundred fifty feet or so.

"It's a chunky pistol," he said. "Here's how you hold it when you're ready to shoot."

He held it out in front of him, pointed at the rose bush in the garden, steadied the piece with both hands in a firm grip, his right index finger set on the trigger. "Use both hands like this because it buys you accuracy. Here, try it."

He stood behind her and placed the gun in her hands, wrapping his around hers. Being so close immediately felt awkward. He took his grip off the gun and stepped back. "Hold it on your own. Both hands." He watched and waited. She winced like she tasted something awful.

"Take a few minutes and get comfortable."

She nodded and shifted the gun, putting her left index finger on the trigger. "I'm left-handed. This feels better."

"Right change," he said. "Now sit in the chair and do the same thing until you feel more confident. You won't have to shoot the damn thing, but looking like you would is important."

She turned the chair around to face out to the garden, and sat down, positioning the gun as if aiming out an imaginary car window. She narrowed her eyes and focused on a rose bush set in the adjacent corner of the garden.

He looked at the time on his phone. "I need to get something from upstairs," he said. "Be right back. Then we'll take off. Try to get there before it's dark."

He raced up the steps to his bedroom, into the walk-in closet and punched in the code to open his wall safe. He stuffed the revolver in the side pocket of his jacket, carefully placed a few other items in the inside pocket, and turned the dial to lock the safe. From the top drawer of his bedside table, he took two small narrow flashlights, sticking them both inside the back pocket of his jeans.

CHAPTER 26:

"It Blots Thy Beauty as Frost Do Bite the Meads..."*

—WILLIAM SHAKESPEARE

A S THEY LEFT THE HOUSE HEADED TO THE JEEP CHEROKEE, SHE FELT the rain start to drizzle down. In all the frenzy, she left her wool hat on the back deck. Drops of rain fell in the creases of her eyelids and slid to her eyelashes.

"Damn, I left my car keys inside," Brian said. He turned back to the front door. "Be right back."

Consuela waited by the Jeep. She removed the long white knit scarf from around her neck and wrapped it over her head.

He came back out the front door, but he was hobbling. He clicked the key fob to open the passenger door for her. Mac stood behind him, wagging his tail.

"You're limping," she said.

"Rough day," he said, and grinned." Mac or no Mac?" he asked, as she scooted into the passenger seat.

---

*   "It blots thy beauty as frost do bite the meads." *The Taming of the Shrew*, William Shakespeare, Act 5, Scene 2

207

"I-I don't want him hurt," she replied, and sighed. "But I welcome his support."

"Right." Brian nodded. "I think the backseat is best for both of you."

She got out of the Jeep, slid into the backseat, and Mac jumped in beside her.

He handed her one of the small flashlights. "Keep this."

"Are you hurt bad?" she asked. "She kicked you so hard."

"I feel like a million bucks," he said, "just a minor hip injury from another adventure."

He drove down the street, headed to the lighthouse, which was set on the ridge about half a mile from Brian's house, not far from the wharf, where he had danced and savored calamari with the enemy. A fucking imposter, he thought, as he turned the corner. I was duped from the start. He checked the time on the dashboard: 6:53. They'd be there in less than ten minutes. The sky had turned a dark gray, laden with heavy gray clouds. The rain distorted the traffic lights, as the drizzle came down, but not enough to warrant the wipers. There would be no sunset after all.

He stopped at the traffic light and glanced in the rearview mirror. Consuela was huddled close to Mac, who rested his head against her shoulder. She rubbed her eyes with her fingers.

Her wool scarf was still wrapped over her head and the tails around her neck, the fringe hanging down her jacket.

She looked like a sleepy little girl. An image of Astrid's face flashed before him, the sleepy look she had when he'd carry her upstairs to bed after reading to her on the "Dora the Explorer" floor pillow.

Brian broke the silence. "When we get there," he said, "you stay in the backseat. Sabrina should be outside somewhere. The museum will be closed."

"Just turn me over in exchange. You may need to do that," Consuela said, her voice shaky. "I don't want Astrid hurt." He could feel her anxiety in the pit of his queasy stomach.

"Stop it. I'm not turning you over to a killer," he snapped. He lowered his voice. "I should notify the police."

"No," she pleaded.

"Okay, okay. I have a plan," he said, but his confidence was diminishing.

"I was such a fool," Consuela said softly. "Leonid was a hero to me—powerful, confidant, charismatic. I was blinded, stupidly infatuated."

"You can't go back," he said. "You'll do better next time."

"I thought of you often, even when I was with him," she whispered.

The drizzle outside had turned to steady rain, which pounced on the dashboard window. He turned on his wipers.

As they approached the lighthouse, the phone call came in. It was Ivy.

"Ivy," he said.

"I'm sorry, but I couldn't call you back until now," she said. "Carl is in the ICU with COVID, but the doctor said he's stable. Not on a respirator and they're hoping he's out of there within the next couple of days."

"What about you?" Brian asked.

"I had the test. It was negative."

The lighthouse was in full view, a few tiny lights around the entrance and the Fresnel lens on top shining out to sea. It was like a mirage in front of him, the perfect picture postcard, the tower white and the bottom section made of brick, a wood deck porch by the entry, and a tall pole with an American flag waving in the wind.

He cleared his throat. "I love you, Ivy."

A few beats of silence.

"Brian, are you okay?"

"I meant to say that a long time ago. I wanted to come up there and tell you in person, but it can't wait. He felt the lump in his throat. "I love you," he whispered again.

He glanced in the rearview mirror and saw Consuela's warm smile beam back at him. He choked up, tears teetered on his eyelids, one losing its balance and slipping down his cheek.

The wipers went into fast mode with the increased pounce of the rain on the windshield.

"I'm sorry. I'm in the middle of something," he said, his tone strained. "I have to go. I'll try to call later tonight. Remember, I love you."

"I love you too," she said, and disconnected.

The lighthouse beacon fanned out to the ocean, the slant of the hard rain illuminated. A pale halo outlined the light like the shadow of a ghost.

There was no movement outside the museum entrance that he could see. It was 7:28. Eight o'clock was the time Sabrina had prescribed.

Where the hell was Astrid? All he cared about was getting her to safety. No other cars in the parking lot or anywhere on the street.

He looked back at Consuela and Mac, who were huddled in the backseat. "I'm going out there. See if she's got Astrid somewhere."

"Be careful."

"You've got that pistol handy?" he said.

He saw the silhouette of her head nod in response.

"Keep it in your hand. Stay alert, but don't get out of the Jeep."

"Okay," she whispered, her eyes wide.

He felt for his gun and the other supplies in his jacket pocket and got out of the vehicle, his left foot landing in a puddle. Without an umbrella and a hat, he was quickly drenched, the least of his worries.

Fucking Sabrina, Savannah Romeo bullshit

He moved to the Surfer Museum entrance at the bottom of the lighthouse. A memory of the last time he was inside the museum flashed through his mind. It was a few years ago on a Sunday afternoon. He was on a date with Ivy just weeks after they first met. They had taken a leisurely walk from the wharf, along East Cliff Drive, down to the Abbott Memorial Lighthouse, also known as the Surfer Museum. It was a day full of perfect weather and casual conversation. He recalled noticing the winding iron staircase at the back of the museum that led up to the Fresnel lens situated at the very top.

He slipped on the first step leading up to the museum's entryway. His hip was acting up. He peered inside the window. No lights. He tried the door. Locked. The bold sign on the window to the museum read, "MUSEUM CLOSED DUE TO COVID."

Drops of water slid down the back of his neck from the portico over the red wood door. A stab of pain shot through his hip. *Maybe she's got Astrid outside by the cliff.*

He pulled the flashlight from his pocket, as he moved slowly around the side wall of the lighthouse, the rain thumping the top of his head. The ocean raged below, visible by the light of the beacon.

What am I doing? He reached for his phone, fumbling with the flashlight. *I've got to alert Tim.*

"Get fuck over here." He heard Sabrina's Russian accent. He could make out the sheen of the wet metal pistol in her hand. She came closer, the brim of the baseball cap shielding her face from the storm. Streams of water dripped from the stringy fringes of her black leather biker jacket.

"Where's my daughter?" he said.

"Inside, you fool. Let's go." She edged behind him and pushed the gun into his lower back. When they reached the entry door to the museum, he placed his hand on the slippery doorknob and hesitated. She kneed him in the left side. A sharp pain ripped through his hip.

"Move!" she said, and pushed the door open with her boot.

He faltered, his knee dipping, but managed to straighten. Inside, a dim light came from somewhere in the back area of the large wood-paneled room. A polished wooden surfboard was mounted on the wall to his left with dozens of what looked like framed photos of surfers set under it.

"Where the hell is Astrid?" he said.

Sabrina slammed the entry door shut behind her and moved around him, the pistol pointed at his chest. "Where's your precious Consuela?"

"I'm not bringing her in until you hand over my daughter."

"Really?" Sabrina laughed; it was a sinister sound that crept under his skin like a blood-sucking tick.

He stepped back and leaned against the museum store counter, where a cash register sat flanked by two metal stands of hanging surfboard-shaped key chains.

"Don't touch anything," she said, and waved her gun for him to move to the center of the room. "Keep fucking hands where I can see them."

His eyes darted around the museum, while he obeyed her request. A movie screen was on the wall to the right. Two more surfboards were on display next to it, a wetsuit framed in glass and a panoramic photo of a Hawaiian ocean scene. Brian's eyes went to the dim light coming from the back left corner, behind where Sabrina stood what looked like a storage area.

"Take gun from pockèt," she said. "Put on floor. Slow."

He could see two legs straight out on the wood floor by the lit area in the back. He recognized the turquoise suede boots.

"Astrid," he called out.

"Shut up," Sabrina said. "Her mouth is taped. Bitch talks too much." She backed up to the storage space, her gun still pointed at him.

"Slide gun to me or I shoot sweet daughter in head." She grinned and aimed the pistol inside the doorway.

He took the .38 from his pocket and slid it on the floor toward the Russian.

She bent to grab it. "Nice piece," she said, and slipped it into her pocket. "Take off jacket," she said.

"Why?"

"Don't fuck with me," she sneered.

"Let me see her," he shouted.

He thought he heard a muffled sound coming from Astrid.

"No, not until you get *my* prize from Jeep. Get her now!"

Brian took off his jacket and dropped it on the floor. "First, I want to see Astrid."

Sabrina kicked his jacket to the side by the wall and stepped out of sight in the dimly lit area.

She pulled on the hood of Astrid's sweatshirt and dragged her up against the side wall just outside the storage area. He could see his daughter. Astrid's shoulder-length brown hair hung in wet clumps, a few strands stuck in the masking tape over her mouth, black mascara smeared under her eyes, her head tilted to the side.

"What did you do to her?"

Sabrina knelt down, and with her free hand, yanked on Astrid's hair, pulling her head back, then releasing it. Astrid's head bobbed down on her chest; her eyes closed. He thought he noticed her eyelids trembling.

Sabrina pursed her lips, and in an American accent, she said in a squeaky voice, "Not a happy girl, is she? Such sleepyhead."

"Fuck you!" he said.

"Hmm, now that would have been nice," she cooed and then narrowed her eyes. "Now, go! Get Consuela. Then you have sorry sack of daughter."

He would text Tim as soon as he got outside. He had his cell phone in the back pocket of his jeans. He turned to rush out the museum's entry door.

"Wait!" Sabrina shouted. She picked up his leather jacket from the floor and checked the pockets. "Give me your phone."

"It's in my Jeep."

"Idiot," she said. "I saw you had phone outside."

He glared at her, took the phone from his back pocket, and held it out.

"Throw it on floor," she said, pressing the pistol to Astrid's head.

He let the phone leave his hand a few inches from the wood floor.

No," she said, and moved to the phone.

"Not like that," she said.

She snatched up the iPhone and held it high above her shoulder, her gun pointed in Astrid's direction. With force, Sabrina slammed the phone to the hard floor.

She gritted her teeth. "Like that!"

The plastic case broke into pieces. He could see that the screen had cracked. Sabrina hovered her black leather boot above the object, and with her heel, stomped hard on it. Shards of glass and phone innards flew.

"There!" she said and smiled.

Brian re-focused on Astrid, propped against the wall behind Sabrina, her chin slumped down on her chest, one of her turquoise boots half off her foot. He saw her raise her head slightly. She held out one index finger from her bound hands, her eyes still closed. *She's listening*, he thought. *Thank God.*

"When I say GO, I will start count to 30," Sabrina instructed, "the number of seconds you have to get Consuela bitch from car. She stood over Astrid. "You fail. Boom! Daughter dead before 31."

He pictured himself barging over to her, ramming her up against the wall, knocking the gun out of her hand, yanking her away from his daughter. *It would be too risky.*

"GO!" Sabrina commanded.

He turned. Before he could put his hand on the doorknob, a short stout handlebar-mustached man burst inside, water spilling off the broad brim of his brown leather hat, his brown jacket tight around his large belly.

Sabrina raised the pistol, glaring at the man. She tightened her finger on the trigger.

"Freeze, both of you," she said.

The man with the dripping mustache, deep creases around his eyes, pushed past Brian. He came up to Sabrina, his face almost flush to the barrel of her pistol.

"Leonid send me," he said.

"You hit man hired by my brother?" She rolled her eyes. "Pathetic." She pulled out her phone and looked down at the screen. "*Da*, it is you. Leonid texted photo. But I do killing. You assist me."

The man nodded, his face stoic. "*Me llamo Javier.*"

"Javier," she said, waving her hand, gesturing for him to move out of the way. She pointed her gun at Brian, but kept her eyes on Javier. "He has thirty seconds to get Consuela bitch from car. Go with him. Bring her. *Andale!*"

Brian felt his neck tighten. The back-up explosives he had stuffed in the inside pocket of his jacket were out of reach, on the floor. How would he ever get to them?

"Go!" Sabrina barked, the pistol pressed to Astrid's head. "Thirty seconds. One...two..."

Brian bolted out the door ahead of Javier.

When he reached the Jeep, he tapped on the side window. Consuela looked up at him. She put her nose to the glass window. Mac tried to jump over her to get out, but Consuela nudged him back. She released the door lock. The face she saw standing over Brian's shoulder couldn't be real. It was Javier, the only man she ever trusted on the ranch in Mexico. Her mind raced. Brian swung the door open.

"Consuela," Brian yelled above the noise of the heavy rain. "I failed you. I'll figure it out. This man is Leonid's hit man. Come, we have to rush or she'll kill Astrid."

Consuela jumped out of the Jeep, her boots sinking in a puddle. The Beretta slipped out of her hand. She glanced at Javier as she reached down for the gun. He grabbed her arm and shook his head.

"*No senora,*" he said, and plucked the gun out of the muddy water. He put it in his pocket while his own gun was pointed at Brian.

Brian grabbed Consuela's sleeve and pulled. They ran frantically back to the museum through the puddles. The pain in his hip sharpened. He pushed open the museum door.

"Twenty-nine," Sabrina shouted, her pistol pressed to Astrid's temple. "Ah, hero!"

"Free her," Brian screamed.

"Do it self after we take care of that one," she said, pointing the gun at Consuela. "Outside now, both of you!"

"What do you mean?" Brian asked.

"You and your young lover, out!" Sabrina said, her eyes cold.

He didn't want to leave Astrid. He caught a glimpse of her just a beat before Sabrina came up close to him. Astrid's eyes were open and met his for a brief second.

Brian started out the door, his hip stinging, Consuela beside him. Sabrina's pistol pressed into the back of his neck.

Outside, a gust of wind hit them in the face. He put his arm around Consuela's shoulder, an attempt to shield her from the beating rain. His gray T-shirt quickly soaked through and molded to his body. Javier walked beside them, the rain sweeping off his wide-brimmed hat.

"Up against wall," Sabrina said, and pushed Brian back to the wall. He could feel the uneven texture of the weathered brick on his arms. "Javier, keep gun on him. I take care of bitch."

Javier stood close to Brian, his gun pointed.

"You," Sabrina said, glaring at Consuela, "stand there." She pointed to the edge of the cliff. "Face me."

Consuela's looked frozen in fear.

"Do it!" Sabrina barked. Consuela's shoulders jumped at the sound. She moved to face Sabrina, and stood at the edge of the cliff.

"No," Brian yelled. He wanted to push past Javier, but knew it could end with a shot to his head.

Sabrina backed away and placed her finger on the trigger. "Perfection!"

Javier moved in fast, bolted in front of Sabrina, inserted himself between the two women, pushing Consuela off to the side. She fell to the mud. Javier turned to Sabrina and grabbed her by the shoulders, pulling her to the edge of the cliff. In the scramble, Sabrina dropped the pistol. Her gun hit the muddy ground and slid off the sharp cliff. She leaned back on her heels, kicked her leg up, a direct blow to Javier's leg, and separated herself from him. He twisted and stood, his back to the edge of the cliff. The pop of her gun echoed. The bullet struck Javier in the chest. He reached out and pulled on the leather fringes of Sabrina's jacket. Her foot faltered. She lost her balance. As she teetered off the edge, her eyes wide, bewildered, she grabbed onto the chin strap of his sombrero and yanked Javier off with her.

Brian and Consuela heard Sabrina's shrill scream, a noise that seemed never-ending, but then was abruptly silenced. Sitting in the muck, Consuela drew her head down to her bent knees, sobbing in the rain. Brian gazed down over the cliff. The lighthouse beacon swept over the dark sea. He could see the leather sombrero bobbing in the swirling water below. Sabrina was laid out on a flat black rock at the foot of the cliff, where the vestiges of a wave splashed over her lifeless body. A flash of her seductive grin looking up at him from the debris in the woods at Wilder Ranch whipped through his mind.

Brian knelt down to comfort Consuela.

"That man saved you," he said.

"He was my only friend in Mexico," she whispered, trembling in the rain, strings of her hair pasted to her cheeks.

Let's go save your other friend," he said, and helped her to her feet.

The first thing they saw when they entered the museum was Mac hunched over Astrid, his teeth yanking at the masking tape that bound her wrists.

Brian snatched his jacket from the floor and took out the pocket knife from the inside pocket. He bent down at Astrid's side, patted Mac, and cut the tape from his daughter's hands, while Consuela gently pulled at the tape on Astrid's mouth.

The front door of the museum burst open.

The handlebar-mustached man limped inside, his black hair and mustache dripping with water, his chin and cheek cut and bloodied, his sombrero gone.

"Javier!" Consuela cried out.

"Perra mala," Javier said, panting, trying to catch his breath. Mac barked.

"He said that Sabrina is dead," Consuela said to Brian, and looked back at Javier.

"But the bullet that hit you?" She pointed to his chest. *"La bala?"*

Javier tugged at his ripped jacket. He undid the buttons, lifted up his shirt, and tapped his fist on the stiff black fabric.

Brian held Astrid close. "Dad," she whispered, her eyes brightening. He looked up at Consuela and Javier, and shook his head, grinning. "Bullet-proof vest, man, you can't beat that."

Consuela said something to Javier in Spanish. Still breathing hard, Javier told her what happened after the fall from the cliff. She wrapped her arms around him and helped him sit down on the floor, his back to the wall.

"You're bleeding," she said.

Javier reached inside his torn jacket and took out a folded wet flowered handkerchief. He wiped the cut on his chin. Consuela's eyes flooded with tears. It was the handkerchief she had pressed into his palm in Mexico to keep as a remembrance of their friendship.

She kissed him on the cheek, stood, and knelt down beside Astrid. She hugged her friend's shoulder, and looked up at Brian. "Somehow Javier managed to grab onto a pipe," she said, shaking her head in disbelief. "He was lucky. Thank God."

CHAPTER 27:

"It Is Not in the Stars to Hold Our Destiny, but in Ourselves."*

—WILLIAM SHAKESPEARE

A S THEY EXITED THE MUSEUM, BRIAN LOOKED UP AT THE NIGHT SKY, his dog Mac at his side. The rain was replaced with a full moon, the sky clear. It was supposed to be a blood moon—that's what he had heard on the radio earlier that day. Consuela and Astrid followed behind him, huddled together, like siblings. Javier trailed, eyes darting from side to side, alert to any new threat.

Brian spotted a male figure coming toward them. *Oh God. What now?*

The man came closer. He wore a black Raiders football cap and held up a gold badge in the air.

"You got a way of showing up in the wrong place," Tim said, shaking his head.

"Yeah, I've got a real pattern going, don't I?" Brian replied.

Tim placed the badge back in his pocket.

---

* "It is not in the stars to hold our destiny, but in ourselves." *Julius Caesar,* William Shakespeare, Act I, Scene 3

"I'm guessing you butt-dialed me," Tim said.

Brian noticed a police car stop at the curb, lights flashing. A young officer jumped out. He rushed over to them, his pistol poised, his knees bent, his gun pointed at Javier.

"Put away your gun." Brian shouted. "That man saved our lives."

Tim waved his arm. "Vega, stand down."

Vega lowered his weapon and stepped back.

Tim took a moment to absorb the tableau of the bedraggled group before him.

"Looks like you all need medical attention."

"Honey?" Brian looked into his daughter's eyes.

"I'm good, Dad," she said.

"I think I'm okay, too," Consuela added and leaned into hug Astrid's sleeve.

Brian looked over at Javier, whose face was bloodied.

Consuela said something in Spanish. Javier shook his head. *"Estoy bien."* He pressed the flowered handkerchief to his bloodied chin.

"He says he's okay." Consuela nodded to Tim.

"What do you mean I butt-dialed you?" Brian asked. "My cell phone was stomped on by that Russian maniac." He pointed his thumb back to the museum.

Tim tapped the brim of his Raiders cap. "Well, I heard a lot of conversation before that happened."

Brian nodded.

"Did she get away? Do we need to go after her?"

"She's dead," Brian said. "Went over the cliff at the side of the lighthouse. Her body is sprawled out on a rock at the bottom."

"Nice work!" Tim said. He looked over at the young officer. "Vega, get some blankets for these people," And notify the Coroner." Vega turned, leaping the large puddles back to the police vehicle.

Tim took out his phone and peered at a photo on his screen. "That was the woman you were with on the wharf, wasn't it?" He held the phone out in front of Brian.

"It was," Brian said.

"Sabrina Petrovsky, the same woman at the bottom of the cliff?"

Brian nodded. "Right. But she pretended to be Savannah Romeo for most of our time together."

Tim swiped his finger on the screen of his phone. "And this is Leonid Petrovsky, her brother?"

Brian took the phone and showed it to Consuela. She swallowed hard, nauseated by his image. "Yes, that's Leonid," she replied.

"I had a conversation with Merida's Police Chief a couple of hours ago," Tim said. "Petrovsky's been arrested."

Brian glanced down at the close-up of the streaked-blond-haired man, his vacant light- green eyes arrogant, the same cold expression Brian recognized from the mug shots of the many perps he had dealt with in the past.

"Petrovsky was under surveillance for weeks," Tim said, "suspected of selling and smuggling weapons. His ranch was raided today by Merida police. Thousands of guns seized. Whole operation busted."

Tears trickled down Consuela's cheeks. Astrid put her arm around her friend.

"Looks like Petrovsky also managed a couple of murders," Tim continued. "Two male bodies found half-buried on the outskirts of his ranch."

Vega returned to the group with a stack of gray blankets. "Coroner's on his way," he said. He placed a blanket around Consuela's shoulders, wrapped one around Astrid, handed one to Javier, and held the last one out for Brian.

"Thanks man, but I'm good." Brian said, handing the blanket back to Vega.

Consuela whispered something to Javier. He nodded.

She looked up at Tim. "I asked him if he would share what he knows about Leonid's operation. Javier worked on the ranch for more than three years."

Vega broke in. "I speak Spanish." He smiled at Consuela.

"Good," Tim said. "If I can have Javier go with Officer Vega to the station, that would help us. We need all the information we can get. He'll bring him back here to his vehicle later."

Vega spoke softly to Javier. *"Yo hablo espanol. Por favor, ven conmigo."*

Javier put his hands out to be handcuffed.

"No need for that." Tim shook his head. "You're not under arrest. You're a hero." He patted Javier on the back.

Vega conversed with Javier, who nodded and followed him to the police car.

"Hey Vega," Tim said, "have an EMT check out his injuries before questioning." Vega nodded.

As Javier and Vega approached the flashing police car, Consuela called out, *"Espere, Javier*. Wait!"

She ran to him and pressed her head against his chest. Vega took out a pad of paper and pen from his pocket and handed them to her. Consuela wrote something and ripped off the page to give to Javier. She kissed him on the cheek, turned away, and with the blanket pulled tightly around her and over her head, slowly started the walk back to where the others stood at the foot of the lighthouse.

"She's broken, but out of danger," Brian whispered to his daughter.

"We'll help her get back on track. Won't we, Dad?"

"Yes, all we can," he said.

"Oh God," Astrid said, looking down at Mac, who sat in the middle of a puddle, lapping up muddy water.

"Oh no. Just what I needed," Brian said.

Looking at the dog, Tim burst out laughing. "You and me, buddy, making life difficult for the one guy we care about."

As Consuela neared, Tim pulled out a small plastic bag from his slicker's chest pocket and opened it. He handed her the gold bangle bracelet with the diamond-centered heart. A ray of light from the lighthouse beacon caught the sparkle of the tiny diamond. Consuela stared at it in disbelief.

"I want to return this to you," Tim said.

Consuela beamed, realizing it was the first time in a long time where she had even come close to a smile.

"Thank you," she said, hooking the bracelet around her wrist, her eyes brimming with tears.

Epilogue

FRIDAY, APRIL 9, 2021: IT WAS EARLY SPRING AND THE SEA AIR IN SANTA Cruz smelled fresh, clean, the sky a cool blue, with scattered light-gray clouds. It was one of those days when the sun went in and out every few minutes without quite making up its mind.

Ivy laced her fingers through Brian's, as they started the walk up the stone steps to the Santa Cruz Courthouse entrance. She was dressed in white satin and held a bouquet of white peonies. They would be married in thirty minutes.

"I'm nervous," she said.

"Your shoes too tight?" Tim's cocky voice teased.

"A best man keeps his thoughts to himself," Brian said, turning to Tim, who walked up the steps beside him and fiddled with the knot of his paisley tie, looking uncomfortable in his suit.

"Easier said than done," Tim said. "But promise I'll keep my mouth shut during the ceremony."

"Sure, you will," Brian said, a smirk on his face, and winked at Ivy.

Astrid and Consuela followed up the steps just behind, dressed in matching cornflower- blue satin pencil skirts, fitted jackets, and navy-blue pumps.

Brian heard Consuela giving Astrid a rundown of her first week with the Shakespeare Theatre Company, where she had been hired to revamp their accounting system.

"And believe it or not," Consuela said, "I'm going to audition for a small role in their summer production of *Midsummer's Summer Night's Dream.*" She laughed. "Am I totally insane?"

"With your passion, you'll ace it. I think you have some real talent," Astrid replied.

Brian smiled to himself, inspired to hear Consuela moving on with her life.

He reached inside his suit jacket pocket, held his breath, and felt for the wedding ring's velvet box. *Got it. Thank you, God.*

At the top of the stone stairs, Brian turned to Ivy. Her eyes twinkled. She looked exquisite, like she was straight out of a 1930's novel, the white retro pillbox, with its delicate veil, shaped above her brown page-boy cut. He squeezed her hand, grateful for the love of a fine woman and for the deeper bond he was developing with his daughter.

The small wedding party clustered together by a tall white column near the Courthouse entrance. It felt good to be without face masks after a full year of the pandemic nightmare. With the wider distribution of the COVID-19 vaccine, virus cases had diminished and life was slowly return- ing to a new normal in Northern California.

"You look stunning," Consuela said to Ivy, and took her hand. "But there's one more thing you need. She unclasped her gold bangle bracelet with the tiny diamond embedded in the center of the raised heart and placed it around Ivy's wrist, clicking it closed.

"Oh, it's lovely but—" Ivy said.

"Please," Consuela interrupted. She glanced at Brian. "Your husband-to- be and my best friend," she grinned at Astrid, "gave me this bracelet on the night before I left for Mexico. Without them, I don't think I'd be alive today."

Ivy nodded and patted Consuela's sleeve.

"What's inscribed on the bracelet is how I feel for you as well," Consuela said. "My heart is always at your service."

Ivy gazed down at the gold bangle on her wrist.

"I'd like you to keep it," Consuela whispered.

Ivy sighed. "Thank you, dear. It's beautiful."

Becky, Ivy's daughter, hurried up the stairs to join them at the Courthouse entryway. The two little granddaughters, Bridget and Tia, were at her side in their pale-blue dresses, blue velvet ribbons braided through their long blonde hair. They both carried straw baskets filled with blue and white daisies.

"The flower girls are here," Astrid announced. She hugged each of them. "You look like goddesses," she said. Consuela peered into their baskets and grinned.

Brian glanced down the steps to the parking lot below where the man with the handlebar mustache leaned against the door of a shiny black limousine. The dogs were in the backseat, up on their hind legs, Mac's snout nudged out of the opening at the top of the window and little Paisley's paws pressed on the glass below him.

"Javier," Brian called out. "Come on, we can't do this wedding without you."

Javier broke into a broad smile, waved, and started up the stairs. The little girls pointed at the pets, which seemed to be cheering them on from inside the limo.

"Look, their tails are wagging," Bridget shouted.

Six-year-old Tia looked up at Ivy and pursed her lips in a pout. "I wish they could come to your wedding, Grandma."

Tim quickly chimed in. "I'll take a video. We'll show it to the mutts later." He winked at the two girls.

Brian grinned, turned, and watched Javier rush up the steps toward them. He thought back to that stormy night at the lighthouse when Sabrina and Javier went over the cliff, smacking into the jagged rocks, headed down into the turbid dark ocean, the bright beacon lighting up Javier's sombrero bobbing in the rolling sea below. That was six months ago, but for Brian, it still seemed impossible that Javier managed to grab onto a slippery drainpipe and claw himself back up the cliff and out of the treacherous scenario, alive.

Luck, Brian thought.

As they entered the Courthouse, he whispered in Ivy's ear, "Have I mentioned today how much I love you?" She tilted her head, buried her face in that space between his shoulder and his chin, and squeezed his arm.

A little luck and a hell of a lot of love, all we need.

About the Author

L INDA S. GUNTHER IS THE AUTHOR OF FIVE OTHER ROMANTIC SUSPENSE
novels:

- *TEN STEPS FROM THE HOTEL INGLATERRA—A woman's romantic adventure in Havana, Cuba*

- *ENDANGERED WITNESS—A San Francisco veterinarian's life turned upside down with betrayal, abduction, and murder*

- *LOST IN THE WAKE—A sizzling thriller set on a luxury cruise liner crossing the Atlantic Ocean*

- *FINDING SANDY STONEMEYER – A romantic murder mystery set in Northern California's Santa Cruz Mountains*

- *DREAM BEACH—A romantic suspense for lovers, dreamers, and trouble-makers set in Tahiti*

www.lindasgunther.com

Made in the USA
Las Vegas, NV
05 January 2023

64878349R00131